Nashville Trade

TJ Arant

Contents

		V
1.	Chapter 1	1
2.	Chapter 2	15
3.	Chapter 3	21
4.	Chapter 4	25
5.	Chapter 5	31
6.	Chapter 6	36
7.	Chapter 7	46
8.	Chapter 8	53
9.	Chapter 9	57
10.	Chapter 10	62
11.	Chapter 11	70
12.	Chapter 12	74
13.	Chapter 13	83
14.	Chapter 14	95
15.	Chapter 15	103
16.	Chapter 16	109
17.	Chapter 17	114
18.	Chapter 18	121

19.   Chapter 19   127

20.   Chapter 20   140

21.   Chapter 21   141

22.   Chapter 22   146

23.   Chapter 23   161

24.   Chapter 24   166

25.   Chapter 25   173

26.   Chapter 26   177

27.   Chapter 27   182

28.   Chapter 28   187

29.   Chapter 29   200

30.   Chapter 30   207

31.   Chapter 31   223

32.   Chapter 32   229

33.   Chapter 33   237

34.   Chapter 34   244

35.   Chapter 35   250

Also By TJ Arant   257

For murder, though it have no tongue, will speak
With most miraculous organ.

William Shakespeare, *Hamlet* (2.2.550-51)

Chapter One

In the mirror I see a face at once familiar and strange, neat and yet unkempt. It is the face of a victim and a survivor, a warrior and a thief, someone who has cheated both death and fate and still lost a life. Eyes green not with envy but with bitterness, with a furious rage, tempered with weariness--I can see the hoods of eyebrows, the strong orbits under which the eyes nest. The ears that jut out, the better to hear the enemy. The beginnings of two parallel creases, worn into being above the nose, between the eyes, testimony to watchfulness and suspicion. The mouth set in a persistent frown, the ends drawn downward like daggers.

No one would see this face, I think, and question it. We see the faces that the world presents us, and we believe they are as they are. We never think to wonder, what was that face before? And how did it come to be misshapen into this?

Mine started the moment I got in-country, at the intake in Ben Hoi, May 30, 1969, and didn't stop until I got on a troop transport back to the world, June 2, 1970. I clerked eight months at Fort Riley, then mustered out. There were no long-haired protesters yelling "baby killer" when I left. I don't doubt that happened to somebody. Like every other story of the war, it's true and not true. I can't judge. It just didn't happen to me.

What happened to me was that my face changed. I went across the ocean at 19 and came back decades more cynical.

Distrustful of people who tell me what to do and how to feel. Skeptical of standards. Wary of anybody telling me that something is right or that another thing is wrong. On guard almost all the time. Against everything.

For a while I fought against it. For a while I won a kind of normal existence. But I never felt like I was really back home. It was as if I had changed in one direction, and Nashville had gone the other.

But when everything came apart again, and with it my life, I could see that I was home. The world really was a place where right and wrong is the same thing most days, where authority is really nothing but raw power, and where people do unspeakable things to each other and somehow get away with it.

I knew I was home when the difference between Nashville and Vietnam was just the subtlety, and when I couldn't really say which was the subtler.

What do you care?

I did a tour in Vietnam. I went in a private and a year later came out a sergeant, not because I was such a good soldier, but because I was a winner in the lottery of attrition. What do they say? In the land of the blind, the one-eyed man is king? I half understood a lot of stuff, which made me a leader.

I got off the plane and there was no one there. We came home to nothing. We spent a year in the bush, in the boonies, and I came home to a deafening silence. Why were we there? Why did we do what we did?

Eight more months doing clerk duty, and I came back and went to school. Nobody challenged me. Nobody said, hey, you're a vet. I grew my hair long and I looked like everyone else. There wasn't a test whose result proved you're a vet, or you're a baby killer, or you're a bastard.

I was just a student. A little older. A little calmer. Maybe.

But what I mostly was, was a little mature. You can't wait for Charlie in the morning, every night, twelve long months, and live, and not think that a Confederate dress up party is just a little lame.

Don't get me wrong. It's not like there weren't scars. I once saw a guy we called Bone Pile, because he was so skinny and uncoordinated, step on a toe popper. A light flashed, and he looked like he was simply falling sideways in slow motion. He didn't know that we all saw half his leg disintegrate. He lay there reaching toward a limb that wasn't there, then broke into sobs when he realized what had happened.

We got him out on a chopper, but he died before he got to a doctor.

And Lester, who said he was from Burnt Skillet, Kentucky, was a rangy and effective solider, vigilant, good to have on your side in a firefight, good to have by your side if you were walking point. He'd grown up tracking, hunting in the woods. He was made for the bush.

One day, his grandpa's pocket watch disappeared. Lester ran all over the camp, throwing gear in the air as he searched, pushing everyone out of the way. After that, Lester got it in his head that one of us was out to get him. He spent the last thirty days of his tour with his back against every rock, sitting with his legs pulled tight and his M-16 ready. His last days were spent believing that there was VC and there was friendly, and that both were out to get him.

On the day he left, he backed up to the chopper, keeping his eyes on all of us, weapon ready. I swear to God I thought he might try to mow us all down. He rolled into the helicopter, assumed a prone position, and kept us in his sights until he was airborne.

I learned a lot. I learned that you can't trust authority as far as you can throw them. The higher ups and the higher, higher ups say to follow the chain of command. Listen, that chain is made to pull you tight and get you blamed before any higher up ever gets in trouble.

I learned that rules are only rules for some people. That means that rules are arbitrary, and you don't really have to follow them. They're just markers laid out to keep us in line.

I learned that nothing is the way it seems. A little kid is as deadly as an NVA soldier. A woman in a rice paddy can blow you up as effectively as VC can. And I learned that if the Army looked like it made sense on any given thing, well, it was a sure sign that it was crazy, and you were too.

If there was a moment I knew I was back, it was when I realized that I wasn't changing back into the guy who went over there. I had learned too much and seen too much. Vietnam, in the end, felt like war as arithmetic. Kill more of them than they kill of ours. Maim them. Don't worry too much if the round finds a kid, because he's probably going to kill you too. It wasn't strategic in any sense. It was just body count.

You couldn't tell if you were fighting in a civil war or a revolution or some sort of global proxy war. You just knew you had a finite time that you needed to stay alive. Usually in a jungle. And always in discomfort. With people you had to believe had your back, but who you never really got to know.

I knew I was back when Nashville felt that way to me too. All the time. It took a while, but it happened. It was a broken idealism, one that could not be restored.

What it was, was 1976. Nashville was changing. Willie and Waylon and the other Outlaws were making Music Row take notice. Opryland was making Country Music feel more like a theme park than a genre. And the Exit/In was booking The Police. It was changing faster than Hubert Davis and the Season Travelers could play Fox on the Run.

Plus, there was an election. The election was everywhere.

And I was trying to figure out how to make a living.

I didn't know what to make of him. He was big, the sort of guy who once would have played linebacker for a small college team. Big enough, but not huge. But then he went to seed, and the guy who was not big enough became bigger than he should have been. He had intelligent eyes, but they were topped by preposterous eyebrows, the hairy kind that need trimming. Old man eyebrows. The hair was gray, and it was two weeks past the barber's visit that kept the butch cut trim. He was wearing glasses, but he had put them down. He was looking at me in a kind of disbelief, I guess. It's not every day that an older man looks at a guy less than half his age and wants help. Especially one who looks like me.

He said, "I don't know much about you, Trade."

I knew something about him. His name was Landon Pittsfield. He was fifty-five, give or take. He had a successful Buick dealership in Indianapolis, and his rented Riviera was parked outside Hannigan's, where I spent too much of my time. His wife was cooling her heels in the Holiday Inn across West End Avenue.

And his daughter was downtown in the morgue. Killed in her off-campus apartment.

"There's not a whole lot to know. I used to work at the University. Now I don't."

"The campus police seem to think highly of you."

I made a circling motion with my hands. "What goes around."

"And now you are a private detective." He smiled a little. I took it as skepticism.

"Not exactly."

"But I thought. . ."

"Be careful what you think. Look at me, Mr. Pittsfield. I'm what most would call a hippie. I have shoulder length hair. A beard. I'm wearing bell bottom jeans and a sweatshirt. If you check with the wrong folks, you'll hear that I have no visible means of support."

"I don't understand." He shook his head slightly, one eye narrowed.

"I have to make a living with the talents I have. One talent is to find things. People have questions. I find answers." I took a long pull on the bourbon in my glass. Sometimes they were just questions about what some kid was doing instead of going to class. Sometimes the questions were a little harder. Sometimes they were questions without answers. Maybe that was the way his question was going to be.

"I see."

Pittsfield was drinking unsweetened tea, which is what non-Southerners drink when in the pickle of what to drink. Hannigan's was a campus eatery that most of campus ignored. It had knotty pine walls that looked like the 1950s. They covered walls from the 1920s. Like all of Nashville, the present covered the past, but the past was there. That's why Faulkner wrote that it was never really past.

It was three in the afternoon on the third Wednesday in October, 1976, and there was nobody there but us.

He said, "I have a hard time asking you what I want."

"I don't know what I can do. Your daughter is dead. The student who did it was arrested almost at once. Then he killed himself. I don't know what else you would need." I took another sip of my drink. His face was resigned. Then, it hardened.

"You're saying the case is closed. Period."

"As far as the police, as far as the courts are concerned? Sure. Done."

"But what about from my point of view?

"What is your point of view?" I asked. "You know her murderer."

"Look, the police see it their way. And yes, perhaps I know her murderer. But there are other things. There are things that knowing her murderer do not begin to touch."

"Like?"

"I want to know why." The look on his face was painful to see. "She was in the very beginning of her life. She was just getting started. Once she came to Vanderbilt, she stopped communicating with us. For the past four years, since she got here, we've known less and less about her. The last time she was home was four years ago. We lost her," he almost sobbed, "and I want to know why."

He was not a comfortable man, at least not now. "She lived in Tolman Hall to begin with. He was a security clerk at the front desk on weekends. From what I've heard, she didn't have a regular boyfriend. He was a little obsessive. He ended up her roommate. That's the story I hear."

"That's the story, I understand." He fidgeted with his iced tea. "Other people say that maybe she was pretty loose." He winced. "She had a lot of men over. She was pretty. They picked up the young man running through the quad, covered with blood, and cursing." He took a long breath. "There's no explanation for any of that."

I got it. It wasn't hard to get.

"Do you see why I have to know more?"

"Sure. Your daughter was lost to you. Now you know something. And now you want to know more."

"Yes."

I understood. It was hard to look at, but I understood. I didn't want to help him. If I say that I'm a naturally unhelpful person, that would be half of it. I'm a vet. I live in a garage apartment for free, so I don't need anything for rent. Mrs. Hannigan spots me a tab, so I pay when I can. My expenses, such as they are, are manageable. They used to be more. They're not so much anymore. I'm 26 years old, in Nashville, with no real means of support.

It's ok.

"Lieutenant Mercer didn't understand. I'm sure he gave me your name because he wanted me to go away."

Maybe. Mercer and I were friends. He threw work my way sometimes.

"But I have to know, I have to understand. What did my girl become? Why is she dead? What in her life made her somebody that somebody wanted to kill?"

Good questions, all of them. Nashville isn't exactly a murder capital, but just in the past five days there had been three murders. And there's no reason for any of them. A man knifed a block from the bus station. An old woman on the north side, hacked into pieces. People say it didn't used to happen. Maybe they're right. Why do people do any of these things?

If there was a reason, if there was even a rhyme to a reason, nobody knew.

"Can you help me, Trade?" He looked smaller than he was. "May I ask you to help me?"

"There's not a hell of a lot I can do, if you want to know the truth. I can nose around. I can try to find things out for you. But I don't expect that I can find what you really want to know."

"I just want to know what became of my girl."

"No, sir. You want a look into the interior of her life. You want to get inside her head. All I can do is find out what her actions were. If I can even do that. I can maybe find out what she did. There's no way I can find out why she did what she did."

He looked a little distraught, the way someone would look if you told him his wife was not the woman he'd been living with all these years.

For some damn reason, I found myself feeling a little sorry for him. "I'll do what I can," I said.

He leaned back into the red plastic of the booth and lit a cigarette. He returned to life, in a way, as he breathed in the smoke and let it out. I lit up too. I drained my bourbon, and signaled Charlie to bring me another.

By the time I was through three more butts and another bourbon, I had filled a couple of pages of notes. She was an only child. She was smart. She had come to Vanderbilt on scholarship and was majoring in history, thinking she would go to law school. She was popular, the way that a good girl was popular. She didn't date much, but all the boys liked her.

How that translated to a girl murdered by a boy in an off-campus apartment was anybody's guess.

And then the picture got complicated when she got to Nashville. They found her harder to contact, and then they found her impossible to contact. She was distant. She didn't come home. She found ways to be unavailable to them.

Another set of parents might have seen this as spreading her wings. A deliberate distancing in order to prove something. A prelude to coming back closer.

What they saw was a girl getting gone.

They had lost touch and hadn't heard from her in seven months. They were worried, but they had settled finally into that uncomfortable space of letting her choose, hoping she would choose correctly.

And then the telephone finally rang. It was Art Blake, Dean of Students, calling to tell them that their daughter, a senior history major, was dead.

High school done at 18, moving away until 21, then dead. It wasn't pretty.

He told me more things I'd read in her file later, pieces of an almost-investigation. Names and addresses and time and things that may or may not have been true. Everything he said, I'd hear again in the next few days. But there was something in his recitation that set me a little on edge. There was something wrong, something I couldn't capture with a note.

"The killer. That boy. I wanted to kill him. But," and here his fist clenched the iced tea glass hard, "he was a victim too, wasn't he? He committed suicide. He was disturbed." He looked up toward a window that didn't exist. "His father is a minister, I believe. His brother too."

"That's what I hear."

"So, it's a good family, the sort of folks you'd want around. I think I'd like to talk to the father, or the brother. But I know that's not a good idea. I know that's stupid." He looked at me for confirmation. "And still. . ."

"You think if you knew them a little better, you could catch up to your daughter?"

"Yes."

Here's the thing. I was pretty sure he couldn't catch up to her. Something changed when she got to Nashville. She flipped a switch and became different, and it was the kind of different she didn't want him in on. But his money would spend the same as mine, and I didn't have a lot at the moment. And I had agreed. Even though I wanted to say no.

"Look," I finally said, "I can do something for you. Maybe I'll turn up something, and maybe I won't. And what I turn up may not be what you want at all."

"I understand that."

"You really want me to start, then?"

"Without a doubt."

"You sure you don't want to hire a firm? They'll work for a set rate and they'll keep it above board, maybe even do something that will help your taxes."

"And you?"

"I'll just take a flat rate. This is something I'm agreeing to do. You have a question, maybe it's a problem even. I will look for an answer. Try to solve your problem." I did it for parents, here and there, when they wondered whether Junior was shacked up with somebody. I could do it for him, too.

"Ok. How much?"

"Give me five hundred. If it turns out to be too much, well, that's how it goes. If I need more, I'll let you know."

I drained my bourbon while he wrote the check. "Just curious. Did you ever think of hiring someone before? I mean, as she drifted apart from you?"

He seemed to shrink before me. "No." He handed me the check. "No, I didn't, and I wish I did. I know, it's like shutting the barn gate now, after the colt has escaped. I could have done more. He looked down at his hands. "So much more."

Maybe he could have, maybe not. I might help him to get closer to the right feeling, but I might not. There never is a right answer when the soul asks that question.

I folded the check and put it in my wallet. "There's one more thing that I want to ask you. It's not appropriate, probably, but there's something I think you haven't told me that you want to tell me."

"Like what?"

"I don't know. Something you left out"

"It's not important, Trade. Really, it's not, if this is your point. She's not my biological daughter. She's adopted. My wife's first daughter." He looked a little indignant. "She's my daughter."

"I understand. It's fine." It told me all it needed to about his feeling of responsibility.

"You're too young to understand," he said. "You don't know what this is about."

"I don't have a child, that's true," I said. "One day I will, and I will want them to be safe. I will want to know that they've had every advantage and that no one will have taken advantage of them.

"Now I have a question," he said. "I feel like I can trust you. Can I?"

"Mercer sent you to me. There's that. I'm well connected, you'll find out if you check. I look like a hippie and you probably wouldn't pick me, if it was up to you, but I'm completely trustworthy. There's nothing that I can't find out. And I don't run my mouth. What I find goes to you alone."

"But why does Lieutenant Mercer trust you?"

"Look. I was an Assistant Dean, the youngest Vanderbilt ever had. I made a bad mistake. Really, you could say that I made a stupid, inexcusable mistake. I lost my job. But the campus police think I know what I'm doing. So, they sent you my way. And here we are."

I sat there after he left, torn between the idea that I could help him and the idea that he was doomed to ignorance. I caught Katie's eye, and she brought me another drink. "Your new friend doesn't drink enough to pay attention to.

"True."

"You have anything to confess?"

"Me? You have to be kidding." I wasn't in the mood for a questioning.

She put her hand on top of mine. "You've been here an awful lot. Had a lot before dinner. Had a lot no matter when you came."

"What's your point?"

"I don't have a point. But you should watch it." She put a hand on her hip. "Maybe you'd be better off smoking a little dope. It might mellow you out more."

"Haven't you heard? Marijuana is illegal in Tennessee. Besides it makes me paranoid, makes me jumpy." I raised my eyebrows. "You don't want me jumpy, trust me. You want me somewhere in the middle."

"You're not in the middle. You spend too much time drinking toward your limit, and then when you hit it, you go over the line.

I had a lot to think of. A busted love affair. A career gone bad. An accusation that, however true it was, wasn't true. And before that, a war that wouldn't leave. "How about you just let me breathe?"

"Breathe. But be careful."

The juke box was playing Gram Parsons. Love Hurts. Emmylou singing harmony.

There was a time I would have had a beer and sung along. Now it felt way too close. Too real.

I got to the bank about closing time and put my five hundred in, kept fifty out. It would be enough for what I needed to do.

I walked back down West End, then stopped where Vanderbilt's campus starts, turned right, and walked around the back of West End Methodist, where the gym entrance was. Inside there were about a half dozen guys shooting hoops, and another two or three just hanging around. I walked over and sat on the part of the bleachers that was pulled out.

In high school, we ran a motion offense called the Auburn Shuffle. It was a way that a bunch of minimally talented, rural white guys could do enough organized movement to frustrate more talented and taller teams. We won our share. More than our share, because we could determine the pace.

Once I got back to the world and started playing here, I found a new motion, a kind of improvised urban intelligence, something quicker that required talent and mostly rewarded it. You could never be sure what would be rewarded the next day because that depended entirely on who showed up and what they had on their minds. Your "good enough" yesterday might be "not even close" today. All you really could do was to be in the flow, go with the game, trust your stuff. You just hoped your stuff was better than whoever showed up that day.

It was a lot like the war.

I don't play now. I don't know why I even come back, except that there's a certain peace you recognize, when you're in a place that makes you feel comfortable. I leaned back and pulled my ball cap over my eyes.

I felt every part of my body go lax. It's enough, sometimes, to feel quiet in your bones. Some people would go to church, to prayer, to get this feeling. I can do it, if I'm on my game, by calming my spirit and letting my breath take over.

The idea is to breath just as much as you need to, and to let the rest take care of itself.

And while I was breathing I tried to make the breathing right for Josie Pittsfield, who would never get to 22. For Mark Simpson, who wouldn't make 21. For my marriage, which wouldn't make 1. And for a war that had ended and would never end.

No breathing for my ex. She had taken the wind out of me already.

Chapter Two

Vanderbilt's police station is in a little house at the corner of 25th Avenue South and Garland. What it had been originally I don't know, but someone's sad bungalow would be a good choice. Rooms that were too small had been chopped even smaller to create cubbyhole offices, each on with a desk, two uncomfortable chairs, and a table with a typewriter. Even Don Mercer, lieutenant and nominally second in charge, had a cramped space.

I like Don. He's a short, slightly paunchy black guy. My age. Vietnam vet. Came back and found a way to make a living. A sergeant in the war, he'd come back and made it to lieutenant on the VU force. He'd done better than I had.

He didn't look surprised to see me. He nodded and motioned toward the second chair. I shook hands with him across the desk and sat down.

"How'd it go with Pittsfield?" he asked. He twirled a pencil between the fingers of his left hand, deftly spinning it through the gaps, first and second finger, then third and fourth, then fourth and second.

"Sad guy."

"True enough. One day he's a dad with a girl in college. Next day," he shrugged, "she's dead, killer's dead, he's outlived a child, and the mom's stunned, he's stunned. Sad would be the least of it. Shell shocked, more like it." The pencil spun a little faster, between each gap, staccato now, fast between, slow in the middle of each finger. "For most people, the death comes, and then police take their time giving them the closure of finding the suspect. Then the courts take their damn time deciding whether he did it. And then the appeal. This was less than a day. She's dead. He's dead. They're alone." The pencil stopped spinning. "If he wants to take a more leisurely trip toward getting used to it, why not you? And you'll make a dollar or two, right?" The spinning recommenced.

"Right. I appreciate it."

"You stroll around her block, talk to some folks. Ask questions. Go down a couple of blind alleys. Before you know it, you're billing him a couple hundred, and he's had time to get used to it. He feels better, and he thinks it's because of you."

"You mind showing me the file on it?"

The pencil stopped dead. "You're not going to see anything there that you don't know. Metro had the boy in custody before they even knew what he'd done."

"You never know."

His eyes narrowed a little, the way I've seen them do in a bar, late at night, when some little something is about to boil over a little. He relaxed, though, and pointed the pencil at me. "You're wasting your time."

"So don't let me waste any of yours arguing with you, Don. If I'm taking Pittsfield's money, I just want to honestly say I looked at it."

"Whatever."

"I'm assuming the Metro report is in there, with the name of the arresting officer?"

"And you want me to make an introduction, too, right?"

"That's the idea, Don." He was spinning the pencil again, as fast as he could, I suspect. Maybe it was the way his brain was spinning too, trying to decide exactly how far along to play.

"He may tell you to go to hell." He rose. "But I'll do it. Just don't let anyone see you looking at the file." He jerked a thumb over his shoulder. "Ross isn't coming in today. You can go in there, shut the door."

A few minutes later I was in a room the size of a closet, Officer Ross's closet, which smelled enough of cigarettes and coffee that I probably didn't need to light up. But I did and began looking. It didn't tell me much I didn't know or couldn't have guessed.

Mark Simpson had been found covered with blood, shrieking various profanities, in the courtyard of Branscomb Quadrangle, the women's freshman area, by a variety of Housing officials and campus police officers. Jermaine Lewis, a new officer that I didn't know by sight, had been on the scene immediately, radioed for backup, and within five minutes Campus Security and Metro had covered and cuffed Simpson.

The Housing folks determined quickly that Simpson was a student and lived off campus. Lewis and the Metro officer, Conrad Dietrich, went to the apartment complex, whereupon they found the Pittsfield girl, according to the report, "naked, with multiple slash wounds from a sharp object, and apparently dead."

Dietrich put the Metro machinery into gear, and before long the coroner's office, the forensic crew, and the picture boys were crawling all over the apartment, putting together the sure and certain knowledge that she was, indeed, dead.

There were a lot more pictures than I needed to see. I could see she was dead from the first one, although what she might have looked like alive was something I couldn't reconstruct. The damage was damn near total. The report basically said she had bled out. From the pictures, I had no trouble believing it.

The coroner's report was next in the file. Dr. Elvin Banks stated that the deceased was a Caucasian female, early 20s, had been slashed thirty-two times with a sharp instrument, that the damage to veins and arteries was complex and fatal, that death had occurred about 3:45 p.m., that the wounds were not self-inflicted, and that she had had oral sex some-time before she died.

As in, right before she died. Monday, October 18, 1976, 3:45 pm.

And so on. Police reports always accrete. Beaches steadily erode with the action of the tide. Police reports are the opposite. With each wave of information, more sand is transported and deposited inside the file folder. The report accumulates a kind of solid order that becomes persuasive. And just like with machines, cases can sometimes get stopped because of one grain of sand left behind.

But this didn't appear to be one. The blood on Simpson was hers. There were plenty of bloody fingerprints, and footprints for that matter, that matched his inside the apartment. No weapon, but hell, he walked the mile or so from the apartment to Branscomb. No telling where the knife was.

Everything I read reinforced the conclusion everyone already had. Josie Pittsfield was impossibly disfigured by Mark Simpson. She had died a horrible death. She hadn't any skin under her fingernails so there wasn't a hint of struggle. She knew the assailant. If she had died quickly, or if she had died slowly, she had died.

"I'd still like to talk to Dietrich," I told Mercer. "I don't think it'll amount to a hill of beans, but I'd like to make sure."

"I told him. He doesn't mind, as long as you buy the beer."

"One thing I don't see. Was she sleeping around? Or hooking? I don't see evidence of what I'd see if she was independent."

"Who knows?" Mercer said. "You look in the closet and there's good stuff. Father wasn't paying for it. Someone was. The apartment was renting for more than your Vanderbilt student could afford." He shrugged again. "Who knows.?"

"So why was she living with Simpson?"

"Jesus, Jackson. That's a whole different question. Maybe she was hooking and carrying him. That way, he didn't have to pay rent. I just don't know. How would I?"

"Was he her pimp, maybe?"

"No. Maybe. Probably. Who the hell knows?"

"But no arrest sheet on them? You or Metro?"

"Nothing."

I let the moment settle. "Here's a thought. If you hadn't found the kid naked and loud, and then moved on to the apartment, the whole thing would have evolved in a more normal manner. Metro would have investigated the whole thing a different way.

"Maybe."

"No judgement, Donnie. But if all this had happened differently, Metro would have investigated the hell out of it."

"What are you saying? That you're going to do the police's job?"

"Not at all. I'm saying that I can give Mr. Pittsfield some peace by doing what you'd have normally done."

What you'd have normally done. That's a phrase that I could have learned earlier. What I'd have normally done, two years ago, would have been to follow the rules. I'd have tried to do the right thing. I'd have asked, if I hadn't known, what the right thing was. But I was following the law of the jungle, I guess, and I was not too worried. I was invincible. I was ten feet tall and bulletproof. I was the baddest badass in the jungle. No one could touch me. You live through combat; you might be excused for thinking so.

And I made mistakes.

Twenty-five years old, an Assistant Dean of Students, and already a super star if I'd just make my way.

But I didn't make my way.

"Are you really saying you can do this better?" Mercer asked. "Because if you don't need my help, screw you."

I put my hand on his forearm. "Listen to me, Donnie. I appreciate the lifeline. I really do. God knows I've messed my life up. I can use the support." I lit a cigarette and offered one to him, which he took. "But the whole point of the lifeline is to be worthy of it. If I can't at least act like I'm doing the job, then what the hell am I worth?"

He took a long breath of smoke. "I guess."

We walked out, down the steps of the bungalow.

"I set it up with Dietrich that you'll come by Linda's tonight after he gets off, gets cleaned up. Look for him around 10."

"Sounds good. I haven't been in Linda's in a while."

"Same awful juke box. Same warped pool tables. He's a semi-regular, so ask Bobby Barkeep to point him out. Remember, he'll expect you to buy his beer."

"Sure. That's no problem." I headed down the steps to the sidewalk.

"One last thing? You saw the report. What could you possibly want to ask him? I mean it. What could he tell you that you don't know?"

"I want to know what it was that Simpson was screaming."

"Is that all?" I nodded. "Simpson was crazy. Simpson is dead. What he was saying is about as relevant as what he was wearing. Which was nothing."

"I don't agree. If he was saying anything, anything at all, then it would be interesting. And it might be significant."

"He's a dead boy, who made a dead girl."

Which might make anything about him entirely interesting. But I just waved to Mercer and walked down the street.

Chapter Three

I went by the Pittsfield girl's apartment. The crime scene was already closed. And the woman who opened the door, the super and not the landlord, she assured me, was about thirty years old. She was wearing cowboy boots, cut offs, and a white dress shirt. She wasn't bad looking at all, in a Nashville way, but she was also full of attitude.

"You want what?" She said it as politely as she could. Twice.

"I want to know about your tenants. The ones upstairs."

"Really?" It was as much an exclamation as a question. "I don't have the slightest idea what they were doing. They paid rent. I booked it."

"I'd really like to have a look."

She rolled her eyes. "We all want something." There was something about her way of answering. She was a little older than I was. It felt like flirting, but I was out of practice.

"Look, I don't want to make a problem. But there's just the possibility that there's more here than meets the eye. Help me out," I promised, "and I'll find a way to pay you back." There's something in the way that people talk to each other, something in the give and take we manage, that gives us the impression that there's more here than meets the eye.

Maybe I was flirting back.

Whatever it was, she answered, "Sure. I can let you have a look. It's not like I care."

We walked up the stairs.

"You knew them?"

"Sure. By sight." She was shaking her hips in front of me. More than necessary, I thought.

"They move in together?"

"No. She was here first. Had a different roommate."

"Another man?"

"Woman. But don't ask me about it. I can tell you the landlord's name. He's the one that would know. I just work here, you know?" She gave me a wink.

"What about Josie?"

"What about her? She was invisible. No noise, no trouble. Not like a lot of the undergrads. Only time I was in the apartment was when they had a leak. I fixed it."

"You're handy, then."

She flicked a blonde lock away from her eyes. "Handy enough." She gave me a look that said more about how handy she could be, but she apparently reconsidered. "What else?"

"What was your impression of them?"

"As a couple? They weren't"

"Yes, I know. What was your impression of them in general?"

"Like I said. Invisible."

"But you formed an impression anyway. Like the story you tell yourself about who someone is, even if you don't know them."

"I have an impression of you. What did you say your name was?"

"Jackson. Jackson Trade."

"I'm Betty," she said, and shook my hand. "You look like a hippie, Jackson. Long hair. Beard. Ratty jeans. But you're wiry, almost muscular, like a jock. And you talk smart. That tells me that you went to college, maybe graduated. But it didn't work out somehow. You're not a cop. You're too young to be some kind of private eye. I don't really have any idea why you're here, or why I'm talking to you."

She had all of that right. "What do you make of me? What's the impression?"

"My impression is that I'm curious. And when I'm curious," she tapped a fingernail on my shoulder, "I generally want to know more."

"I might satisfy that," I said. "But what about your impression of Josie and the Simpson boy?"

She concentrated, brows together. "Not sleeping together, for sure. Like family. When they talked, they talked quietly, like they were keeping separate from the world." She put her hand on my arm and looked toward the door. "Can I get you a cup of coffee? Or a beer? It's late enough for a drink."

I had rinsed my mouth out with bourbon at Hannigan's before I rinsed with Listerine. Maybe she couldn't tell. "I've got somewhere I need to be. After I get a look at the apartment."

The apartment was cleaned up. "The father said to keep the furniture, that he didn't need it." If there had been blood everywhere, as surely there must have been, Betty or her cleaning crew had made short work of it. "This is about how it looked the couple of times I was in here."

I walked to the kitchen counter. A dishtowel with an embroidered cat was folded neatly, next to an empty butter dish. A vintage knife block sat on top of a cutting board. Two slots were missing knives. One of them, probably, was the missing murder weapon.

It was the sort of place her father would have approved of. Safe. Not on the bottom floor. Double dead bolts. "You clean everything?"

"Told you I'm handy. Didn't tell you I work pretty hard too." She grinned. "At everything I do, Jackson."

I laughed. "Are you working hard now?"

"Can't you tell?"

"You're not sweating."

She crossed her arms, placed a finger on her chin. "Want me to?"

This is what inevitably gets me in trouble. There's me. There's a woman. There is flirting. There is drinking. We end up making out. We end up in bed. Or on the couch. Or on the floor. It doesn't really matter. And then there is hell to pay, because I never, ever do this with the right woman. The only one even close to the right woman was my ex, and she turned out to be the wrong woman too. I like the game, but what follows is never as good as that. And it's never predictable. Except that it won't work out.

This time, I'm smart. "Not today. I want you to have an easy time of it today." I motioned at the door. "I have an appointment to get to."

As we walked down, side by side, she bumped me lightly twice. It wasn't enough to comment on, but it was more than enough to notice.

At the complex door, she pulled me to her and tiptoed a kiss, light on my cheek. "You're cute, Jackson. Anytime you want to stop over for a beer, well," she grinned, "just come on over."

She winked at me and shut the door.

I could smell just the trace of her on my face. It might be a scent I'd like to bury myself in, but there were other things to do first.

Chapter Four

Linda's was a dive. That's probably generous. It was a decade past being a dive and had entered the territory inhabited by places you probably didn't want to go. It smelled of piss and beer, and if you tried a little you could probably, way back in your throat, catch a little vomit stench. The mop had left the final unpleasantness, the sourness of an unhygienic slap applied without interest or success. It wasn't a place you would want to drink in, unless you didn't care much anymore where you drank.

Even the bartender was past the dive bar stage. Bobby had pulled drafts all over town, from the downtown dives to the west side taverns. I knew him from around.

"What are you drinking, Slick?" Bobby called everybody Slick. It kept the problem of remembering names at bay.

"Give me a Pabst longneck." I didn't want to take a chance on how clean the taps were.

Bobby wrenched the top off the bottle and gave it to me. "Guy over there in the corner said you'd be looking for him."

"What's he drinking?"

"Draft."

"Pour one. I'll take it to him."

Bobby held the plastic cup sideways to keep the foam down, then expertly topped it up so it had a nice head on it. He pushed it toward me, and I paid him.

Conrad Dietrich looked up as I came toward him. He was younger than me, I'd say. His haircut was sidewalls with a shock of unruly black hair on top. It had the same uneasy look, an almost homemade manner, as he did. When I handed him the beer, he took it with long fingers, like a piano player's. I wondered if he'd come to Nashville to be a musician and then fell into law enforcement. Some days, it seemed like almost everybody came to town for music. Almost none of them made it.

"You Jackson Trade?" His dialect wasn't from Tennessee. Maybe he did come to be a musician.

I nodded. "Why here?" We were the youngest in the bar by a good thirty years, and most of the rest looked like they lived here.

He drained his first cup and took a drink from the one I'd brought. "Beer's cheap. Jukebox isn't too loud. Nobody knows me here." He took another drink. "One-Two-Three."

"Might could find a place that smells better."

He snorted. "Places I end up in, you can't tell much difference."

I didn't know if he meant the places he ended up for work, or if he meant the places he drank. I wasn't sure I wanted to know.

"You know why I wanted to talk to you?" I sat down across from him. I could feel a spring about to come through the booth's seat.

"Don Mercer said you wanted to talk about the girl."

"That's right. Her, and the boy."

He turned the plastic cup in his hands. He stopped his rotation, and the red embossed "Miller," with "Champaign of Bottled Beers" below, faced me. "I don't know that I want to talk about this with you."

"I thought Don had this set up. You got a problem talking about it because it's a police matter?"

"Not sure it's right."

"You thought it was fine when you talked to Don."

"I thought you were in the brotherhood." He looked up and down at me. "You're not a cop. The way you look, hell, you look like the guys I bust all day."

"Well, this is awkward," I said. I could have said, the way you look, you look like the guys that didn't do well in my unit back in combat. But I didn't. I waited. "How much death have you seen in your line of work, Dietrich?"

He drank his draft down.

"Is this the first one?"

"I've been on emergency calls where I've seen dead bodies. Car wrecks. Heart attacks. Not the same as this one."

"Tell me why, Dietrich." I motioned to Bobby to bring another draft. "How was this one different? They're all dead."

"You know why." He looked like the sort who would be an angry drunk, mostly because he looked half-drunk and pissed off already.

"I'm serious. What's so different here? You don't look like the delicate type, so it can't be because it was murder. That's like a nurse who faints at the sight of blood."

"I didn't faint." He shot Bobby a look as he brought the beer and grabbed it out of his hands. "You don't know what you're talking about."

"Didn't say you fainted. I just asked what was different about this."

Dietrich looked down at the table. "I don't want to talk about it."

"Why? Are you that distrustful of me? You thought I sounded fine when you talked to Don. Now? Because I have long hair? Because I'm not a cop?" All the time I was peeling the label off the longneck. "Because I can't change that, Dietrich." I waited a beat. "You know what I think? I think you need to talk about this."

He didn't look up. "I don't need nothing."

"I think you do. You saw something that spooked you. I've seen the pictures. You saw a scene, and you didn't know anybody could do such a thing. You can't tell that to your buddies on the force. You can't tell anybody."

He shook his head.

"You thought I was a cop, and you were willing to talk cop shop. That's because you can keep your distance. But you don't want to keep your distance, Dietrich. This whole damn thing bothers you. You want to talk."

He pointed a long index finger at me, staring hot into my eyes. "Listen, damn it. I don't need some long-haired punk telling me I need to talk it out. I'm a fucking cop. I don't need therapy from you. Who the hell do you think you are anyway?"

"I'm a guy who's seen his buddies blown up in a rice paddy, officer. I'm a guy who's put men on a chopper, knowing they'd never make it back home." I leaned toward him. "I'm a guy who's sent the enemy home to visit mama-san with M-16 holes through them." I drank the last of my Pabst. "If you think I'm asking because I want to save you, forget it. I can't save you. I can't even save myself. But trust me, brother. You need to talk."

The jukebox whirred. "I Fall to Pieces" came on. Patsy Cline. God, Nashville changes, but it never changes. It played songs that haven't been on the radio in fifteen years.

"Your call, Dietrich. But you won't get a better offer. Not in this stinking pit."

He let out his breath, and looked over my head, as if there were someone there whom he couldn't quite make out. Then he looked back to me. "I'm sorry, man. I was out of line."

"Not a problem." I held out my hand. "Start over?"

He grasped my hand, and we shook. "Ok." He stood up. "Get you another?"

"Sure."

When he returned, he was easier in his mind. "It was bloody, man. I mean, you think of blood as red. Because that's what it looks like, right? You cut yourself shaving and put a piece of toilet paper on the cut, and the blood is bright red. But this was dark, Trade. The blood was like a brown that was red, like it had come from an organ." He shuddered and took a drink. "Never saw anything like it, and it was everywhere. On the floor. On the sheets. Everywhere."

"Like I said, I saw the pictures. It was bad." I offered him a cigarette, which he took, and we both lit up. "What about Lewis, the campus cop?"

"He was downstairs, interviewing neighbors. Thank God, too. I nearly lost my lunch."

"What did you think about the boy, Simpson?"

"I think he must be one crazy mother to do what he did."

"What did he say when he was screaming?"

"It was hard to make out, a lot of it. He was sobbing and screaming."

"That's not a good combination," I said. "Could you make out any of it?"

"He was shrieking. "Dead. Motherfucking dead." Once he settled a little, he kept saying, "Not again. Not again." Kind of like a chant."

"What did you make of that?"

"First thing I thought was that he'd done this before. But I don't think that was it at all."

"Really? That seems like a reasonable thing to think."

"But then he went off on another screaming fit. I think he could feel himself losing control. I think he was settling down, felt it coming on again and didn't want it to happen again."

"Seems like an awful lot of self-awareness for somebody who's crazy."

"You know what, Trade? I'm not sure he was crazy."

"What would you call it? Guy butchers his roommate out of the blue. Runs right toward a place he can be caught, screaming. Sounds crazy to me."

"Oh, that's all true." Dietrich exhaled smoke straight up, then looked directly at me. "And I don't doubt he's insane."

"Isn't crazy just another word for insane?"

"Not to my way of thinking. The way I see it, insane is a 'put you in the nuthouse thing' because you can't be in human company. Your mind doesn't play by society's rules, and that makes you dangerous. Crazy is when you don't have any rules at all."

"You a cop or a shrink, Dietrich?"

"I'm a cop." He finished the last of his beer, took a drag and stubbed out the cigarette. "But I'll tell you what. Mark Simpson wasn't crazy. He was playing by some set of rules."

Chapter Five

I had a head start. That's true. I worked my head start pretty hard. And then I screwed it up.

That's the truth.

But then I found a way to admit what I'd done.

Art Blake was the Dean of Students. He was the man who'd fired me. For good reason, I might add.

But he'd left the door open. And I walked in.

He lived on West Side Row. They were some of the oldest buildings on campus. They were the apartments of some of Vanderbilt's student leadership and some of its administrative leadership. C1 was Art's place.

And that's where I went.

I wasn't there to ask for something that was none of my business. Instead, I was concerned about what I could find out regarding Simpson or Josie. I didn't know what I didn't know. But I did know that Art could answer questions.

He was seated, as usual, behind his desk in the study, his bourbon in a smaller glass. My bourbon was in a larger one, with more ice. I picked at his paperclip tray, hooking one to another.

Blake had started young in the business, and twenty-five years in, he was still under fifty. He stood six-six and had a red handlebar mustache, impeccably waxed. His eyes were always active, intelligent but hard. He was beloved by some, detested by others. In other words, he did his job right, and didn't much worry about the consequences.

He'd have done well in the war.

"The whole thing about student deaths," he said, "is that they're endlessly unexpected. Everyone thinks they're going to live forever."

"And then they die," I said. I took a sip of Jim Beam. It was about a sip more than I needed with all I'd had.

He shook his head. "It's not really that they think they'll live forever. It's that they think, and there's good evidence for this, that they're bulletproof. They know they're mortal. They just don't think it's today they'll get caught." His tie was loosened, and the top button undone. "You know how it is, Jackson. You had the best part of two years chasing them down most nights and every weekend."

"And two years before that as a student." I'd bought into the profession as an undergraduate, working as a resident advisor, then a Head Resident. It's where I got my taste for connecting dots. Or rather, it's where my natural tendency in combat got domesticated, tamped down to a more housebroken use.

"They really do appear to be bulletproof. They drink until daylight, brush their teeth, and show up for their 8 o'clock class, unshaven but not that hungover. They don't get so much as a sniffle living a lifestyle that would kill me. Hell, it might kill even you someday." He raised his glass as if in toast, and then drained it. "Another?"

"I better not. Already been at Hannigan's and Linda's." My paperclip chain was an even dozen.

"You're right. You've been living like an undergrad." He set the empty glass on its coaster. "What is it you're here for? It's clearly not the bourbon, and it's not usually about the company."

"More often for the company than you know, boss. But I'm helping the Pittsfield girl's father out. Trying to help him understand what had been going on with her."

"She was an unknown to me."

"What about the boy?" I began a chain of paperclips to the chain I'd already made.

He made a steeple of his fingers and looked away. "He was not an unknown, but he was not, apparently, what he appeared to be either." I waited for another sentence. "He worked for us last year as a desk clerk in Tolman Hall."

"Right. I know that. She lived in Tolman. That's how they met, I gather."

"I don't know so much about that. I do know that young Mr. Simpson was dismissed with some prejudice before the end of spring semester."

I knew something about how that might go. "What'd he do?"

"He was entertaining his boyfriend at the security desk."

"He got fired because he was gay?"

Blake narrowed his eyes and leaned forward. The left side of the handlebar twitched a little. "You know better than to say that." For a moment, I thought he might throw the empty glass at me. "No, the boyfriend was not a student, for one thing, and was a little too noisy and flighty with the Tolman girls. Simpson had been warned, but the boyfriend came in, one last night, tipsy. They got into a quarrel, and Simpson kicked the chair the boyfriend was tipped back in. He crashed down, the chair broke, and the Tolman Head Resident, whose room, you'll remember, is next to the security desk, heard it all. He was fired the next day."

"He was violent, then?" My paperclip chain was starting to look a little like a necklace. Or a noose.

"No. I didn't have that impression at all. He kicked at his boyfriend's chair during an argument. I don't think he meant to hurt the boy. But you can't have that going on when he's supposed to be watching for male reprobates sneaking in to steal girls' panties."

He laughed. It was a line I'd heard him say before. It had always seemed to me a way to make Vanderbilt seem like it was still the 50s, and any moment now Buddy Holly would be on the radio. Panty raid! And the boys would come from Barnard and steal underthings.

"Did anything happen after that? Did your office get involved?" Blake ran student discipline, among other things. His was the court where people got serious time.

"No need to. If I got involved every time there was a romantic argument, I'd never get to the real crimes of passion. Like this week, when A-Train Wilson got brained by a baseball bat at the High Life."

"A-Train's head gets in the way of all kinds of things." He'd been a football player, until he lost his eligibility.

"Thus, young Mr. Simpson was dismissed from his post, and he became as unknown to me as the girl. The remainder of the story is a good illustration of the fact that, while I know a great deal, I mostly know what is presented to me, face to face." He leaned back, more relaxed again. "On the other hand, you seem better at sorting through what is not presented in so clear a way."

"If you say so. I know that a girl was killed in a grisly way. The evidence points to a young man, who is her roommate and who is arrested. He proceeds to kill himself in jail. The police are satisfied and close the case. That's as clear as the presentation gets."

"Your presentation is a little less sure than what's making the rounds. Boy kills girl, gets caught because he's acting deranged, and then kills himself. "

"No matter how you say it, the problem is why."

"Because the boy is nuts." Art Blake laughed. "I'm sorry. I would be more circumspect in public, as you know. But you've got a maniac here. I don't know when he turned into one, or if he's been one all his life. But he was one that afternoon. That's what the police said, and I saw him in Branscomb. He fit the bill."

I finished the Jim Beam, the ice having diluted it enough to swill down. I stood and felt just a little drunk. Not so much that a ten-minute walk to my apartment wouldn't sober me up. I tossed the paperclip chain onto his desk. It fell in a heap, the shape it had in my hand, a necklace or a noose, disappeared.

"You ok, Jackson?"

"Fine. I just need some sleep."

"No doubt you do. You might want to go a little easier." He saw me out the door. "You're not as bulletproof as you think, my friend."

"I'm not bulletproof. I know that." I put my hand on the doorknob and half-turned. His face was a little flushed. He'd had more than a couple too. "But I'm smart enough not to get shot at."

"Keep it that way," he said. He waved as I shut the door and went into the October night.

For whatever reason, that's the last I remember of the night. I don't remember walking home. I don't remember undressing or getting in bed. And I don't remember getting shot at.

As we used to say as we bivouacked after a day patrol, good enough.

Chapter Six

I woke up with a mouth full of cotton and gauze around my brain. For a minute I didn't know where I was, then I realized that the sun was coming in through the one window in my apartment, above a garage no longer used by Carl and Gemma Bucket, my landlords. They were in Florida now, and that's where they'd be for another three months. I got to stay in the apartment because I looked after the house. Which is to say, I checked daily to make sure the doors and windows were locked, and I picked up the mail.

For all I did for them, their letting me stay in the apartment was a kindness to Art Blake. It certainly wasn't a real job.

And I wasn't much of a tenant, to be honest. The place smelled of stale smoke and the pile of dirty dishes in the sink never really got any smaller than it was now. Not that I cooked much. I rooted around in the mess to find the least dirty coffee mug. I rinsed it out and wiped the coffee ring until it disappeared.

Then I boiled water and put some Folger's Instant in it. My head didn't exactly hurt, but it wouldn't take much to put it over the edge. The coffee helped some, and a shower helped more. After about an hour, hair back in a ponytail and ironed white shirt on, I was presentable enough to go out in the world.

I walked down Reidhurst toward Elliston Place. I had phoned Mercer to ask him to vouch for me with the management company handling Josie Pittsfield's apartment. He had and phoned back to give me Chet Ervin's name.

Elliston to Church, and then over to 18th, and up to Patterson. Along the way I stopped at a Krystal, ordered 4 square burgers for a dollar and a coffee. It would give me indigestion, but it was as cheap a meal as could be had in town.

Ervin's company was two doors down from the Krystal, so I found myself knocking on his door right at 10 o'clock. To his shouted "Come in!" I entered to find a skinny man with a Fu Manchu mustache, about 40 years old, with hair parted on the side and down to his shoulders. He didn't look like a rental management agent, but nothing looks like it used to. Sometimes it's like Haight-Ashbury finally came south without bothering to overcome all the redneck traces everywhere.

"Trade?" He stood, nodded, and motioned to a chair. "Policeman told me what to expect, otherwise, I wouldn't have even known where to start with you. You can smoke if you like," he said, lighting up a Camel unfiltered.

"Just put one out," I said. "You know that I'm interested in Josie Pittsfield?" He nodded again. He was the sort of guy who would nod at a tree blowing in the wind, as if the fact that it could move would have just occurred to him. "She's been there less than a year?"

He shuffled some papers. "No. No. That's not what ..., well no. She had the apartment since, here it is. She signed the lease October 1, 1973. Annual, renewable. So, she had just recently signed a lease to end on September 30, 1977." He pushed his hair up over his eyes and looked at me. "Why did you think she had just moved in?"

Now I was the confused one. "My understanding was that she was living in the residence halls until summer school, this summer, when she moved out. You're telling me that she's been there, what, three years?"

"Yep. Going on four."

"Who else is on the lease with her?"

"Nobody. She's the lessee."

"Why would you rent an apartment, for what, $200 a month? To an 18-year-old freshman without a job?"

He shuffled more papers. "Doesn't say she is unemployed. Says she has references. Says what her monthly income is. She met the requirements."

"Chet? Can I call you Chet?" He nodded again. "This is all news to me. This is a young woman from Indiana who would have been a freshman at Vanderbilt. She's not allowed to live off campus. She lived on campus for three years, only getting permission to move off-campus this past summer. Where does it say she worked?"

"Wait a minute. I've got that here," he said shuffling more papers. "Says here she worked as a secretary at Huddleston Tire, over on Shelby Avenue, other side of the river."

"Does that make any sense to you, Chet? Living in Green Hills and working over there?"

"Might not. Wouldn't have been a question anybody here asked."

"You check the employment and the references, right?"

He nodded. Again. "Sure. But you know how that goes. The phone rings. Someone on the other side verifies the information."

"You verified her employment with this tire company, though?"

"Again. You call. Someone answers." He picked up a set of eyeglasses and put them on. "The only reason we ever get upset is if someone misses rent. If they're going to the trouble to lead us down a trail, what do we care?"

"They why would you bother?"

"Most people don't bother to lie."

Clearly he didn't hang around with the people I did. "Who was her reference at work?"

"Doesn't say. Just that employment was confirmed. I know you're going to ask, who was her personal reference? Says here, Donald Sebring. Want the phone number?"

I said I did, although it wouldn't tell me much. I had a feeling Donald Sebring didn't exist, at least with that name.

He nodded. Again. Like a slow-motion puppy on the dashboard. "I bet he doesn't go by that name either."

This time, I nodded too.

I went down to the pay phone on the corner and found the number for Huddleston Tire. The person who answered had never heard of Josie Pittsfield. I could have asked who worked there three years ago, but that wouldn't have got me anywhere. I did ask about Donald Sebring, but the person said that wasn't a name she knew.

My next dime went for the number where Sebring had answered, three years ago. It was disconnected, not in service.

I didn't have much to report, and what I had to report wouldn't help the parents. Still, it was time to check in. My third dime went for the Holiday Inn on West End. I left a message on their room phone to meet me at Hannigan's at 3:00.

I found myself at Dead Ringer, a bar halfway to Hannigan's. I sat down to have a bite to eat, and it ended up being more than that. In no time at all, I had three empty shot glasses lined up in order. A fourth one was in my hands. And I was playing Old Home Week in my mind, reliving my past.

I ended up in Nashville because that's where Vanderbilt was. I got a scholarship, and my GI benefits paid the rest. It was the biggest city near where I grew up and I felt almost comfortable. But somewhere around my junior year it started to change. Maybe it was the music changing. Maybe it was the country changing. And maybe I just started to notice. But Nashville stopped being a backwater, and it started being harder to figure out.

Don't get me wrong. There's always been a lot of bluster and showmanship. There's a stereotypical way to walk through life in Nashville. You're a songwriter, and ready to make it big. Or you're a singer, and ready to make it big. Or you have some talent that supports one of those, and you're ready to make it big. Or you can be faking one of those things, and you'll never make it big. Or you might. Fortunes have been made on no talent at all.

Lately it seemed like there was more fakery than usual.

I was sitting at the bar contemplating this when a woman said to me, "You know anyone important?" she swayed as she asked it, so I took the question with a grain of salt. "Seriously, I mean, seriously, can you get someone in this town to take me seriously?" The word seriously came out a little more sloshed each time.

I raised my hands in surrender. "I got nothing, lady." She was about four foot eleven, but she had on high heel cowboy boots that made her taller. She had on a tight miniskirt, and there were little sparkles woven into her pale green sweater. It went well with her blonde hair. She looked like a budget version of Barbara Mandrell.

She made a nasty sound with her breath. "They told me you were a gatekeeper, man!" She swept her hands backwards, toward some imaginary someone. "You really don't have contacts on Music Row?"

"Not a one." I felt a pang of sorrow that I didn't. I invited her to sit on the stool beside me. "Happy to buy a drink."

She sat down hard. No doubt she was already half of three sheets to the wind. I ordered her what turned out to be a tequila and freshened my bourbon.

She leaned up hard against me. "You really can't get me a contract?" Her face was too close by half to mine.

"Can't do a thing that way. Anything else I can do?"

She was good looking. I was just asking.

"Not him, you ditz," said a voice over my shoulder. It belonged to a guy with a beard, a bandana, and a cutoff Levi jacket, notable mostly because it served to bare a fairly impressive set of arms. "Him," he said, pointing to a much older man, who looked every bit the part of an agent.

"Aw," she said, leaning up against me with her sparkles. She gave me a peck on the cheek. "You look like more fun, but you can't do anything for me."

I looked up at the bandana, raised my eyebrows, "Story of my life, man."

"I wouldn't worry too much, partner. By mid-afternoon, she'll be sleeping it off. And he ain't no agent anyway. He's just a buddy of mine." He bounced a fist off my shoulder, gently. "She can't sing worth a damn."

I watched the fake agent interview her, give her some pointers. I think he even gave her a business card, which meant that maybe he was a better fake than some of the real things. But the bandana and the sparkle left after about fifteen minutes. He gave me the thumbs up as they left, with her walking a little uncertainly in the lead.

By that time the lunch crowd was gone and the after-work crowd hadn't showed up. I ordered another bourbon and mused about Josie Pittsfield. I couldn't think of any reason, other than the obvious, how she would have pulled off having an apartment by herself. Maybe Hillsboro Village, which was nice, and it was centrally located. But she'd moved more upscale, to Green Hills. Far enough you'd need a car, which freshmen at Vanderbilt typically didn't have unless they're trust fund folks.

There must have been some sugar daddy footing the bill. So that was mystery number one.

Mystery two was Simpson's role in all this. A gay man. Living amicably with a young woman who seemed to be, if not in business, then certainly attached in a commercial way to a man with money.

It didn't make sense at Chet Ervin's and five shots hadn't made it make more sense. So, I stopped, paid my tab, and walked down Elliston Place to Hannigan's.

I was nursing a beer when Landon Pittsfield walked in. A day hadn't done much for his expression. If anything, he looked more hangdog than before.

"We're leaving tomorrow," he said. "My wife just can't take being here, what with," he gestured hopelessly, "you know."

"I can't even imagine," I said, and I meant it. "I have found some interesting things. I should check them with you."

He wasn't really in the mood, I could tell, but he was curious. How are you supposed to feel when your daughter has turned into someone you didn't know, couldn't connect with?

"Josie has had that apartment since her freshman year." It was a blunt instrument. I hoped it would knock something loose.

"That's just not possible," he said. "She lived in Branscomb her freshman year, then moved into Tolman Hall. She only moved in there this summer."

"I've seen the rental agreements. She signed a lease in October, 1973. She's renewed it three times."

A thousand thoughts probably went through his mind, but all he said was, "Somebody else paid the rent."

Bingo. "Any idea who?"

He dropped his head, his hands around the glass with unsweetened tea. "Not a clue." He spun the glass slowly, and the ice rattled against the glass. "But you think that's, what, her. . ." he looked at me helplessly, looking for a word.

"You could call it her patron. Her supporter. Someone who befriended her and set her up."

"That's way too kind, Trade. I'm talking about a pimp." He looked with wide eyes at me. "I don't know what I mean. How could what the papers are saying, how could it be true?"

"We don't know that. It could have been a lover." I knew that, either way, it was hard for a father to hear. "We just don't know anything. Except that she had the apartment from the beginning."

"What's next?"

"If you could give me a friend, someone who she talked about."

"None of that. She didn't talk about anyone specific. We worried that she wasn't fitting in, or not making a lot of friends."

"Did she go anywhere with anyone? Maybe on spring break?"

"Her freshman year she went to New York for break. With a girlfriend. I can't remember the name."

"Did she write you? Or was it always phone calls?"

"There were letters, yes, at first. I could see if we've still got them." He looked doubtful, either about finding them or about their value.

"When you get home, check." To be truthful, I doubted there would be any value there, even if he could find them. But there was a chance, and it gave him something to hang onto. "Was she a good student, Mr. Pittsfield?"

"In high school, she was. One of the very best. To be honest, I don't know how she did at Vandy. Her grades came home the first semester, and they were fine, but after that they came to her." Easy enough to check the Registrar on that, I knew.

"Why don't we leave it this way. I'll try to reconstruct her life here, trying to figure out the day-to-day of her existence. You look at home for letters, anything, that can give me a clue. Does that sound right?"

He smiled. "We're grasping at straws here, aren't we?" I started to protest, but he continued. "Please don't think I don't appreciate what you've done in 24 hours. But I have a feeling that Josie has covered her tracks pretty well."

I finished my beer. "I know I don't look like Lieutenant Columbo, Mr. Pittsfield. But I have an advantage here that no-body else does. I know VU. I worked there. I know everybody there. And no matter how you think I look, most people see the person they've known for seven years, from the time I was a freshman to now. And like I said when we met Wednesday, I have a knack for finding things."

He waved me off. "Don't take it the wrong way, Trade. We'll do it the way you're proposing. I just don't think there's going to be much anyone could do." He looked out toward the window. We were sitting in the front of the restaurant, near the money pinball machine. Once the night crowd got started, this would be a noisy, crowded place. In the afternoon, it was the quietest place in the restaurant. "Where do you suppose your talent for finding things, as you put it, comes from?"

"Pretty simple, really. I'm curious. And it's hard to satisfy my curiosity."

"I know people like that. I might call them nosy."

"Nosy is sticking your nose in other people's business. Curious is different. If you're good at being curious, people don't even know you're in their business."

He laughed a short, raspy laugh. "Unless you've been invited into their business. Like now."

We said our goodbyes. He would head back to Indiana with his wife, and he would search for letters. I flagged Charlie down for another beer and an order of fries.

What I had said to Pittsfield was true. I believed I could get some answers for him about his daughter. If she had still been taking classes, and I believed she had, I could get a transcript from the Registrar, talk to professors, get a feel for how she went about her business on campus. Vanderbilt classes can be large, sometimes, in the first year, but after that they tend to get much smaller. Hard for her to hide. And there was the whole ruse with living in Tolman. She had been there at least initially, and maybe for some time after. Blake could give me the resident assistant roster, and I could find what her dorm life was like.

After that, it was less clear what I could do. But that's what curiosity is. Or rather, that's what being hard to satisfy is about. It's about figuring out what's next. Maybe that's what I can apply to my own life, too.

Chapter Seven

There's not a damn thing you can do about an election year. Ford. Carter. There's a sense that "a ray of Blanton sunshine" is less obnoxious than presidential politics. But really? Not really. Jim Sasser. John Jay Hooker. The Nashville Tennessean and The Nashville Banner arguing daily in editorials, one in the morning and one in the evening. Howard Baker playing the sage in DC. Al Sr. and Al Jr. trying to figure out how to jumpstart phase two of the Gore train.

It was a year of decision for the city, the state, and the country. I didn't much care. My personal decision had been made eleven months earlier. It had exposed who I was, and while I didn't much like what it showed, I had to admit that it was the truth. It had cost me my job, which was going to be my career, I thought. It cost me a bunch of friends.

Lynn and I had married right out of undergrad. We'd had a fast romance spring of senior year, after having known each other most of our four years. We'd always been just at the edge of each other's social circles, partly because I was older. But things roll downhill fast when you're getting ready to enter the world of work, and we went from friends to lovers to inseparable in record speed.

She was not what you'd call beautiful, or even pretty in a way, but she had a bristling wit and an intelligence that made her attractive. It also helped that she was built for speed. Long legs, strong butt, and a shape that turned me on. She knew how to dress, and she knew how to carry herself. She was a hell of a lot of fun to be with.

I took a job as Assistant Dean and we lived in an apartment on campus. I found the days were full of work, but so were the nights. Three, four nights a week I was late getting in. Usually she was asleep, but after a while she was just as likely to be still out herself. The advantage of going to college in a city is that, after you graduate, a lot of your friends are still around. She was working part-time at the Chamber of Commerce. But in retrospect, I left her waiting around a lot.

I shouldn't have been surprised when I found her, one afternoon, in our bed with a friend of ours. I was surprised when they both just laughed at being caught. His name was Bob, and he was more a friend of hers than of mine. Obviously.

"Get dressed, Bob. Then come out to the living room. I want to talk."

"We'll both come," Lynn had said.

"No, please don't do that. I just want to ask Bob a question. After that, you and I can talk."

I had waited in the living room of the apartment, hearing them rustle around. I was pretty sure I had heard them gig-gling. We'd been married a few months. Maybe it didn't seem too different to her than before. God knows, she was sleeping with another guy before we became close.

But that's what I think now. What happened then was that Bob came out and sat down without looking at me. He picked up a magazine and flipped through it. Finally, he looked up. "What's the question?"

"How long?"

"A while now." He stood up, straightened his hair with his hand, and adjusted his belt. "That it?"

I walked over to him. He was a few inches taller than me, but he had narrow shoulders. He had good hair, and he certainly had a long pedigree. "Depends. You coming back?"

He laughed. "Not your say, is it?" He turned to say over his shoulder, "Call me, Lynn."

I don't think of what followed in regular speed. In my mind, as it was that day, I perceived it all in slow motion. I stepped toward him and planted my foot hard, throwing a punch that broke a couple of ribs. He made a sound like air escaping in a flash, then doubled over and fell to the floor. As he rolled onto his back I drove my knee into his stomach and grabbed his good hair. I felt his nose break with the first punch, saw the blood start to flow with the second.

Lynn was screaming.

"You're not coming back, Bob."

It was over in thirty seconds.

In fact, it was me who was not coming back.

After considering whether to file charges, he decided to let it go, reasoning that someone caught in bed with a man's wife might not get the entire sympathy of a jury. That, and his name was well enough known that, should he want to follow his father into the politics game, sleeping in another man's bed might not be a good look for the future.

Lynn, of course, moved out that night, but not before telling me over and over that, if I ever laid a hand on her, I'd die in prison.

I had no intention of laying hands on her. Maybe I'd neglected her. Maybe I deserved what she did. At least that's what I thought.

I moved out about a week later. Blake heard about what happened and called me into his apartment. "Lord, son, you broke two ribs and a nose, they're worried you've perforated internal organs, and there's some talk he can't see out of one eye."

"He's an ass. I snapped. It was over quickly."

"Thank God it didn't go longer. But better it shouldn't have happened at all."

"He got what he had coming."

"Maybe that's right. But I can't keep you on my staff. If anything ever happened again, and it might, there's no defense for the University. We'd have kept a violent man on staff and let him run loose." He walked to a wingback chair and sat down. "I don't know that I can do anything for you, except give you a week to move out."

It hadn't taken that long. Blake introduced me to the Buckets, and they installed me over their garage. That's where I've been ever since.

So, when they say it's a season for decision-making, it rings a little false. Seems like I made my decision already.

And when I say that all that ruckus cost me friends, it doesn't mean that it cost me every friend. Wendy Williamson was the Assistant Dean whose area contained Tolman Hall. When I told her about Mr. Pittsfield and my task, she set up a meeting with Angela Dussault, the RA who, it turned out, had Josie's floor for two years.

We met for coffee at 4 pm at the Campus Grill, directly across from the University library. It was time for a shift change, and all around us the sounds of waitresses and dishwashers and cooks changing places, arguing over the transition from day to night, even though the actual fare served would not change. Either you were having eggs, or you were having a burger. Angela and I were just having coffee.

Angela was a young woman who, in another time, would have been called spinsterish. She wore round glasses and had her long hair pulled back. She had a bit of a hawk nose. She had on sensible jeans and a white twinset sweater. On the surface, she looked every bit the kind of person who wanted to be an RA because she wanted to tattle on the bad girls.

But as the coffee arrived, she popped a pack of Newports out of her bag and lit up. She took a long, slow drag and expelled it slowly through her nose. She looked out on the traffic on 24th. "I've got a P-Chem midterm Monday, so I can't really stay long." Somebody in the kitchen let out a string of adjectives, followed by a verb. He wasn't pleased.

"Pre-med?" At VU, you're either pre-med, pre-law, or already rich, sometimes two of those three though never all three, unless you're lying. Vanderbilt was like Nashville that way, just with different stakes.

"Yeah." She took another drag, then a sip of coffee. "The bitch of this whole thing with Josie is that everybody knew who she was, but when you ask anyone something specific, some detail, they just can't come up with it."

"Such as?"

She stirred her coffee. "Ok, here's one. The day it all happened. I went around, asking about the last time anyone had seen her. You know, a week ago? A couple of days?" She tapped the ash off the Newport. "Everybody would say, oh, sure, like a week ago, I think?" But when you push more, like what day, it gets vaguer and vaguer. Honestly, I don't think anyone's seen her all semester, push comes to shove."

"And you? When was the last time you saw her?"

"That's easy, I saw her in my anthropology course the Monday before it happened."

"She was going to classes?"

"Well, she was going to that one. We laughed about it because it was our last distribution requirement, and we'd put it off. Hard class, too. Should have taken a different one."

"What was she like, Angela? How did she dress? Did she seem happy?

She took a final drag and stubbed it out. "There's a lot in that question. She was always really well put together. I mean, you know how campus is. There are freaks who dress one way, and sorority girls who dress another. Every group kind of has its own uniform to wear. But she was, I don't know, professional. Not haughty. But just well put together."

"And friendly?"

"Sure. But not in a teenager way. And not like sorority girl friendly." She held her mouth sideways as she thought. "You know, it's like she knew she didn't have to be friendly, so if she was, it was genuine. But it was never over the top. She would smile, and say it was good to see you. And you felt like she meant it."

"You know the boy? Simpson?"

"I didn't know his name. I saw him a couple of times after class. He and Josie would walk off together. I didn't think too much of it then."

"Just thought he's a boyfriend?"

She snorted. "God, no!" She covered her mouth, self-consciously. "I'm sorry. That was rude. But no, he didn't look the type."

"Meaning? You thought he was gay?"

"No, not that. He was just not in her league. That's all. She seemed to have it all together. Looking at him, you could tell he didn't have anything much together.

"Were there any rumors about her, Angela?"

"Like I said, everyone thought they knew who she was and where she was. And yet it seems like nobody knew she wasn't there, and nobody had a clue what she was up to."

"Like she's invisible."

"Like she's invisible but has us convinced we can see her." Angela shook her head. "That's a hell of a talent, isn't it?"

She thanked me for the coffee and went back to study for her physical chemistry midterm. I let the waitress refill my coffee and sat there, smoking and watching the daylight die.

I was no closer to knowing why Simpson had killed Josie Pittsfield, and not a lot closer to understanding the life Josie Pittsfield was living. The young woman Angela described was one that Josie's parents certainly would have been proud to have raised. She sounded indeed like someone who had found a way to be mature without being condescending.

But at the same time, she seemed to have materialized out of thin air everywhere she went. Tolman Hall. The management agency. The apartment house. She had all the reality of a substantial person. She left traces of substance everywhere. Grades. Friends. Rent checks. Employers.

And all those things were like smoke.

And Simpson, after killing her, went up in smoke himself, taking his testimony to the grave.

But he presumably wasn't smoke before that. And maybe he was even fire. That's what I needed to find out.

Chapter Eight

Mercer had told me that Simpson had ended up working at Brophy's, a bookstore on Division not that far from my walkabout. I'd phoned ahead to ask Mr. Brophy to speak with me. He'd said yes.

Mick Brophy was athletic. He wore a Led Zeppelin tee shirt that was half a size too small for his chest, and it stretched tightly over his biceps. He didn't look like a guy that would own a bookshop like Brophy's but then, what should he look like? Vincent Van Gopher? In a beret with a monocle? If a guy who looked more like a bodybuilder wanted to run a bookstore, who am I to say?

"The boy was exemplary in every way," he told me. "I don't have a bad word to say about him. He showed up on time, and he did everything I asked."

"On the day of the incident, he left early?" I wanted to extend the conversation, to the extent it was useful.

"As I recall, he came back from lunch complaining of a migraine. He had them once in a while. I told him to go home."

"When was that?"

"No idea. I don't work people on a clock. I'm sure he wrote it down. He always did. But all I care about is getting the work done. And he did. So, if he's not able, then he's not able. I sent him home." Getting the work done did not extend, it seemed, to housekeeping. The bookshop was piled with books, making the place a little claustrophobic. And dusty.

I sneezed. "Were you surprised?"

"Shocked. I mean it. Shocked. It's not the sort of thing you come across, is it? I still can't imagine it."

"You knew he was living with the girl?" I sneezed again. The afternoon light filtering through the window showed just how much dust was in the air.

He disagreed. "No. I mean, I knew he said he was living with a girl. But come on. He was a gay man. He didn't need to tell me that. I'm gay myself. "

I hid my surprise, then felt a little ashamed. I should know better than to stereotype. "He knew that, then?"

"Leave it at the fact that we knew. We didn't need to have that conversation. I wasn't his mentor. I wasn't his lover. I wasn't his anything. He was here to work, and I was glad he was. His living arrangement was of no concern to me."

"Was he happy?"

"Define happy. He was a guy who was struggling. You could see that. But was he able to cope? Was his life ok? Yeah. I think so."

"You think he could have done what they say he did?" Brophy had continued unpacking the box of books. I could see the dust in the shaft of late day sunlight. I sneezed again.

There was a long pause. "I have no idea. Maybe. Like I say, you never really know anybody. But if you ask me, in the absence of everything else, I'd say no."

"Why?"

"In the end? He wouldn't have the balls to do it." He shrugged. "Some folks do. He didn't."

"Everybody's saying he was crazy."

There was a long silence as Brophy sized me up, almost as if he was deciding whether he should tell me something. "He wasn't crazy. He was sensitive. That's the best way I can put it. Not delicate, but he bruised easily."

"Weak?"

He shook his head. "No, not weak. But he felt things deeply."

"Somebody like that might be sent over the edge, right?"

"In my experience, any one of us, even you or me, could be sent over the edge."

He had that right. I was proof. "Ok. Fair enough."

"I can tell you that once he moved in with her, he seemed a little more centered. A little less bruised. So, the idea that he did what they say he did? Well, it takes a lot to get to, in my mind. I just don't see it."

I walked down Division to Mack's Café for a bite to eat. I'd been going to Mack's since I was a freshman and, while it never qualified as haute cuisine, it was the cheapest meat-and-three place in town. Sometimes you might bump into a minor country star or session player. But mostly you sat with a lot of folks who wanted to get full for $2.99.

I ordered chicken fried steak, mashed potatoes with gravy, fried okra, and butterbeans, with cornbread and coffee. I was reading the Tennessean when someone flicked a hard finger into the paper.

I jumped.

The finger belonged to Mercer. He was with a tall, busty brunette I recognized but didn't know. "Go get us a booth, sugar," he said. "I'll just be a minute here."

"She's an upgrade from your usual," I said as I watched her walk away.

"Fuck off," he grinned. "Seriously," he said, sitting down across from me, "I have a name for you if you want it. You still up for a little work on the Pittsfield thing?"

"Sure." I brought him up to speed on what I'd found out.

"Well, that's interesting, I guess. Doesn't get you anywhere. And this might not either." He handed me a folded piece of notebook paper. "That's the phone number of the public defender who was assigned to Simpson. I understand that he spent some time with him before he killed himself." He stood up and found his brunette friend. "Might be worth a call."

I thanked him and went back to the paper. Ford in the news. Carter on the campaign trail. Tennessean endorsing Carter. Which means the Banner will endorse Ford. Howard Baker sounding diplomatic. Sasser ahead of Brock by 10 points in the poll.

But it wasn't all politics. Church Street renovations are slower than expected. Opryland continues its record setting first year pace. New waterfront park proposed. Vanderbilt signs two local basketball stars. Talk of a minor league baseball team.

I looked up. At the table next to me, a guy alternated bites of food with drags on his cigarette. Talented guy. Probably can pick a banjo at the same time, too.

All around, life continued, just as it had. Except for Josie Pittsfield and Mark Simpson. Things had stopped for them. Forever. And I didn't know why. Maybe a public defender would.

Chapter Nine

His name was Anthony Ellis, and he cut a fine figure, as they say. Robert Redford blonde hair, cut stylishly and just long enough for the ladies and short enough for the judges, a three-piece pinstriped suit, the lapels wide enough for the clubs and narrow enough for the courtroom. I was pretty sure I'd seen him around campus, and it turned out I was right. BA 1971, Law 1974, and two years in the firm of Hawk Burnham Marks.

"I mostly do civil law and I don't do much litigation, but we all have pro bono we have to do. I pulled duty on Mark Simpson. I had every expectation that the family would eventually hire someone to defend him."

We were in a rich oak and mahogany conference room. I sate in a chocolate leather chair that matched the one Ellis relaxed in, that was a brother or cousin to twelve more in the room. The conference table cost more, I'm sure, than everything I owned.

He sat across from me, and his pants leg came up to reveal a brand-new pair of Tony Lama boots, the shaft decorated by a red, white, and blue eagle, wings spread. Custom. Also probably worth more than everything I owned.

"Thanks for seeing me," I said. "You didn't have to."

He leaned back and chuckled. "It's not a problem. Lawyer client privilege is pretty much moot when the client is dead. Besides, I didn't do much for this one."

"You saw him at Metro, I understand."

"I did. I was doing my due diligence, even though, like I say, I was sure I'd be replaced."

"What did you think of him?"

"Troubled fellow, for sure. Although if you ask me, not the murdering kind."

"Why do you say that? Just about everybody says he was crazy. Crazy people are the murdering kind, aren't they?"

"Not all of them. Or even many of them."

I thought of that old geometry aid: all squares are quadrilaterals but not all quadrilaterals are squares. "Aren't all murderers crazy, though?"

"I mostly do civil cases. Who knows? But my impression of Mark Simpson was, crazy or not, he was not a murderer."

"Didn't he confess? I thought that's what I heard."

He re-crossed his legs and the other eagle peeked out. "Not exactly."

"That's a strange answer."

He smiled and put his elbow on the leather arm. He was a man who was comfortable in his own skin, probably because his skin was rich and white and comfortable to be in. He had an easy manner with those he considered like him. I doubt he was as comfortable with those he considered outside that lane.

"He was distant. I mean, he talked enough. Especially about trivial details. How long he'd lived there with her. Where he was that day. How he got back to the apartment. He was there with me, and he was participating. But he had a look on his face that said he wasn't there at all."

"Thousand-yard stare," I said.

"What? Oh yeah. Like soldiers get."

"Exactly." I knew it. I'd seen it. "It means that you've disassociated from the world. The horror of battle. You cut off all feeling because, if you let yourself feel anything, you'll end up howling in the night." I had a feeling that Ellis could have F-4'ed out of combat. He wouldn't know. But he might recognize that in Simpson. "That sound like him?"

"No. I mean, not really." He shifted again, and both eagles disappeared. "We were having a conversation, and he was there. But he was somewhere else too. He kept reaching toward something with his hands." He looked at me, raising his eyebrows. "You see? He was reaching for someone."

"How do you know that?"

"He asked me if I couldn't see her."

"Was it the Pittsfield girl?"

"That's what I thought. He didn't call her by name."

"Did he seem happy to see her?"

"I wouldn't call it happy. It was more like pleading."

"What was he pleading with her about?"

"He said, 'Now you understand, don't you?'" Ellis got up and walked to the window. He fiddled with the blinds, as if to straighten them. "He wasn't crazy, Trade. He was traumatized, yes. But that is not an expression of guilt." Satisfied with the blinds, he turned back toward me. "So, no. He did not confess."

"Was he traumatized by the blood? There seems to have been a lot of it. Do you think he freaked out when he saw how much blood there was?"

He stared out the window. From his Broadway window, you could see the Beaman Pontiac logo outside. The flowing hair of Chief Pontiac, frozen in neon, hadn't been Pontiac's emblem for years. That hadn't changed the Nashville sign, though. Nashville was changing, but some things wouldn't.

"I suppose. But I don't think the blood bothered him."

"There was enough blood to bother anyone. I talked to the officer who found the scene. He was bothered."

"Yes, but he had blood all over him."

"Of course, he did. He killed her."

He walked back to the chair and sat across from me, elbows on his knees. His mouth was set, a straight line that would, over time, turn into a sour, sad mouth. Now, though, it was a mouth that was taut with sadness. "That's not it. He was bloody for another reason."

"I don't understand."

"He told me that he held her in his arms. That's how he got so bloody."

"Now I know he was crazy. He killed her, then cuddled?"

"He said, I wanted her to know I love her. I didn't do that before."

"Before what? Before he killed her? As in, 'I love you, but I have to kill you'?"

He put his chin in his hands. "As in, he felt great tenderness for her." He closed his eyes. "The kind of tenderness that means he wouldn't have killed her."

"All right. How would you have gone about proving that to a jury, counselor?"

He opened his eyes and leaned back into the chair, once again the comfortable, rich, upcoming attorney. "I wouldn't have even tried. I would have argued diminished capacity and tried to get him the best deal I could. But," he pointed a finger in my general direction, "I would not have given up on him. He may have done it. But I don't think that he thought he'd done it."

"Crazy person has a black out?"

"Maybe." One eagle was fully exposed now. "Or maybe not."

When I left Ellis, I took a side street to The Dusty Road, a downtown bar with cheap bourbon and a bad reputation. I had a couple of bourbons and left as daylight faded. I stopped further down Broadway at The Hideaway, had a bourbon and talked to the bartender about how hopeless Vanderbilt football was. Two hours later I was on my third bourbon at Hannigan's when I finally ordered a cheeseburger on French bread, medium rare. That got me to 10:00, and I walked the mile past Centennial Park to the High Life, where I had three more beers and a pickled egg.

I don't tell you this to impress. There are a lot of young men who can drink all day and stay relatively functional. I tell you so that you can understand that, as I left the High Life, and walked back toward my place, you'll know that I'd had more than enough. That may be why I thought I saw someone following me. There's enough sidewalk traffic after midnight on West End Avenue that it's not unreasonable to believe someone was indeed walking behind me.

But this felt like it was something different. I turned at least twice, figuring to catch some figure in my line of vision. But each time, there was no one.

Centennial Park was dark as I passed its gates, and yet again I looked behind me, sure I'd see someone. Or something. But the sidewalk behind me was empty.

I walked quickly until I got to my street, and as I turned into the darkness I broke into a trot, then slid behind a hedge. At the end of the street, two men appeared. They stood at the end of the street, one pointing, the other raising his hands, as if saying he didn't know. They stood a minute more, then moved off.

I waited a few minutes, then ran to my garage apartment and locked the door behind me. Downtown around Commerce Street, I would have had my head on a swivel constantly. But Nashville was changing. It looked like I'd have to treat the west end just like downtown, and that was too bad.

Chapter Ten

I'd tried for two days to contact Simpson's brother, a preacher like their father. Paul Simpson was pastor at an independent church out on White Bridge Road, several miles from campus. I got my Chevy Impala to start and pulled into his driveway. It wasn't impressive. In fact, it gave you the impression of a startup church. When I rang his doorbell, a good looking, entirely respectable woman answered. "Yes," she said, "Brother Paul is expecting you." I was shown into a comfortable enough living room.

I sat down in a comfy chair, with a fireplace burning fake logs. There were books in a row on three wide bookshelves. They looked semi-real, at least. The walls were knotty pine, or at least a reasonable facsimile thereof. To be completely honest, the whole thing looked like someone's idea of a study, someone who had no idea what a real study was.

I sat for a few minutes before I heard his footsteps. He was older than I was, but he carried himself with a weight of weariness that was a decade older still.

"Mr. Trade." He said it with a faint air of disdain. Or did I imagine that?

"Brother Simpson." I stood and shook his hand. "I'm sorry for your loss."

He gave me a look that was between sanctity and remorse. I don't know what it meant. But he motioned toward the chair and we both sat.

"I don't know how I can possibly be helpful to you, sir. Your client wants something that I'm afraid I can't help with."

"But do you know what he wants?"

"I assume he wants to know why my brother killed his daughter. I can't possibly know."

"Help me understand your brother better. That will go some ways toward the goal."

"Let me be clear, Mr. Trade. I have no sympathy for the girl. None at all. The newspapers suggest she was a prostitute. There's nothing there for me in terms of her. A woman who will sell her body can have no place in my heart."

"That is an interesting position for a man of the church. What's forgiveness for, anyway? Remember Mary Magdalene?"

"Mary was different. As far as I know this girl didn't ask for forgiveness. As far as I know, she died without asking for it."

"And your brother?"

"My brother, as you no doubt know, was living a homosexual lifestyle. That is a sin and an abomination before the Lord. I wish I could find a way to absolve him. But he didn't ask for it, and he didn't even, as far as I know, think it was a problem."

I didn't say anything. I didn't know what to say. He was punching the air as if he were hand-punctuating a sentence I couldn't see.

"Understand. I loved my brother. I love all my fellow men. But you cannot sin against God and expect a good result."

"Were you close at all?"

"We are imperfect, Mr. Trade. There are always things that we can do better. One of the things I could have done better was to shepherd my brother. He did not have to choose the lifestyle he chose. He did not have to live with the woman he lived with. I regret he made the choices he did. But he made them. I pray for his soul."

"Sounds like you should."

"You're a little sarcastic, I think."

"Not at all. I was raised Methodist. I understand your theology, even if it's not mine."

"Then you understand that my brother, whatever his flaws, is a human who could have found grace. It pains me that he never looked for it."

"'Are you so sure of that?" I found myself in a real conversation with him, even as I doubted that he was having a conversation with me.

"I am sure that, if he sought grace, he would have found it. And I am sure that he didn't seek it."

We sat there at a temporary impasse, he because he was saying words that made him feel righteous, I because his words were empty, just markers put around his perimeter to keep people out. He walked to the fireplace, seemed to wait for the fake fire to warm him. I thought the room already hot enough. He adjusted a picture frame on the mantle, and then walked back and sat.

He looked at me a long minute. "You said you were raised Methodist. What are you now?"

"Nothing."

"Are you an atheist? Or are you just unchurched, waiting for the opportunity to return?"

To return would imply that I was ever there, but I let that slide. "Does it matter?"

"If you are lost to God, then that is your sin and your failing. If you only let grace enter your life through Jesus Christ, you can be born again. What do you believe?"

"I don't believe either of those things," I said.

"Do you even believe there is good and evil in the world?"

There was ample evidence for that. I saw enough in Vietnam to know. "Yes."

"Then understand, even if you do not believe it yourself, that my brother had evil in him. And that girl, whether prostitute or not, was evil herself. Mark might well have found his way back, perhaps even found his way back from his evil lifestyle, but for her. That is the way I see it, sir. There is no other way to see it, if you believe the right way." He was near his preaching voice now, and I could easily imagine its power over a group who wanted to believe what he was saying. He pointed a muscular finger at me. "She took something from her family with her actions, and she took something from Mark. He killed her, yes. But she put him in the position to do it by her own life. I feel some sympathy for her parents, I suppose, though she was not put here evil on the earth. Something made her that way and that usually is the fault of poor parenting."

"Is that why Mark was gay, then? Poor parenting?"

His jaw clenched and he took a breath. "Mark was not a homosexual by nature, if there is such a thing. All that nonsense started after he got to Vanderbilt."

"Ok." I said it to placate him, but also to move to a different topic. "You're a bit older than your brother, right?"

"Ten years." He looked suspiciously at me.

"Just wondering. You weren't there, then, for a good chunk of his teenage years at home." I knew they'd been raised near Waverly, about halfway between Nashville and Memphis.

"That's true. I came to go to college at Horace Williams. I took up my calling here."

"Just as your father took up his call."

"I don't understand your question. My father has served the same church for thirty years. He is a faithful servant."

"Was his expectation that you and Mark would follow in his footsteps?"

He got up and walked to the window. He drummed his finger on the frame. "I suppose we always knew that was the expectation, though I came to Horace Williams and majored in business. The Lord calls you to ministry and, if you hear, you have to respond. Mark did not hear that call, and his goal was, at least at first, to become a lawyer which, before you ask, our father fully supported."

"Is your father's church big?"

He turned from the window. "Not at all. About a hundred on the rolls."

"How does a man like that afford Horace Williams and Vanderbilt? Private schools. Very expensive."

"I played basketball at Horace Williams, and I worked. Mark had an academic scholarship. He worked too."

"And your father and your mother were proud of you both, no doubt."

"Our mother died when I was sixteen." He turned back to the window, as if looking for something. "Mark was just about to start first grade. It was hard for us all."

"And hardest for Mark?"

"I don't know that. Our father was devastated, of course. I was hurt, but we all knew the fact of heaven and the certainty of her salvation. We knew she would be waiting for us. All earthly time is soon, Mr. Trade. All God's time is eternity."

"Did Mark get over it that easily? Six-year-olds Thadon't usually have that grasp of eternity."

He moved to the fireplace and sat with his back to the fire, facing me, closer in proximity than we'd been since we shook hands. "That's true. That's an insight. I see it every day in my congregation. That's why we have children's church before the worship gets started. That way, the younger ones can hear, in their own way, about the evil of the world and the grace of our Lord and Savior Jesus Christ. But you're right. Mark had a longer, harder time than my father or I did." He reached to turn the fire off. "You're warm enough?"

I nodded. I thought it was hot enough to be oppressive in the room. His was an interesting narrative. A father and two boys left too soon by a mother. It wasn't too hard to believe that the older one had recovered by moving out and getting on with life in the city. It also wasn't hard to believe that the younger one felt deserted, first by his mother and then by his brother. "Did your father remarry?"

"Never did. And I can see what you're thinking. He raised Mark in a single parent household. But you must understand the nature of his congregation. Mark had many, many mothers. The women of the church treated him as one of their own."

"Actually, I wasn't thinking that at all. I was wondering if your father, given his responsibilities and his burdens, might have found being a father more taxing than when he had a partner in that work."

"Well, that never occurred to me. If it was, he certainly didn't say anything about it."

Our conversation never got any deeper than that. He didn't trust that I could really understand how righteous he and his father were, and I never really thought he had enough insight to understand why his brother might not be sinful. But the interview ran to a natural conclusion, with him telling me what he remembered of Mark's life from age 6 to when he came to Nashville. It wasn't much. Stories of Christmas vacations and summer visits.

"And then he came to Nashville. You saw him often?"

"No. He made it clear he wasn't interested in seeing me. I suppose he didn't approve of the way I regarded his friends."

"You met some of them, then?"

"Queers," he said. "And then her."

"You met Josie Pittsfield?"

He gave me a level gaze. "Once. He was working in the dorm. She came into the office."

What was that conversation like, I wondered? So I asked him.

"I asked her to leave my brother alone."

And what did she say?

"She just laughed at me. Told me to mind my own business. Called me a Christian moron."

"And then you didn't see him again. Until you saw him in jail?" He nodded. "I assume that conversation was different."

"I've never been on the inside of a jail, Trade." The preacher was gone now. In his place was a quieter person. One that was pitiable. "It was an awful experience."

Probably worse for his brother, I thought. "What did he say to you?"

"He admitted he killed her. He was distraught with the knowledge." He seemed visibly limp.

"Did he say why he killed her?"

"I think it's just as you read in the papers. He didn't know exactly what caused him to do it. He flew into a rage, I suppose. He felt possessed. What do they call it? A crime of passion?" His voice was flat.

That's usually what they call something different from this, but I let it go. "With a crime of passion there is generally a great love that gets twisted somehow." I waited for that to sink in. "What great love was here?"

He looked away from me. "Where God's love is rejected, there is no great love, and there is no greater love." He turned back toward me. He had his preacher face back on, the one that leads the mourning at funerals. "This was of the Devil and was mere evil. I'm sad for my brother, as I said, because he forsook the grace available. I am not sorry for her. And I can't be sorry for what he did."

On leaving, I had known what I needed to do, but there were a couple of things that had prevented my doing it. I needed to spend some time in Josie and Mark's apartment before the complete clearing out of personal effects happened, but I really didn't want to see Betty to do it. I also knew that I didn't want to get busted for breaking in. It's the sort of conundrum that can make you wait too long to do the thing you need to do. So it's best just to get on with it.

Betty was out, as were the first-floor tenants on the other side. Floor two had one empty apartment and one where an elderly couple lived. Third floor was Josie's and a Middle Eastern couple, probably graduate students. Fourth floor was where I wanted to be, since Betty had said that the tenant, a resident at the hospital, was on rotation in Memphis until December.

I looked at the locks. There were two of them, one the regular snap lock that locks the knob when you close the door. The other was a beveled deadbolt. I don't even know why they bother to sell the things. I took out a strip of celluloid and slid it between the jamb and where the beveled plunger would be. Both popped backwards and the door was open.

So much easier than Josie's place, with its double dead bolts, neither of them beveled, would have been.

Once inside, I relocked the door and went to the window where the fire escape was, went out the window and went down one flight. The window in Josie's apartment was unlocked, and so I was inside, one floor down, in about five minutes.

An hour later, I reversed the procedure, relocked the door, and exited the building. I could hear the television in Betty's apartment. I could smell bacon frying. I could hear a couple speaking a foreign language excitedly, as if they were either agreeing or fighting, just like in Vietnam. You couldn't tell the difference. Maybe there was no difference.

I walked down the street to where my Impala sat, started it, and drove home.

Chapter Eleven

I started my morning in a phone booth, calling Wendy Williamson again. "Did a girl named Elyse Hyde ever live in Tolman Hall?" A few minutes later, the phone in the booth rang, and Wendy confirmed that a girl by that name had indeed lived in Tolman. She was a senior when Josie was a sophomore. Then a quick call to the alumni office. Yes, they had a recent class note citation on Elyse Hyde. She had married Brad Thursdale, class of 1971, and they were living in Franklin.

I called directory assistance for a listing of Thursdale in Franklin, Tennessee, and got a single number, which I called. A pleasantly Southern female voice answered.

"Mrs. Thursdale?"

"I am she." Perfect grammar too.

"My name is Jackson Trade. Can you spare a few minutes to talk about Josie Pittsfield?"

"Are you with one of the papers? I don't know anything about what happened to her. Plus, the student who killed her turned around and killed himself. What could I possibly add to that?"

"I grant you, maybe nothing." I told her how I came to be involved in this, and how Josie's father wanted somehow to connect the dots of his late daughter's life. "You were there for a part of it, Mrs. Thursdale. You can help."

"I don't see how. I have to go."

And she hung up on me. Lovely talking to you too.

It wasn't hard to put together why. For one thing, she had a new life. Old mail in Josie's hall closet had Elyse Hyde's name and that address on it. So, Elyse had been the woman who had lived there before Mark. Elyse had married and moved to Franklin, an up-and-coming suburb in Williamson County, about thirty miles south. Perhaps she'd married one of the many medical school or law school graduates from Vanderbilt. Maybe she wanted to protect that life. Maybe there was something in the relationship with Josie that made her think she had to protect that life.

I called again. She let it ring four times, then didn't answer at once when she picked it up. When she finally said hello, I said, "Don't hang up on me again. Do you understand? If you do, I will come out there during dinner some night, knock on your door, and ask you my questions in front of your husband. Do you want that?"

"You wouldn't do that," she said.

"Do you want to find out?" I could hear her breathing on the other end of the line. I fancied I could hear her heart beating faster too. "I didn't think so," I said.

"Very well. I can't do today. And there's no way I can come into town tomorrow. I have several appointments in the morning."

"I can come to you. Do you have plans at lunchtime?"

"I really don't know. I cannot be seen with you. Do you understand?"

"I understand well enough. You pick the place."

"Not here. How about up in Brentwood. There's a Steak and Ale just off I-65."

"I'll see you there at noon."

"How will I know you?" she asked.

"I'll be sitting out front waiting for you. I have long blonde hair." I didn't tell her the rest. It wasn't necessary. People like me weren't in the Steak and Ale, for lunch or any other time.

What I'd found in the apartment was negligible. Yes, I'd found the envelopes that led me to Elyse Hyde, but there'd been precious little else. A few keys. Pens. Receipts from the drug store. Mostly the detritus of a life, things left behind. What I'd done for most of the hour was to sit and listen, sit and try to feel Josie and Mark in the small space. It was clear from the arrangement that she had the apartment and that he was simply staying there. The one bedroom was hers; the sleeper sofa was his. There was a clear hierarchy of space allocation. She had the bathroom and the counter space. He had a spot to put his deodorant. It wasn't even clear that his shaving materials could stay out; they were put away neatly in a drawer. Her clothes were in closets, arranged in a way that let me know that she took good care of her things. His were folded, with geometric precision, in a dresser.

Where all that shifted was in the kitchen. There, you sensed a different vibe. She may have been an omnivore; who knew? His was a more Spartan diet, and everything in the kitchen suggested that his was the dominant personality. Like his clothes drawers, the kitchen was a place of order and precision. Even the knife block, and even missing a couple of knives, was clean, its implements old but cared for. The overwhelming impression was of a household well run and agreeable to both parties.

I had sat for a while in the apartment, trying to intuit what possibly could have gone on. Not just with the report, but also with my own knowledge of what was happening. Even with the cleaning Betty had done, I found blood stains here and there.

I could feel something there. It was not a feeling of something terrible about to happen. In fact, it was more the feeling that these were two happy people, making their way. I didn't understand their arrangement, but it appeared that they understood it. There was a domesticity to it, the way Betty had described it as brother and sister, that made me doubt even more the apocalyptic Reverend Simpson.

Sitting there, it was clear to me. These were not evil people. They had carved out something rare in this world, the art of being fully in place. They were domesticated, whatever else they were doing. She might, in fact, have been a prostitute. Just as he might, in fact, have been a promiscuous gay man living with a prostitute.

Their life was tidy. Until it was not.

I needed to find out why.

I watched out the window. The blue wasn't a blue. It was broken up by low clouds that raised themselves into the upper atmosphere, causing dark pink striations to punctuate the sky. Below there were banks, first of bright blue, then orange, then yellow. Finally, at the place where the tree line gave way to the horizon, there was the white light of sun just then gone. The brightness was almost more than you could bear. And then, in a minute, it receded into a toasty yellow, and the other layers began to fall away, one by one, into the deepest blue. Looking west, the radio tower was lit, then was a shadow, and then gone, as if it had disappeared from the earth.

As if it were unselfconscious of itself as metaphor, which of course it was.

Chapter Twelve

When I got back to my garage apartment, there was a message on my phone from Mr. Pittsfield. He was interested in knowing what I'd found, if anything. He'd also found, as I had requested, the last couple of communications they'd had from Josie. So, the next day, I opened a can of Pabst and sat down to call him. He was out to lunch. I told the receptionist at the dealership I'd call him later.

I would find out more, I hoped, from Elyse, but the central mystery remained: how had Josie afforded the apartment in Green Hills as a freshman at Vanderbilt? The reigning suspicion, from VU police to Metro to the newspapers to Simpson's brother was that she was a prostitute. That may certainly be a possibility. But it's hard to fathom how a girl from Indiana could have so rapidly found, her freshman year, how to start hooking and making a decent enough living from it.

It made far more sense if she was being supported, what used to be called a kept woman. It was still a stretch, but it made a little more sense that, instead of hooking, she was being kept by one man, probably one who had a reason to be considerably more invisible in her daily, college life than a regular boyfriend would be.

The apartment reference at Huddleston Tire came up again, in my mind, as a possible place. Chet Ervin had treated it as a facile lie that was par for the course. Maybe, though, it had more utility than that.

I called the number for Huddleston Tire again. "Hi. This is Joe Ford from the Nashville Banner's business section. I'm updating our files on business ownership."

The helpful voice on the other end said, "How can I help you?"

"Pretty simple. For some reason, our files are completely blank on your business. Can you tell me the owner? Is it a Mr. Huddleston?"

"Mr. Huddleston died four years ago. His wife owns the business."

"Oh, that's too bad. How old was Mr. Huddleston?"

"I don't know exactly. Pretty old, though."

Scratch him off the list, then. "And who manages the business? Were there children?"

"No, no," said the friendly person on the other end. "Mrs. Huddleston runs the business. She was always quite involved." There was a pause before she said, "Is there anything else?" She was ready to finish the call. You could hear it in her voice, even if she didn't remember my fake name.

"Ford. Joe Ford. From the Banner. One more thing. Do you remember anyone working there named Josie?"

"In management? Not at all."

"Anybody. Wouldn't have to be in management. I have a scribbled note here in the file that just says 'contact Josie'."

"That's not a name I know from here at all."

We hung up. Strike two with Huddleston. Maybe that was even strike three. It would seem that Mr. Huddleston's dying would make it impossible that he was the sugar daddy. And now two people had said nobody named Josie had worked there. So maybe Chet was right, and the reference lie was so facile that it worked, if nobody had checked it out.

I had checked it out, from three years away, and it seemed to lead nowhere.

I left the apartment again, this time walking the quarter mile to Hannigan's. The place was quiet, the lunch rush over, and

Katie smiled at me and brought a bourbon. I waved off the menu, saying, "Not yet, anyway," and she nodded and took it away. I sat in the dark corner next to the pinball machine.

What did I know, after several days of walking around and talking to people and one completely illegal break in? I knew that Josephine Pittsfield was a decent student who planned to graduate. She had moved into Branscomb Quadrangle as a freshman, into Tolman Hall as a sophomore and junior, but had never really lived in either. Instead, she had rapidly found an apartment in Green Hills, had Elyse Hyde as a roommate for some period of time, then Mark Simpson, who had been a security clerk in Tolman until he got fired, for another period of time. Mark had worked at Brophy's Book Store on Division and had continued in school. At some point in what appeared to be a stable life, Mark showed up in Branscomb Courtyard covered in blood and screaming profanities. The blood was hers, and he was arrested for her murder after she was found mutilated beyond recognition in the apartment they shared. He subsequently killed himself, after telling his brother that he had killed her.

I knew some detail. I had filled in a little color. But I had nothing substantial that I didn't have when I started. I knew little more than Don Mercer had told Mr. Pittsfield the day he arrived from Indiana.

I knew that someone set her up in that apartment. I needed to know who did it.

I sat there for what seemed the better part of several hours. The sky grew dark outside, and a storm blew trees and rain sideways. Dan Miller on Channel 4 even disappeared for a few minutes when the television went out. I had several more bourbons, then ordered a salad. By the time the nighttime crowd came in, the storm had passed, and I'd had enough of Hannigan's. I waved at Charlie, who by this time had taken the register, and told him to put it on my tab.

"You going to be able to put something on that soon, Jackson?" He didn't say it so anyone else heard, but he said it all the same.

"I'll come by tomorrow." I knew about what it came to. I knew I didn't have it in my wallet now, and I didn't have checks with me. "I can get most of it then."

The streets were wet, and limbs littered the sidewalk. The storm had been the kind you see in October in middle Tennessee. All it takes is a warm and humid atmosphere, a cool upper atmosphere, and a wind shear that makes a vortex take off like a thing possessed. It had been humid during the day, around 85 degrees, and now, after the front had passed, it felt a little more like fall. A wet one, and one that wasn't yet ready to turn the corner toward winter, but seasonal. I wished I had a jacket on.

I crossed West End at 26th Avenue South, in front of the park, and walked the south side of the street down to The Top Hat. It was quiet inside, as it was once the dinner rush was over. I took a table and asked the waiter to bring me a bourbon.

The thing about The Top Hat that was different from my usual dives was that, first, it was no dive. They had white tablecloths and real napkins. The second was that, notwithstanding my friend Richard Elliott, who had graduated and left for law school, there was precious little to attract an undergraduate crowd. The food was above average, but not good enough to cause people to drive to a small building with little parking. It was just a touch too far for the undergraduate to walk, and especially too far to walk with a date wearing heels. Thus, The Top Hat struggled along, probably barely able to make its expenses.

But the attraction it had for me was the quiet. There was classical music playing in the background. Except for an older couple finishing dessert and a harried-looking business type chowing down, probably before running back to a back office at Health Corporation of America, I had the place to myself. The waiter looked like he could have been a graduate student at VU, but he also could have been a local who was trying out a new gig.

I ordered a second bourbon. I was starting to feel the alcohol in my eyes. They weren't adjusting to dark that well. But my mind was still working well.

It was working well enough to wonder, for the first time, whether there shouldn't be a car.

The working assumption was that she and Simpson took the bus in from Green Hills. It certainly made sense. It was a straight shot to campus and only, what, five or six stops? In a big city, that would be nothing. Walking, it was three miles, certainly doable, but why would they have done that? Only poor people in Nashville walk three miles. Vanderbilt students? Never.

Josie had a nice apartment. Why wouldn't she have had a nice car too? It was something I could check on with Mercer in the morning. If she had a car and she drove to campus, it stood to reason that she had a parking sticker.

I remember a fleeting sense that I was done for the night. Everybody should get one good idea a day, and I had mine. It had taken a lot of bourbon to get it, but I had it at last. I paid the bored waiter in cash and walked out into the night.

The air was cold now and raw. The front had passed entirely and left in its place a feeling that winter could be right around the corner. I walked down West End, the breeze at my back sending a small chill through the thin tee shirt I'd started a warmer day with. The bourbon wasn't helping keep me warm either. The headlights on wet streets caused a glare and made looking up toward the traffic painful.

I heard two car doors thump closed behind me. "Hey, buddy. Hold up a minute," said a voice. I turned to see two men, one larger than me, one smaller, coming up toward me. The short one was lighting a cigarette, and the smoke curled around his head. Both had on stocking caps that reached over their ears. The short one had on a denim jacket, the other a longer coat.

"Yeah?" I heard myself saying, just as they drew even with me.

Shorty blew smoke toward me. "Made a night of it, bud?"

"It's not quite eleven," I said. "Hard to make a night of it before midnight."

"You figure on heading somewhere else?" said the larger one. I'm 6'2; he had me by three inches, maybe four.

I didn't like the question and I didn't like the odds if this was going somewhere physical. I backed toward The Top Hat's entryway. It was a good thirty yards back. I didn't figure to make it there if they really wanted to keep me from it.

"Hey, man," the shorter one said. "We're just checking on you. You been hitting it hard all day. Just trying to help a brother out." The taller one was moving to my side. Unless I moved quickly, he was going to outflank me and cut me off.

I put my back against the building and moved to my left, back toward The Top Hat, shuffling as fast as I could.

Shorty threw his cigarette down and advanced toward me. The tall one loped two steps and got completely to my left. They had me trapped.

"What do you boys want with me?" As I said it, I could hear the slur in my words. I didn't feel drunk. I felt completely energized. My nerves, if they could have, would have been standing on end. I was alert, on the balls of my feet, ready for whatever I needed to do.

"Aw hell, man," said the taller one. "We're just trying to get you home in one piece. You been drinking all up and down West End. Come on. Get in the truck. We'll take you home."

I readied myself for some kind of tussle. Knees bent, hands out, ready to fend them off, body balanced. "Mama told me not to take rides with strangers," I said.

I heard the snap come from Shorty. He had a blade out. "I think your Mama didn't know us. But that don't mean we're strangers." He was grinning.

I have seen this play out before. Usually in a bar, sometimes at a frat party, one time even in a 7-11. There's something tense going on. A weapon is introduced. And then nothing good happens. Somebody gets hurt. Sometimes several people get hurt. As an Assistant Dean of Students, I saw it more weekends than not. But not usually with a knife involved.

I moved as quickly as I could to spin so that my back was to the street. Now they were on either side, but I wasn't pinned in. "Hey now," I said. "No need to bring your knife into this."

Shorty's breath was visible in the newly chilled air. "If you get in the car, there's no knife in play." A Metro black and white went by and he put the knife by his leg. "Come on, man. Take a little ride." He pulled the knife away from his leg so I could see it.

"Take it easy, man." I kept my eyes on one, then the other.

"Just get in the goddamn truck."

"Ok, ok," I said. "Just put the knife down. Geez, man."

He was about five-six, and though he looked wiry I had thirty pounds on him, easily. I took a step toward the taller one, then sprinted as hard as I could into him, driving him into the wall of the building behind him. As he hit the wall, I put my forehead as hard as I could into his nose. I heard the crunch of his bones and felt him collapse. The knife flew into West End.

The taller one had been slow to react; he had already taken a step toward the car. Now, he froze. Shorty was moaning. Blood was coming from the corner of his mouth and from his nose.

I was a little out of breath, but I could feel the adrenaline. "Pick him up and put him in the truck," I said. "Either that or race me out in the traffic for the knife. But I'll plant you before I let you get to it."

"You're a crazy mother," he said, putting his hands up.

"Come for me, and you'll see what a crazy mother looks like."

Shorty's breathing was shallow. I suspected a few things were broken. I knew he wasn't going to be a threat tonight. I walked toward the taller one. He backed up. "All right. Just let me get him out of here," he said.

He was backed up against a parking meter when I rammed him. He spun around the meter and took a swing at my head, glancing off my nose. I kicked hard against his knee and heard him yell, then grabbed his shoulder with my left hand and spun him, throwing my right hard. I was aiming for his nose, but he was taller than I thought, and I swung through his jaw. He went down, covering his face. I fell with both knees on his midsection, then grabbed his hair with my right hand. I pulled my left fist back. "Do you want this?"

He didn't answer.

I let go of his hair and his head fell to the ground. I put my hands around his throat. "I don't know who you are. I don't know why you're after me. But you better stay away." I leaned down to look in his eyes. "And if you decide to bring something besides knives next time, just know that I'll be ready." I tightened my grip on his throat. "You understand?"

He understood.

I listened to the rain, the sound of it alternately lashing the window, then pecking at the metal gutter. For hours it had been thus, by turns stormy and then merely wet. Outside the temperature had dropped again. It was October, but winter was coming.

I had awakened from a drunken sleep. My head still throbbed, telling me that the "just one more" attitude of the night before had been a mistake. I pride myself on being able to hold my alcohol, to be functional when others couldn't be, but what's the point of that pride?

My right hand hurt. I had put two guys on the ground last night. What was that about? I knew what I thought. They were trying to get me in a car and take me, but where? Who were they?

Or did I have that right? What if they were trying to help a stumbling drunk get home?

But no, that couldn't be. There was the knife. There was a knife, right? I didn't imagine that, did I?

I looked at the clock radio. Four in the morning. I walked to the bathroom, opened the medicine cabinet, and shook out four aspirins. I chewed the bitter tablets, feeling the grainy bits as I swallowed them down. I put my mouth underneath the faucet and drank.

Chapter Thirteen

I wasn't sure what the next move was. If they were the guys who had followed me two nights before, and why wouldn't they be, what did they want? Were they going to take me to see someone else last night? Or were they just going to throw me in the Cumberland River? And either way, why? Was it just that Nashville was turning into a city? With senseless city crime?

I stripped and turned on the shower. Twenty minutes later I was clean but hardly sober, still. I could taste the sour residue of that last bourbon on my tongue.

I brushed my teeth, drank a glass of water, and crawled under the blanket.

I awoke to someone pounding on the door. For a second, I incorporated it into my dream, but it didn't go away. I rose, pulling my pants on as I went. I could hear Mercer's voice. "Jesus, Jackson, open the damn door."

I found my jeans from the night before. They were stiff enough to stand on their own. I grabbed a flannel shirt from two days ago, draped on the kitchen chair. It was good enough to answer the door in.

I opened the door to find a uniformed Mercer clearly ready for day shift. He brushed past me into the apartment. "Morning, Donnie. You look chipper."

He stood in the middle of my apartment with his hands on his hips. "Where were you last night?"

"Are you asking as my friend? Or as a cop?"

"Between 11 and midnight."

"I'm just making coffee. You want some?"

"Because someone at Linda's saw you running down West End. And that same person looked up West End and saw a couple of guys crawling into a pickup truck. One of them looked to be in pretty bad shape. That's what I hear anyway."

"Well, those are two dots that are not connected. It's a type of logical fallacy, Donnie. Post hoc, ergo something. Just because I was running doesn't mean anything about other people."

"Why were you running?"

"You know how cold it was last night? I had a tee shirt on. I was cold. I wanted to get home."

He rubbed his chin, probably trying to decide whether to believe me.

"Who saw all this?" I asked.

"You remember Dietrich? The Metro guy? He called me from Linda's."

"Did he go check on the other guys?" If he had, he wouldn't have got much.

"I don't think so. A Metro cop with three beers in him will usually just sit tight."

I shrugged, stirred the Folger's crystals into hot water and tasted it. The water wasn't hot enough, which gave the coffee the taste of murky dishwater. I put the cup down. "You didn't come over here before work just to see about me, right?" Mercer sat in the comfortable chair. "Make yourself at home, Donnie."

"There is a little girl missing the past few days, from a house up on Acklen." He looked at me to confirm I understood where that was.

"Nice little neighborhood."

"Yeah. Between Natchez Trace and 32nd. Anyway, she was delivering Girl Scout cookies before dinner three nights ago and didn't return. There were people who saw her on Acklen, even one who saw her on Natchez Trace, but nothing after that."

"Where was she delivering the cookies?"

Mercer looked around the small apartment. "Don't you have a television? This has been on every station in town. Jessica Settles, the weekend anchor on 5, even went out to try to get the parents interviewed. I mean, this has been major, Jackson."

"I don't have a tv here, and I don't take either paper. Plus, I've been busy."

"You have been busy drinking, at least for the past couple of days."

I had enough of a hangover not to argue. "I've been busy following up on the Pittsfield thing."

"Sure. There's that." He gave me the side-eye. "So anyway, last night, while you were running home in the cold, Metro found the body, much to the chagrin, I believe, of the FBI and the state boys who were helping out. Anyway, they found her body in a neighbor's outbuilding. She'd been raped and strangled. Then cut just for the fun of it."

"Jesus. Not a nice little neighborhood after all." I took another sip of bad coffee. "I guess Metro has hundreds of people out looking for who did it. Do they know?"

"There's a suspect. Kid in the neighborhood."

"Why a kid? That's a hell of a thing."

"Somebody took the cookies and the change she was carrying. That's got juvenile written all over it."

"Downtown, people will take your cookies just for the hell of it," I said. Maybe on West End Avenue too, it turns out.

"This is Hillsboro Village. They don't even lock their doors over there."

"Maybe they should." I poured the coffee out in the sink and put the kettle back on to boil. "It's still a hell of a thing."

"Everybody on radio and television is all in. Channel 4, Channel 5, they're running nonstop breaking news reports.

The afternoon talk guys on WSM radio have been having a field day, and now Metro is turning this kid loose."

"They know about the suspect?"

"The Assistant DA has let it be known that they're close. Probably a good idea. Otherwise, that side of town would be scared to let their kids out of the house. They probably are, anyway."

I could see that. West Nashville was a sleepy place, full of middle-class folks, caught between Belle Meade and its mansions and the grit of downtown. To its south, 21st Avenue turned into Highway 431 pretty quickly, and you didn't get much but country until you got to Franklin. A dead girl, and one raped besides, was not a usual thing. "Well, thanks for the report, Don. You saved me buying a Tennessean today."

"There is one more thing, Jackson." He had a grin on his face that didn't match the keen look in his eyes. "Something that you will be interested in."

"Do tell."

He shook his head. "You will be interested to know that in the sweep of the neighborhood, something odd turned up." He got up, as if to leave. "Yes, you'd be interested in this."

I wasn't biting. "If it's so interesting, just tell me."

"You're not much fun." He sat back down. "Ok, so our murdered girl. . ."

"The Girl Scout? Or Pittsfield?"

"Good. You're tracking me. I mean Miss Pittsfield. She lives in an apartment in Green Hills. How does she get to school every day?"

"Did I call you about this last night?" I asked. Honest to God, if I did, I was way drunker than I thought.

He looked surprised. "You didn't call me at all."

"Go on, then. It's just interesting that I think we ended up in the same place."

"Ok. Did she walk? It's three miles, so it's possible, but she doesn't seem like the type."

"Agreed. She could take the bus. It's, what, five stops, six at the most?"

"Again, she doesn't seem the type. So . . ."

"So. you looked in your parking permits to see if she'd registered a car on campus, so she could park."

"Not quite. Or at least, not next. What turned up in the neighborhood sweep was a tan Ford Torino, a four door, registered to Miss Josephine Pittsfield."

"Where in the neighborhood?"

"About halfway between Acklen and the Pittsfield girl's apartment."

"What's that? Maybe half mile away?"

"More like eight tenths of a mile. It was found on Blair Boulevard, so closer really to Acklen. But close enough to walk."

That didn't make much sense. "Why would she park the car almost a mile away from her apartment? That's almost as far as it is down 21st to Vanderbilt. She might as well have walked to school."

"I don't disagree. But I thought you might find something interesting about it."

I pulled the kitchen chair over in front of Mercer, spun it around and sat with my forearms on its back. "It's pretty strange, you know. I had convinced myself last night that she must have had a car. I don't know why it took so long for me to get there."

"Maybe you're not as sharp lately."

"Nice try," I said. I did my best to make it sarcastic, but I think I mostly just sounded tired. "You didn't think of it until you knew there was a car. If I'm not sharp, what are you?"

"Not interested." He kicked at my leg. "I've handing you a bone. It doesn't fit the skeleton they're constructing at Metro. I don't know if you can use the bone or not."

He got up and headed toward the door. "Thanks, Don. I appreciate it." I stood up too. "You know where the car is now?"

"Still over on Blair as far as I know. Nice car too. Looks like a V-8, 360."

"Lot of car for a senior at Vanderbilt."

"Plenty of car for anybody. Especially if they're dead."

I let him out. He was still chuckling to himself about too much car for a dead girl. I didn't think it was that funny, but then I don't do his line of work. Maybe it goes squirrely after a while.

What I did know was that I had a couple of odd facts. The car, certainly. Why was it parked in the wrong neighborhood? And Mark Simpson may well have been living a lifestyle, as his brother put it, but where was the evidence of that? Certainly not in the apartment. Was he gay? Or did everyone have that wrong?

There was only one way I knew to find out.

I went where I knew there might be answers.

Nashville had always had its gay bars and drag cabarets but, unlike a city like New Orleans or Atlanta, the gay scene hadn't been much above ground. There had always been the threat, and sometimes the reality, that a pair of men caught holding hands could find themselves hauled downtown, jailed overnight, and the record of arrest published in the paper the next day. It was not an easy town to stay closeted in, as the fifty-nine men arrested one night in Centennial Park in 1962 found out.

The Jungle never had as many run-ins as the other bars because the owner was a cousin of a deputy sheriff. But every other gay bar in town had to be on its watch to make sure either that a raid found only upstanding, though entirely male, customers, or that, in the case where they were hauled downtown, they got bailed out quickly. That was especially true of Juanita's, over on Commerce.

Juanita's had been legendary. Check that. Juanita herself had been legendary. Miss Juanita was known, when a raid emptied her entire establishment, to march down and pay the bail money for each one, then lead the parade back to the bar. When the police chief finally got tired of the back-and-forth, he entered into negotiations with her, and the result kept the police off her back for close to twenty years. It was a good thing too, since there were always plenty of prominent Nashvillians in Juanita's place.

By 1976, though, Commerce Street was pretty rough, both in terms of the customers passing through and in terms of the grifters and hard cases hanging out on the street. More than once, a gay man was robbed, and a couple had been killed. The general feeling was, "that's what happens." Not that many gay men were going to go to a cop because they had been hassled. And there was a suspicion that some Metro cops weren't going to look that hard for somebody who'd robbed somebody coming out of Juanita's.

So I didn't figure to start downtown. That was an area way too rough for Mark Simpson. It would have been easy enough to get out to The Warehouse in Berry Hill but, from what I knew of its reputation, the vibe there would have been a little loud and a little aggressive for him. I opted for Other Times at 7th Avenue South and Broad.

It was a white building with three distinct spaces. A space on either end with loading dock doors, and the club itself, with a narrow door and no distinguishing marks. The explosion of gay Nashville had begun to happen, but it was not an explosion that had many visible markings still. Juanita's to the contrary notwithstanding.

I walked in and let my eyes adjust. It was a place where the night crowd, with cologne and drinks and noise, would have ignored any deficiencies of the building. In the early Saturday afternoon, with sunlight filtering through the windows at the top of the cinderblock, you could see the lack of cleanliness.

Instead of cologne I smelled sour mop water. It wasn't the most pleasant place. Last night, and tonight too, it would probably be raucous.

At the bar there was a bartender watching Wide World of Sports and a single drinker, an older man with what looked like a tumbler of bourbon and a newspaper. Neither paid any attention to me.

I walked to the bar and waited for the bartender to turn. "What's your drink?" he said without looking away from the television. Some kind of event with lots of snow was on the screen.

"Bourbon. Like that guy's," I said, "Fill it up to the top."

He turned from the television quickly enough. "Jackson Trade," he shouted. "You son of a bitch. My God. What the hell are you doing here?" He said all that quickly, then came out from behind the bar to give me a hug. A chaste hug, for the bourbon drinker. "Damn, man. Where you been?"

Jeremy Winston and I started Vanderbilt at the same time. He was so closeted that he was the freshman class candidate for Homecoming Court. Nobody knew. But he was on my freshman floor and those of us on the far end of 4th floor Curry Hall knew that Jeremy was not exactly like the rest of us.

He had gone to a good prep school in Richmond. He was friends with all the pretty girls. And he was absolutely not going to bed with any of them. For a Vandy freshman, that was a dead giveaway.

"Things going ok, Jeremy?" I asked.

He motioned to the bar. "What could be better? Got a gig. Got a place. Making a little money. You?"

"Know this young man?" I put a picture of Mark Simpson on the bar.

"Sure. It's the boy in the papers last week. Why are you asking?"

"That's the ten-dollar question. He ever come in here?"

Jeremy leaned up on the bar. "I'm not sure. I mean, that's what I thought when I saw him in the papers last week. You know? Like, that's a familiar face. But then you get distracted, and I just let it out of my mind."

"So you're not sure?"

"Seriously, Jackson, I'm not trying to be difficult. Let me think."

He went about his business for a while. He was cleaning glasses and refilling the lemons and limes. He got the bourbon guy another bourbon. Then he returned. "I mean, the first time he was here I asked him for ID."

"But not since then?"

"Look. I'm not sure. Let me think about it. I didn't take him home. I know that. But I think he probably went home with one or another of the regulars. I can ask."

I drank the rest of the bourbon. He had poured me Maker's Mark. It was the least he could do, I'm sure he would say.

"Give me a ring." I left my business card. "Or maybe I'll stop by again. It's pretty quiet in here and you could get some thinking done."

He smiled at me. "You get in the habit of coming down here, and there'll be more than some thinking, Jackson. People will start thinking they know something."

I made more rounds. The Toolbox was probably out; he didn't look like the leather boy type. The Jungle, but that was more the older guys, and I didn't have him pegged for that. Who knows? People at neither place could put Mark Simpson there, though everybody said come back at night. That's when the crowd's there. And this was Halloween.

Great. It'd be full.

The only place left was Juanita's on Commerce. It sat like the cockeyed crown jewel of a tough part of town. Dingy hotels, dive bars, pawn shops--they all coalesced, not because of drinking or whoring or gambling, but because that was where the Greyhound Bus station was. Every day, all day long and all night long, people from the countryside got off, some with guitars ready to become famous, and others just looking to leave behind a little town that cramped them. For probably too many of them, the cramp was evangelical and hard, and for no small portion of them, the answer was either drinking or sex, or drinking and sex. That hadn't really changed for years. The only thing that had changed was that the city had written Commerce off. Sin City. Let it be.

Juanita's was there to provide for a certain clientele, and I didn't think it was Mark's type either. But it couldn't be discounted.

Unlike the rest of the bars, Juanita's in the daytime had customers, probably owing to its word-of-mouth in the gay community, and partly because of its proximity to the bus station. I sat at the bar, drinking bourbon, and showed Mark's photo to several people.

A businessman in a three-piece suit looked at me with doubtful eyes, narrowed and held sideways. "You do not look like a cop. Are you undercover?"

I explained a little of my business.

"You think this boy killed her, then? That's what everyone thinks?"

"I'm not really trying to find that out. I'm trying to find out why he was living with her."

He relaxed comfortably on the red barstool. "There's a good question. Why do any of us live with who we live with? Me, I have a wife in Franklin. We have two kids. There is nobody in Franklin who'd be caught dead on Commerce Street, and that's why I'm here. But I live with who I live with because we have a life. I'm trying not to mess it up."

"Sounds a little dangerous, your being here, if what you want is to protect that life you're not wanting to mess up."

He signaled the bartender to bring him another. "You want one?" I shook my head. I had plenty already. He waited until the drink arrived. "I didn't know, or I couldn't admit, that I shouldn't be married until it was pretty late in the game. I knew I was supposed to be married. That I was supposed to have a family and be successful. Or maybe it was that to be successful I needed to be married and have a family."

"Does it matter?"

"No, it doesn't. It doesn't matter that the life in Franklin doesn't really fit me. But it matters that twice a month I come to town for a meeting, and along the way I end up down here, where no one will know me, and I usually find someone who fits me for an hour or two."

"Your wife knows?"

He looked pained, then smiled. "God, I hope not. It would make all her church friends and club ladies pity her. And she really shouldn't be pitied." He turned slightly to face me. "Does that sound harsh?"

"A little."

"It's not directed at her. But the people in our circle are no different from me. We're all hypocrites in one way or another. It's just that I practice hypocrisy twice a month on Commerce Street. Who knows where they're doing their thing?"

I retraced my steps to Other Times. It was getting close to seven, and a crowd was starting to trickle in. Jeremy spotted me as I came in and waved me to the corner of the bar.

The sour mop smell had been replaced with something musky and vaguely masculine. I guess it comes in an industrial strength spray.

"Got lucky," he said.

"I don't care about your sex life, Jeremy."

He slapped my hand. "Very funny. I got lucky finding one of your young man's suitors."

"Where is he," I said, looking around.

"Already left. Just came in for a toot before dinner. But he had some interesting things to say."

"Spill."

"Your young man was a regular on Thursday nights for about six months. He would come in about eight, work on one drink for the entire time, and usually, but not always, leave with someone."

"I thought you said you only saw him once or twice."

"Thursdays are my night off. Have to rest up for the weekend," he said. "Anyway, the story from this one guy is likely the story of them all. Your young man was diffident throughout the entire encounter."

"Your Vanderbilt education must be better than mine, Jeremy. Diffident?"

"Unsure of himself. Very modest. Not very confident."

"He was young, Jeremy. Lots of young guys are not very confident."

"Not the ones in here, son. Young bloods in here are ready to ride and roll."

"You mean rock and roll."

"I know what I mean," he said. "It appears young Mark was just not that into it." To my look, he added quickly, "I don't mean he wasn't gay. I mean that he just seemed not to want what a young man gets into here."

"You said he came in for six months. When did he stop?"

"About a year or so ago. Just vanished. My guy says they figured he went back home. That's what happens with a lot of them. They come for a while. Then they leave. Who knows where they go?"

I thought to myself that a few of them probably go to Franklin. But I didn't say anything.

Chapter Fourteen

A lot had happened since I'd called Elyse Thursdale, but I thought it was still worth the drive to Brentwood. The Impala had trouble starting, and it belched a little blue smoke out the back as I began the trip. I knew it was on its last legs. It was certainly no Torino.

I took Franklin Pike south. It's a pleasant enough drive, all nine miles of it. I could have done the trip on I-65, but that would have taxed the Impala more than I thought she needed. Franklin Pike was four lanes but not four lane crazy like 65. I was a little early when I pulled into the Steak and Ale lot.

It looked like every other Steak and Ale in the United States. A faux Tudor exterior, a dark and wood interior, and a menu for "lords and ladies." I know that the vibe was supposed to bring forward some idea of English countryside tavern, but when you have something on your menu called Mushroom Mishmash, I think it's hard to take it seriously. Besides, why would anyone take the trouble to go out to eat, if what they really wanted was a little Mishmash?

When she came in, I knew it was her. Though she was older than Josie, it was mostly the way she dressed and carried herself. The description I had of Josie was that she was well put together. Elyse Thursdale was very nearly matronly in aspect, if such could be said for a woman still in her twenties. She wore a gray skirt that was mid-calf, and a white jacket over a pink blouse. She had on what looked like pearls and had a matching bracelet. Her pumps were sensible. Her bag was, too. But it was all better than what you'd buy at Castner-Knott. It quietly all spoke of money.

"Mr. Trade?" She was letting her eyes adjust to the darkness of the steak house. "I hadn't really expected someone so . . ."

"Young?" I offered. I could have offered "so hippy" or "so unkempt," but I didn't.

"I . . . ," she stopped.   "I just thought you were more like a detective. You seem like you're just out of school. If you are."

"I'm older than I look. Let's get a table, shall we?"

We were ahead of what little lunch rush the place would have, so we were able to request and get a booth in the back, away from most of the rest of the tables. It was heavy with quasi-Tudor furnishings, and it was even darker in the back than in the front. I ordered a beer. As the waitress was walking away, Elyse thought for a moment, then said, "I'll have a glass of white wine." The waitress nodded and returned a few minutes later with the drinks.

"Cheers," I said.

"Cheers to what?" she answered. "You call me up, threaten to come to my house, and make me come here to talk. I told you that I can't help you."

"I know. I'm evil. You can see it in me, even in this light." I smiled. "And as to the young part, I'm actually 50. I'm so evil I made a deal with the devil. It's a Dorian Gray thing."

Despite herself, I think, she smiled a little. "I just don't know what on earth I could tell you."

"Just talk about Josie. Her father wants to know about her, about her life in Nashville. You were her roommate for a while. You should know." I waved down the waitress again, asked for another beer and an order of fries. "You want anything?"

She shook her head. "We weren't close, Josie and I. I wanted to be out of the dorm. She was already out. She offered a space for not much rent. That's about it."

"You didn't run in the same social groups, then?"

She twirled the stem of the glass, leaving little beads of condensation in a circle on the table. "Not really. I'm Tri Delta, though I went inactive around that time. But I had my friends, yes, and she had hers."

"What were hers like? Who were they?"

She looked up at me. Her eyes were a bright blue, almost unnaturally so, and they were set attractively apart, but they were topped by eyebrows that slanted down, giving her a slight look of distrust, even, I suspect, when she was completely open to trust. "Josie did not really have friends."

"Was that because she was an escort? That seems to be the prevailing theory."

Her laugh was high pitched, something like the sound of crystal breaking. "No. She was most definitely not an escort." She took a long drink of wine. "Where on earth did that come from?"

I finished my beer and pulled the next one to me. "The Tennessean has all but said it. I'm just connecting the dots. She moved from Branscomb freshman year into this apartment. She had no job. Her parents didn't give her the money. She had no visible means of support. Yet, she had this apartment. Nice clothes. That seems to equate to escorting. Or at least to being a kept woman. Some man's mistress."

She adjusted herself in the booth and made a little swishing noise as her skirt glided against the leatherette seat. "I could see how that might occur to someone."

"But it didn't occur to you, I take it?"

She frowned and took another sip of wine. "I wondered how she could afford it, of course, but she let on that her parents rented it for her. They weren't impressed by campus housing or by her assigned roommate, so they just paid it out of pocket."

"They were well off enough to pay for Branscomb and an apartment?"

"It's Vanderbilt, Mr. Trade. People do all sorts of things. Money isn't much of an object for a lot of them."

"Tell me about the folks she hung out with. Or the folks she didn't."

She waved the waitress for another glass of wine. "Look. It's not like she was a problem. She was just a girl. She told me I could go halves. So, I did."

"But you weren't friends, and you weren't in the same social group. Why were you roomies?"

"Like I told you, it's pretty simple. I needed a place."

"I don't get the connection," I said. "If you didn't have a relationship, where's the connection?"

There was a long silence as she finished her glass of wine. "I don't know, really. There was something about her."

"Like what?"

"She gave off an aura. Like there was something more to her than what you saw."

"Was it sexual?"

She hesitated. "Kind of?" There was a moment of hesitation. "There was a time, right before I moved out, when we were hanging out. We'd had dinner. A couple of drinks. She reached over the side of the couch and kissed me."

"That the sort of thing you have experience with?"

"Not at all. She kissed me. I kissed back. It was kind of nice. But that was the end of it."

"You're saying she had girlfriends, instead of boyfriends?

"I don't know what I'm saying. Except that I kissed her."

It was novel, certainly, and it didn't blow up the escort or mistress possibility, but I didn't know what to make of it. "Were there other women?" I studied her face. The eyebrows were pointed downward, giving her face an angry look, but the lines around her mouth were those that come from smiling. It made her expression an enigma.

"She didn't have a job, but she was gone a lot. Some of it, I think, was when she went to Tolman. I think she used that room as a study space when she was on campus. By then, I was working, and I was dating Jack, the man I married. But there were also nights when she didn't come back to the apartment."

"What did she say about those nights?"

"You never met Josie?" I shook my head no. "Then you don't know how easily she could flip a conversation on its head, just by answering and changing the subject. Once, I noticed that she came back one morning with a pair of shoes I'd never seen. A very expensive pair of Ferragamo loafers. I made a comment about midnight shopping."

"And?"

"She just laughed and said, Italian Weejuns, that's all. And then, what's for breakfast? She moved on. And you moved on with her. Like I said, there was something about her that made it easier just to go with her flow."

I ordered another beer and another white wine. Elyse began to warm to the conversation, and I began to get a better idea of Josie Pittsfield. Sometimes the phone would ring, and she'd take a message. It wasn't anything much. Dry cleaning that was ready. A dentist's office follow-up. At first, there wasn't anything too strange. But it was always a woman who called. "You'd think once in a while a man would be on the other end, right?"

"This was before she kissed you?"

"That's right. It just seemed a little weird but nothing else."

"Any chance it was always the same woman?"

She pulled a pack of Salem cigarettes out of her purse, shook one loose, and lit it. "I only do this when I'm drinking." She took a long drag and held it, then pushed it out through her nose. "Maybe. I don't know. When you're not already thinking that, and when it's so long ago, you just can't tell. But I suppose it could have been."

"And if it was, what do you make of that?"

She flicked an ash into the ashtray and took another sip of wine. "I don't know how to explain Josie. She was absolutely a grown-up woman, even at nineteen. She dressed like a woman, she held her own in conversations. She was well-rounded and secure. Everything about her screamed that she was going to be somebody."

"Sounds like she had it together."

"It does, doesn't it? But if you were with her for any amount of time, the façade had cracks in it. If she was well-dressed, it almost seemed like dress-up, as if she was compensating for something. If she talked about Proust or Plato, there was something, somewhere, that almost felt a little desperate, as if she wanted to be sure to say the right thing just the right way. But she covered those cracks so quickly, so effortlessly, that you didn't notice unless you were with her a lot."

"Like a roommate."

"Exactly. But I had the feeling, more than once, that she needed me there to see the cracks. Does that sound strange?" She put out her cigarette and excused herself.

While she went to the women's room, I ordered a couple of cups of coffee. I felt like I knew Josie a little better, but what I knew opened onto more dark alleys. If she wasn't an escort, or a mistress, was she gay? If she was gay, was she being kept by a female? And if so, was it the female keeper who was paying the tab, on everything from the apartment to the Ferragamo loafers?

Elyse came back and thanked me for the coffee. "I don't need that much wine, especially not at lunchtime."

"So how did the end come? Why did you move out?"

She looked down at her hands. She pulled a napkin out through the space between a thumb and forefinger. "After that night we kissed, I withdrew a little, I guess. It unnerved me."

"That she was gay, or might be?"

"No. That I might be." She kept her eyes on the napkin, drawing it back and forth between her hands. "There was nothing to it, I told myself. I felt nothing. We were a little drunk. But that wasn't the truth. Or at least not the whole truth." She looked up finally. "It was thrilling, actually. Do you know what I mean?"

"I think so. You were afraid you were different from what you thought you were." We all have that instinct. When it turns out that our carefully constructed narrative is mostly, or even partly false, we react. Sometimes the reaction isn't flattering.

"What I thought I was." She shook her head and looked down again. "I thought I wanted to get married to a successful man, be a successful woman, live in a nice house and have wonderful children. I didn't want to live in an apartment with a nineteen-year-old whose kiss gave me goosebumps."

"So you moved out."

"I had to."

"How did she take it?"

"It was the only fight we ever had." She glanced up and shook her head at the waitress's silent offer of coffee. When the waitress was gone, she said, "She cried. She said she'd pay the whole rent, that I could stay there free."

"To stay and be her lover?"

"No, that wasn't it at all." She smiled distantly. "I don't think that kiss meant very much to her or, if it did, it was more sisterly than sensual. In retrospect, her kissing me was tender, like an acceptance of me into her life. But to me," and here she hesitated, "it threatened everything I thought I was."

I waited for her to continue. When she didn't, I said, "Why was she so upset then?"

She looked for another cigarette, but the pack was empty. I offered her a Marlboro, which she declined, then took. I lit it for her. "She trusted me, I think. Whatever was going on with her, and I think there was something, I didn't ask too much. I let her be. If she came home late, I could be brushed into a different topic. If people called, I just relayed the message."

"If she lives alone, nobody asks any questions either."

"True, but there's nobody to relax with. Nobody to talk with. Nobody to have a glass of wine with." She studied the

Marlboro and raised her eyebrows. Even though they still pointed down, the effect was expressive, open. "She needed companionship. In Branscomb or in Tolman, there would be more than companionship. There would be invasion. But here, with someone like me, there would be something that, I don't know how to put this, something that gave her comfort."

It was an interesting picture that was beginning to emerge of Josie Pittsfield. I left a ten and a couple of ones on the table and we walked out into the sunlit parking lot. We both squinted as our eyes adjusted. "Did she ever talk about her parents?"

"She never brought them up." She put on her sunglasses. "I asked her once, and she absolutely shut me down. 'Let's not talk about them,' was all she said."

"What did that mean?"

"It meant I never mentioned it again. Like I said, you go with her flow."

Chapter Fifteen

I finally got back to Nashville after a stop at a Sunoco on Franklin Pike to relieve the pressure of a liquid lunch. I pulled into the Bucket's driveway and walked up the stairs to my apartment. Someone from Terminex had put a "we were here" note on the doorknob. Wonder if they were trying to tell me something.

Inside, I sat down and called Pittsfield at home. When he answered, he said, "I thought you'd lost interest. Been a few days."

It hadn't been that long unless I'd lost a day or two. "Did you find the letters?" I was doodling little circles on the paper in front of me. Circles. Like the ones I was running in.

"Just a couple of postcards. The one time she went to New York City, we got a postcard from her, with a note. "Having a wild time in the city." That's all it says."

"What's on the picture side?"

"The Drake Hotel. Park Avenue and 56th."

"And the postmark?" Making my circles bigger.

"June 18. Three years ago."

"What's the other one?" Putting little circles connecting to the bigger ones.

"December 22, same year. Blue Seas Motel, Miami Beach is the postcard. Her note says, "Hope you have a wonderful holiday. Love, Josie." He paused. "That was a hard one to get. We'd hoped she might come home. It was her freshman year."

That would have been a bummer. But it also meant that she cut the cord quickly.

"Does it suggest anything to you?" He didn't sound desperate anymore. Just curious.

"Without a few more pieces and parts, it doesn't. Except that she was traveling. And staying in nice places."

"The picture of the Blue Seas doesn't look like anything but a motel."

"Is it on the ocean?" Putting feet on my circles. It was starting to look like something. A rodent?

"Yes, it is."

"Then it's plenty nice." I had been to Florida on Spring Break once. I didn't have any money and it was plenty nice. If Josie was being funded, it would have been pretty great.

"Do the postcards tell you anything?"

It told me that she probably stayed in the Drake, and that's a nice hotel. It told me she had found a way to be oceanfront for Christmas. All this was after she had moved out of Branscomb, for all practical purposes, and into the apartment on Lombardy Avenue. If it told me something I couldn't have guessed, I couldn't see it.

He asked me if I had anything else to share. There was a tension in his voice that he covered with a cough. I brought him up to date on what I knew for sure. I didn't say anything about the things I could only guess about.

"This Elyse girl. Did she shed any light?"

"I got a few hints of Josie's personality, but nothing that helps me understand what she was doing with her life." I lied. "A name came up a couple of times, though. Does the name Huddleston mean anything to you?"

"Huddleston?" There was a pause on the other end, then, "I don't think so. Is it important?"

"It's the name of a tire company in town. Josie claimed to be working there when she filled out the lease application." Putting a longer tail on my circles. Looked more like a squirrel now than a rat. "Oh, one thing, Mr. Pittsfield. Was Josie at all domestic?"

"You mean, was she good at housecleaning?"

"No, no. I mean more like homemaking. Cleaning, yes, but cooking, decorating. You know, the sort of things that men are not supposed to be good at." I looked around my apartment. Maybe it wasn't a stereotype. Mine wasn't very clean, and the decorating sense was Early Cave Dweller.

His chuckle broke the tension that had been in his voice. "God, no. We used to joke that she would need a meal plan in college because she couldn't possibly eat toast for every meal. That's all I ever saw her make and eat. As for housecleaning, we never asked her to. We have a woman who comes in. I don't think Josie ever had to pick up for herself." He paused again. "Pretty lucky life, right?" You could almost hear the weariness in his voice.

I told him I would be back in touch when I had more. I sat looking at my doodle. What had started as random circles had grown a spherical body, then ears, then feet, then a tail. I had thought it was a mouse, then the tail seemed to make it a squirrel. Now, as I looked at it more closely, it was just a bunch of random circles. If there was anything else, it escaped me.

I called information and got the number for the Drake Hotel in Manhattan. After a few misdirections, I finally got the assistant manager. I told him I was Don Mercer, a police officer in Nashville, and I was investigating a disappearance. I asked if he could verify a registration in mid-June, 1973 for Josephine Pittsfield. I held while he looked. Actually, I think I held while he waited for me to give up and break the connection. And I was just about to when he finally came back on the line. No, he said, there was nothing in that name for that date.

The manager was nicer at the Blue Seas, and much quicker. His answer was the same.

I wasn't surprised. I was almost certain that Josie wasn't footing the bill herself. But I didn't have another card to play. I was sure there was another name; I just didn't have it.

I went to the refrigerator to get a beer. There was nothing inside except some lunchmeat and an apple. The apple was shriveled, and I didn't remember when I had bought the lunchmeat. Instead, I poured myself two fingers of Jim Beam, and thought about riding the afternoon out on the couch.

I had dragged enough ground to stir up dust, but I didn't have much more than dust to show for it. I had some feel for Josie Pittsfield, but not enough to really tell her father what she was doing, what she was like, and why this happened. Why not just lie low and wait for time to go to Hannigan's?

Except I was restless. The apartment's dinginess combined with the depressing state of affairs in the refrigerator, made the place feel smaller and more confining than it might have. Or it was a pretty accurate reflection of just how bad things were. There was a guy paying me to do something. My reaction was to have a drink and wait out the afternoon. I didn't like the way that made me feel.

I got up, I locked up the apartment, and left on foot for the Hillsboro Village street where Mercer had said Josie's car was. One of the keys I had collected in her apartment was made from a blank, but it had the right length to be a spare Ford key. It would be a nice break if it was.

I remember when I first came to Nashville as an undergraduate. Freshmen acted like the five block walk up West End to Arby's was a long trek. They thought you needed a car to get all the way to Lower Broadway, and nobody ever thought about walking to the neighborhoods the other side of Blakemore. To the undergraduate brain, there was nothing back there. Just houses where people lived. And even though I had hiked through what seemed like half the jungle in southeast Asia, I didn't walk that much as an undergraduate either.

Now, with a car that only worked sometimes, walking around the west side of town was nothing. I walked down 25th, cut over to 24th past the VA Hospital, walked past the elementary school, and twenty minutes later I was walking down Blair Boulevard. It was a nice street, with craftsman houses. Midway down the block, I saw the tan Torino.

It was the middle of the afternoon, so there wasn't a lot of activity. Everybody was inside, probably watching the NFL. The Raiders were hot, and they were playing the Broncos. Everybody would be watching Stabler carve up the Denver defense. The NFL was changing like everything else. We used to watch the Packers play the Bears on frozen sod. Now the Raiders played in bright sunshine, and long hair fell out of players' helmets.

I took out the key and put it in the lock. Success.

The car had been kept clean. She may not have been a housekeeper, but Josie didn't dirty up her car. The seats were like new, and the floor mats looked freshly vacuumed. I leaned over to the glove compartment and found it locked. The key made that an easy solution. Inside, there was the car registration. Josephine Pittsfield, 2053 Lombardy Avenue, Apartment 2A. There was nothing else in the glove compartment, not even spare Kleenex. I locked the car and opened the trunk. Also clean. Showroom new.

There was nothing there. Somebody bought it for her, but that someone must have given her the money to buy what she wanted. I hadn't seen the title in the apartment, but Betty could have cleaned that up without meaning to. And there were no clues in the car. She didn't even leave a stray strand of hair in the car. If I hadn't seen her name on the registration, I wouldn't have believed she'd ever even been in the car.

I retraced my steps. By the time I got to Elliston Place, it was time to resume my usual post. I waved to Charlie about the time I realized I had said I'd pay my tab. I reached into my wallet and gave him what I had. Then I went back out the door and walked to the High Life. They wouldn't be calling my tab today.

Chapter Sixteen

The High Life is a dive. It has a bar, a jukebox, pickled eggs, two kinds of drafts, and a lot of cans. There are booths lined up along the wall opposite the bar, and several money pinball machines near the window.

Money pins was the reason I was allowed to run a tab at Hannigan's and at High Life. In my misspent undergraduate days, I had picked up the taste, then the talent, for the machines. No flippers, not much in the way of flashing lights, but all the variations had twenty to twenty-five holes, each protected by a bumper or pin, making landing the ball in the hole an exercise in futility. At least that's what it was like for the uninitiated. If you had spent enough time, and I had, you had a deft touch on the plunger so that you could get the ball launched to the right point, and you had a good sense of how much, and when, to punch, jiggle, and otherwise influence the ball. As I said, I had spent too much time on this.

If you're used to regular pinball, the kind with the flippers, you would look at something like Casino Grand or Double Bingo and say, there is just no way you can play this game. And why would you, if what you wanted was to smack a silver ball around a board and make it ring and whirr? But money pins had a more important feature even than the dexterity it took to land a ball in a hold with just skill and gravity. Money pins were at once much simpler and much more complicated for this feature.

That feature was the odds. On the vertical face of the machine, where the regular pinball displayed your score, was a complex arrangement of the numbers represented by the numbered holes on the board. You could win games by getting three, four, or five balls in the row. The 16 hole was usually in the middle on these machines, and it was protected by devious bumpers. You could get one in there, but it was murderously tough. Still, you could win games with three in the row, so you didn't always need the sixteen.

If you put more quarters in, you could change the odds. For instance, if you won games of 4-6-8 for three in a row, four in a row, and five in a row on a quarter play, you could put another quarter in, and your odds went to 8-12-16. More quarters put bigger payouts in play, but you still only got five balls.

With big enough odds on Grand Casino, you could begin to change which numbers were in which rows. With even bigger odds, combined with enough free games on the counter, the bumper guarding the 16 hole depressed, leaving it wide open.

Think of it as the perfect game for an infantryman. You spend your money to increase your odds. But there's no amount of skill, and no amount of luck, that can keep you in the game. In the end, you never know how much of each you'll need. You only know you have to manipulate everything at your disposal. You have to know when and exactly how much to work the machine. You have to be comfortable with the notion that you may tilt it all, if you judge wrong.

I remember the first night I won big. I kept hitting three and four in a row, racking up free games. I wasn't spending my own money at this point, just using free games to jack the odds up, then getting three or four more in a row, which gave me more free games on the counter. When I got the counter up to eight hundred free games, I could have stopped and cashed out. At a quarter a play, that would have been two hundred dollars. Since I had only put in five dollars' worth of quarters to get going, it would have been my biggest payout to date.

What the hell, I thought.

I ran two hundred games off on the odds, pushing them as far to the right on all four colors of rows--green, blue, red, and yellow. I had 1,296 games for hitting a five-in-a-row. And I had moved the sixteen to the top corner, with the 1 hole in the center.

One is a good number for me, always has been. It takes a light pull on the plunger so that the pinball dies against the first bumper and slides into the one hole. And that's what I did.

Next, I needed to hit the nine, which is second row, under the two. That took a gentle punch to the left side of the machine just as it slid past, causing the pinball to rotate up and right, into the nine.

I missed eighteen the first time, but salvaged the ball because I needed the twenty-two, below and to its left. The move for that is a short punch on the left and a light pull on the right. On some machines, and some nights on this machine, that can get you a tilt. Not that night, though.

I canned eighteen with the fourth ball, and only needed the seven for a five-in-a-row payout. The seven was my nemesis then. It is far right, first row, and you almost have to pull the plunger all the way back to have a chance at it. But if you do pull it all the way back, you risk careening off the top bumper and having it fall straight down. My luck was good that night because I gauged the needed pressure just right. The last pinball spun, but then nestled into the seven hole.

The machine began to click, the counter moving with the metronomic regularity. It kept going. It kept going. It kept going long enough that people came over to see. One thousand two hundred ninety-six games counted off. Add the two hundred that I had banked and not used, and the payout was $374.

A guy who can hit that can have a tab because $374 cleans out the cash register. That's why Hannigan's let me run one. And that's why the High Life did too.

I had been messing with Laguna Beach, which was a new machine at the High Life. I was trying to get the hang of the way the odds moved and the feel for the machine. I was three Blue Ribbons into the process when I decided to give it up for the night.

I took a seat at the bar and listened to an old guy two stools down explaining why Nixon had got a raw deal, and that Ford had done right to pardon him.

"I don't know," the bartender said, "he always seemed kind of shifty to me. I mean, I don't even think Ike trusted him when he was vice president."

"Whaddya mean," the other guy said. "You can't expect guys that get that far in politics to be clean. They're all paid off one way or another." He turned to me. "Ain't that right, bud?"

I shrugged. I find that it's usually best for long haired guys to look apolitical in a redneck bar.

He jerked a thumb toward me. "That's what you get with the younger set. Now that Vietnam's over, they don't give a rat's ass about politics." He got up and leaned over toward me. "What's your angle, bud? What do you care about in this political year?"

I could have said what I thought. I really don't give much of a rat's ass who wins. Either one would have sent me to war. The economy is down. Prices are up. I don't have a job. Ford or Carter? Carter or Ford? Pretty much whether you want the one in Washington or the one who wants to be in Washington. Six of one, half dozen of the other. But that's not what I said. What I said was, "You think any of them are honest? You think Howard Baker is? Or Ray Blanton? What about John Jay Hooker?"

The Tennessean thinks Blanton is, The Banner thinks Hooker is, and they agree that Baker is a saint. But the old guy, drains his mug and slams it down. "By God, it's Baker. The other two are damn Democrats and will lie like a dog, anytime and every day."

I toasted him with a raised can. "Spoken like a true Republican, sir."

He took a step toward me. "You a Republican, boy?"

I tried to measure how drunk he was. Drunk enough, and I could just buy him a beer as if we had cemented a friendship. Not drunk enough, but garrulous, and I could be in for an unwanted and long conversation, no matter whether I was a Democrat or a Republican. Not drunk enough, but drunk enough to fight, and I probably didn't want to say much of anything.

I decided he was drunk enough. "You're all right, pal. What are you drinking? I've got your next one."

I was wrong. For the next thirty minutes I had a fast friend with some of the most irregular views I had heard. That Jim Sasser, who was running for Senate, owned a hotel outside of town that everyone knew was a den of prostitution. That he was running for Senate so that he could make it legal in Tennessee, just like in Nevada. I learned that Ray Blanton, the governor, was selling liquor licenses and that it was just a matter of time before he was found out. And I learned that Howard Baker's daughter was going to drop out of college and become a line cook at the Loveless Café.

Or maybe I was drunk enough. I finished off my Pabst and clapped my political friend on the shoulder. "You take it easy getting home, mister," I said.

"I've got my truck," he said. "I can give you a ride."

I like my odds better when I know my machine. "I don't have that far to walk," I said.

Chapter Seventeen

Monday broke cold and dismal. Rain spattered the window next to my bed. In spring and fall, it was the right placement for the bed, if a Tennessee breeze was stirring. Now, with winter bearing down early, the chill made me pull the blanket up to my nose.

Not even the instant coffee warmed me up. It wasn't until I was in the shower, with steam rising and fogging the tiny bathroom window, did I feel like my blood was finally flowing. Showered, hair tied back, jeans and flannel shirt on with wool socks and boots in place, I felt adequately put together to face the day.

Today's task was to figure out who gave the car to Josie. A young woman with no job does not afford a brand-new Ford. I figured I'd start at the DMV, which the phone book told me was on 2nd Avenue South.

It was too rainy to walk. Or too cold. Or both. I stood out on West End waiting for the 3 bus to take me downtown. I got on, dropped my coins in the slot, and took a seat next to a suitcase which presumably belonged to a black woman across the aisle.

"Ok if I sit by your bag?" I asked. I smiled. I didn't want her to think I was anything but friendly.

She took a long look at me. She was wearing a black raincoat that had a plaid patch on the elbow. It looked like a home-made job, and it gave a splash of color to her otherwise drab appearance. She smiled back, a gap in her front teeth showing. "That's all right. You don't want what's in it anyway."

"Never know," I said. "I might be the Great Nashville Suitcase Thief." The bus hit a pothole that must have had its own zip code. We all lurched left, then right.

She laughed out loud. It was more like a hoot than a laugh, and it caused the sleeping man in front of me to startle awake. He shot her a look over his shoulder and leaned his head back against the window and shut his eyes.

"You ain't no thief," she said. "A thief has a certain look, and you ain't got it."

I put my knee up on the seat and turned to face her more fully. Her gray hair was neatly cut in a way that suggested it was, in fact, a wig. Her eyes were framed by black glasses so thick that they obscured her eyes. But the eyes were sharp and bright, nonetheless. Not much got past her, probably. "How do you know a thief, then?"

"Can't see one. Not at first. You got to feel him first. The way he stirs the air. The way he smells. Once you get his scent, then you can see him."

"Sounds like you have to be a bird dog, like one I used to have growing up. He could smell what you were hunting before he could see it."

"Yep, that's it," she said, approvingly. "You don't ever see a thief. That's why so many people get robbed. They might be looking but they ain't seeing."

I got off at 8th and Union. I caught the downtown express, which let me off two blocks from the DMV.

DMV's all look the same. They have tile floors, long lines, and unhappy people behind bank teller windows. It's designed to communicate one thing: you don't want to be here. The people who work here don't want to be here. The people in line don't want to be here. Even the furniture looks like it wants to be somewhere else.

I was in line behind a young couple arguing about whether they could afford the car they had already bought. It seemed a little late to have that conversation, but what do I know?

Fifteen minutes later I was face to face with Clerk Number Four. Or rather, she was at Window Four, so I assume that was her title.

"I am trying to locate a title."

"Is the title in your name?" She said this while appearing to read a sheet of paper in front of her. The paper was a form, and it had boxes everywhere.

"No, I don't know whose name is on the title."

She stopped reading and looked up at me. She was about thirty years old and had missed a part of her upper lip when she had applied her lipstick. "I beg your pardon?"

"I am researching a fraud case, and I need to know if the name on the title of the car is the same as the name on the registration."

"I can't help you." She looked over my shoulder. "Next."

I didn't move. "Seriously," I looked at her name badge, "Jan, I need some help with this."

"I don't doubt it," she said. "But the DMV is not the place for that kind of help."

"Don't you record titles here?"

"We do not. Next."

"I just saw a couple come here and do that."

She looked at me directly. She set her mouth as if she was about to do a very hard thing. "I told you. I can't help you. It's not your car. Now, you really need to step aside." She exhaled. "Next."

"Better move along, mister." I felt a hand on my arm. A stocky Metro officer about two inches shorter than me had me by the elbow. "Ok?"

"Thanks for nothing. Jan." I looked at the officer. He didn't seem to be angry. He was only insisting I move aside. "Maybe you know," I said.

His eyebrows raised. "Know what?"

"I am researching a fraud case. There is a car involved. I know the name on the registration. I believe the name on the title may be different."

"So?"

"How do I find out the name on the title?"

He scratched the side of his head. It was the stereotypical quizzical gesture, but it looked odd on him. Maybe it was the way he leaned his head into his finger. Like he enjoyed it more than he expected.

"You might try the county clerk's office. If you do a title transfer, that's where you do it."

"Not here?"

"Not in Tennessee. County clerk handles property transfers. If you think there's fraud, you'll want to know if the property was transferred legally. That's the county clerk."

The rain had stopped, but the chill was in the air. It didn't signal a good winter.

The County Clerk was in the City Hall, about a mile and a quarter back up 2nd Avenue South. I put my hands in my pockets and walked quickly, getting a little body heat generated. Before long, I was staring up at what once had been a building of its time, maybe even a landmark of a sort. Now, forty years on, it was a little dingy and looked like it could use a thorough wash.

It housed both the courts and various government offices. No doubt, the merger of Davidson County and Nashville into the Metro had caused functions to be merged and no doubt some of those functions had been imperfectly put together. The County Clerk may have been one of those.

I went to one window manned by an elderly woman with a scar that ran across the bridge of her nose. When I told her what I was looking for, she wordlessly pointed across the lobby.

The second window housed a young man with acne and eyeglasses that seemed too large for his face. There was a shock of hair that would not stay in place, perpetually doomed to fall across his eyes. I told him what I wanted.

"Sure. Let's see your POA." Without looking up, he held his hand up to receive something.

"My what?" I knew DOA. I knew MIA and POW. Once or twice, I came close to KIA. I knew EIEIO. But not POA.

"Power of attorney. You need power of attorney to get the title of a car that doesn't belong to you." He looked at me the way my third-grade teacher used to, as if anyone with a brain could do long division in his head.

There were all kinds of things I could probably get if I tried hard enough. Power of attorney for a girl already dead didn't seem like one of them. "Are you sure? I mean, I'm just trying to do a job here."

"If you're doing a job for a lawyer, you'd know that you can't just walk up and have me pull a title on a car you don't own. Only one person can do that. The person on the title. You aren't the person. You need power of attorney from that person." Satisfied that he was perfectly clear, he put his head back down and held out his hand. As if the explanation would have produced a document.

"It's not a matter of public record?"

"Not here, it isn't." He had given up on trying to corral the shock of hair. It hung in front of his left eye.

"Look, man. I really need to see the title to this car. It could end up saving someone a whole lot of hassle. Isn't there any way?"

"Sure. Go get a court order. If you find a judge who believes you are doing what you're saying, and he can certify it, then he can issue a court order that we'll obey." His voice was getting more nasal as he talked.

"Not my first choice," I said. "For one thing, that sounds like it'll take too much time. Never mind the cost."

"There's your option. If you don't have POA, then you need a court order. "

"I don't get it," I said. "I can go across the room to her," I pointed at the old woman, "and ask to see a deed book. I'll know who owns a property. I'll know who used to own that property. I can get the entire history of a piece of property. I come on this side of the room, and you tell me that I can't know who owns a piece of automobile property unless I have a legal ruling or a legal right." His shock was all the way across his face now. "Why is that?"

"I'm not a lawyer," he said. "But I can tell you that you can't see the title to property over there. Deeds, as I understand it, are the record of title transfers." He tried, one last time, to get the shock of hair to stay put. He failed.

"Can I see the title transfer then?" I thought I was finally making progress in understanding this.

"Nope."

"But you just said--"

"Automobile title transfers are recorded on the new title. Which is what the owner has. We have records of title transfers, of course."

"Can I see that, please?"

"Not without POA. Or a court order."

I sighed.

"Look, man. I can't help you. You might try DMV."

I could see out the window that it was pouring rain again. I didn't want to go out again, but I couldn't see much reason to stay. "DMV sent me here. You are sending me to DMV. Listen. If I wanted to see if a car I was about to buy had a clean title, how the hell could I find out?" I admit I was a little peeved. "Without a lawyer or a judge."

"I can't help you with that."

"There are probably a thousand cars sold in Nashville every day. You mean to tell me that nobody knows whether any of those vehicles has a clean title?" Before his shock of hair could fall again, I knew the answer.

Chapter Eighteen

There's nothing like a jolt of recognition to make you realize that you're banging away at something the wrong way. Somebody always needs to do a title search. But it's not some long-haired guy with a VIN number and a story. No, it's a used car salesman needing to do a title transfer when he makes a sale.

My problem was that I didn't know any car salesmen. But Wendy Williamson did, and she put me in touch with a guy named Marty Blake at We-Sell-Em off Dickerson Pike. It took me a while to get back to my Impala, and then longer to drive out to East Nashville. When I did, I found Marty waiting for me.

Marty was a character out of a movie. He was clad in polyester, head to toe, from his red jacket to his royal blue pants. He had on a white shirt open halfway down his chest, with a gold chain signifying his absolute disco coolness. In country music Nashville, he was a splash of Memphis, or New York, or wherever they dressed like that.

"Wendy bought a sweet little Triumph off the lot from me," he said. "Best car on the lot. Good judge of cars, Wendy is. And she says you have a problem."

"Not a problem, per se. I just need to do a title search. And the DMV and the county clerk's office are working me back and forth. According to them, they can't do anything.

"Well, there you go. They can't. But I can. I have to do a title search anytime I'm taking or selling a vehicle." He smiled a smile I knew would cost me a little money.

"I have a hundred that says you can do just that." I felt like I was dumping quarters into a machine that Marty knew how to play.

His eyes sparkled. "For a hundred I can probably remote start that car over there. But let me see what you've got."

I gave him the VIN and Josie's name. He called into somewhere and waited. After about five minutes, he said, "Thanks," and hung up.

"The registration is Josephine Pittsfield. You knew that." I nodded. "Title was Josephine Pittsfield as well. No big deal there."

"But the title will tell the previous owner. What do you have there?"

"It does indeed. The title transfer was from Marie Huddleston. Know her?"

I could make it where I did know. I could argue that it cleared a lot of things up. Or I could argue that it muddied everything up. The only way I'd know was to find Marie Huddleston and ask some questions.

I found myself putting another dime in a pay phone across the street. When the girl picked up at Huddleston Tire, I asked for Marie Huddleston. She wasn't in, so I left a message. I told her I wanted to pitch a business proposition. I didn't mention Josie. I didn't see much reason she would talk to me if I did.

It had been a long, cold day. I drove back to my place, then walked down the street to Hannigan's. I turned a five-dollar bill into quarters, played some money pins, and after twenty minutes cashed out 100 games. Fifteen dollars' profit, and enough for a cheeseburger, fries, and a couple of beers.

I was just finishing up when Mercer walked in. He was in his out-of-uniform uniform of jeans, tee shirt, and a leather jacket. He wasn't a motorcycle cop anymore, but off duty he rode his BMW bike. The only time he was in a car was at work. He got a beer at the bar before coming over.

"Isn't it just a little cold, riding on a night like this?" I knew it was. His hands looked cracked, frozen.

"Beats walking," he said. "Beats driving a Chevy Impala, for sure." He took a long pull. "Know what I mean?"

"I know who you mean. Where's your female companion?"

"She's working. You know we hired her to dispatch?" I didn't know. "She's working second shift." He sat down. "What's happening with your little project?"

"That's a good name for it. Got a break today, but it took a whole day of running around, standing in lines, being lied to by county employees."

A couple of guys I recognized at Metro cops walked in and he waved at them. "County employees don't lie, Jackson. They stall. If they talk while they stall, it just seems like lying."

"Ok. Then I got stalled most of the day." I waved at Charlie to bring me another beer. When he returned, he brought a fried chicken plate to Mercer. I picked an onion ring off the plate. "If everything on your plate is fried, you'll have a heart attack."

"If your dinner is liquid, your liver will explode."

"Hey, I had a burger. And this onion ring."

"All fried. You're going to die anyway."

"We're all going to die, Donnie. Just a question of when." I took a second onion ring.

He took a leg quarter in hand and pulled the leg from the thigh. There is something about eating meat with your hands that recalls the animal essence in humans. It doesn't take much to conjure up a cave and a fire when you're watching a man rip flesh with his teeth.

"What was your break?"

He demolished the leg quarter and started on macaroni and cheese, this time thankfully with a fork. I explained the ping pong of DMV and County Clerk, then the car lot and the answer to my question.

"Nice touch with the car guy. But you know DMV and the county were both lying to you. They could have given you the title information if they wanted to."

"I figured. But they were just stalling, right?" He finished the macaroni and started in on the turnip greens. "Do you always eat things one at a time?"

"I eat in the order I want things. I wanted chicken. Then cheese. Now I'm just cleaning my plate." He took an onion ring and wiped the plate. "What do you do with this point of information?"

"I called her. Told her I wanted to discuss a business opportunity."

"Maybe that will work." His look told me he didn't think so.

"Thanks for the vote of confidence. It's not like I can roll up in a squad car and flash a badge."

Mercer pushed his plate to the side and leaned on the table with both elbows, his fingers dangling the longneck. "That's true. You don't have the same tools somebody like me has. You have to have a little cunning. You have to skirt around the truth some."

"I have to stall?"

He laughed. "Fair enough. You have to stall. Or speed up. You have to control the pace of the game. If you're not in charge of the tools, you have to be in charge of the game."

I got the analogy. It's just like playing the Auburn Shuffle when you don't have enough talent. I didn't see, though, how it was accurate for me. "There has to be a game in order for somebody to be in charge. I don't see the game right now. I know about Marie Huddleston, but I don't know how she connects. I don't know about Josie. I really don't know about Mark. Every fact I find out, like what I got from her old roommate, just muddies the picture."

"Hear what I'm saying, Jackson. You're acting like this is an investigation. But you're not a cop. You don't have police tools. You don't have police instincts. And you don't have an investigation."

"If you're trying to cheer me up, it's not working."

He shook his head. "None of this is a surprise to you. You have a dead girl's father who wants to know more about his kid. He's asking you to do research. That's all. You've got a college degree, right? You did research papers. It's not police work. It's research." He tilted the bottle and drained it. "The crime is solved. You have to solve the girl."

He was right, of course. The idea was to solve the girl. It was a simple command, and a complicated proposition. Josie couldn't answer any questions herself. I was trying to make others speak about her, but what I needed was someone to speak for her. I needed to hear something about her voice that was silenced now. "Don't detectives have to do that too?"

"I guess. Most of what we do is cut and dried. Sure, we have to use our imaginations, but it's much more like a lab experiment. I have to have evidence. I have to connect pieces of evidence. The final lab practical is the courtroom. If my experiment works, if my evidence holds together, I have done my job. You're not doing that. Your crime is already solved."

"My crime is yet to be committed, my friend."

He saluted with the empty bottle. "As you wish. But the crime against Josie Pittsfield is solved. Your job is to describe who she was when she was killed, or how she got to be that way."

"And if I don't have police tools, what do I use? Besides cunning."

"The father wants you to tell her story. If you want the truth, then it's a newspaper writer's skills. If you're going to make it up, you're just a storyteller."

"Great. All I have right now is a bunch of fog."

"That's probably the beer," he said. "Which I'd advise is a good sign to slow down."

Chapter Nineteen

It appeared that November was going to begin its 1976 reign on an absolute tear.

I woke up with a hangover, and wind whistling through the window by my bed. I must have cracked it open before I went to sleep. Now the wind's icy bristles shocked my face when I peeked from beneath the covers. I slammed the window shut and pulled the covers over my head.

I thought about what Don had said the night before. Act like a journalist. Or just make up a story. You're not a cop, so don't think like that.

Was that what Landon Pittsfield wanted from me? Did he want some sort of investigative journalism? Or did he want a story, true or not, that comforted or confirmed?

I had to admit I had no idea. "I need to know about my girl," he had said. If he wanted the truth, if that's what I found, could he handle it?

I braced myself through a shower that started colder than I felt and ended so warm that I didn't want to leave. I dried quickly, dressed quickly, and got out of the apartment quickly. Walking against the wind, I went to the Krystal on West End and drank their bad coffee instead of my own.

I grabbed a Tennessean from an empty booth and flipped through it. Carter was back home in Georgia today, Election Day. Ford was in the Rose Garden dedicating something again. I had to admit, once he figured out that he was President,

Ford was doing a lot of things to make himself look like a president. Tennessee was excited about Carter, though, his being a Southerner and all.

Below the fold on the front page was a headline: Suspect in Baldwin Murder Released. The story said that the juvenile, unnamed, was released after questioning. Police spokesperson relayed that the investigation was still active and that the suspect remained a person of interest in the matter.

I bet everyone in the neighborhood knew who he was. I hoped, if he wasn't the killer, he had a good place to hole up, preferably a place not in the neighborhood.

I had a couple of items on my agenda today. If I was going to get a better feel for Josie, I was going to need to settle the matter of the car, which I assumed was going to be the same as settling the matter of the apartment. And which I assumed would settle the matter of who Josie, so far a cypher, had become.

And since I assumed all of those paths led to Marie Huddleston, I was going to have to find a way to have a talk with her.

I dropped a dime in the payphone and dialed Huddleston Tire. A sleepy male voice informed me that Marie wasn't in yet. I didn't leave a message.

I set out on foot for Blair Boulevard to have another go at the Torino. I had been pretty quick in my initial search and knew that I hadn't spent the kind of time on it I should have. Cars don't have all their secrets in the glovebox and the trunk.

As before, the street was quiet, and few cars were parked on the street. This was a neighborhood where most of the houses had driveways. It was serene, the way Acklen Avenue was serene. No wonder the murder of a child had people so shaken.

I unlocked the car and checked under the floor mat. Nothing. I sat in the driver's seat and shut the door. Methodically, I checked under the seats, behind the visors, in the console. I turned the engine and the big V8 came to life. The radio was tuned to KDF and the Rolling Stones were seeking satisfaction. I couldn't get any either, seemingly. I punched the station presets. WRVU, the college radio station came in feebly. Even this close to campus it was almost out of range. Not so WSIX and WSM, the full power country stations. The last preset was public radio. Her taste was eclectic, at least.

I got out and popped the hood. I didn't expect to see anything, and I didn't. It was a remarkably clean engine. I closed the hood and walked around back to inspect the trunk again. I pulled the cover to find the jack, the spare, and nothing else. I shut the trunk and got back in the car. It had the badge of Wyatt Johnson Ford on the outside. Low mileage. Less than 3,000 miles on it. Probably hadn't even had its first service call. I could call out to the dealership to see, but I didn't know what they would prove. I was just trying to feel, when she was in this car, who she was.

Did she even know it had to have regular service? With that kind of mileage, did she even need it?

You wouldn't have had this kind of problem with the Impala. It was like a version of me, an extension of my life. You could tell from empty Tex Ritter bags and Krystal sacks in the back that I ate on the run too much. There were empty beer cans, and a full six pack left from a trip to Percy Warner Park last month. The ash tray was full. It needed an oil change and a wash. And all that served as a spare tire in the trunk was a doughnut that I should have replaced after I used it for 10,000 miles last year. It was a good bet that the car needed a valve job that would cost more than the car was worth on the market. And it burned oil like it burned gasoline. It was an extension of my messy life. It might even be a metaphor.

I gave the engine some gas and felt the pleasant rumble of power. It wasn't a Mustang, but it would move. Was she that kind of driver? Or did she move timidly, afraid of Nashville streets, afraid of cutting someone off? She had left no trace of who she was in the car. I couldn't really imagine her in it.

I switched the engine off and sat. The sun streamed through the front window and gave the car a pleasant warmth. I was tempted to drive the car to Huddleston Tire and hand the keys to Marie Huddleston. I was sure she was the benefactress. Or sugar mama. Or mama to a sugar daddy. Who knew about any of that?

In the end I decided I was better off walking back to my garbage dump of a car and driving it.

I walked back, cleaned up and put on a coat and tie, then pulled the burger bags and beer cans out of the back of the Impala. I drove across the river to Shelby Avenue and pulled into Huddleston Tire's parking lot.

There were six service bays with cars on lifts, and another half dozen cars in the service lot, either finished or about to be worked on. Big displays reminded me that radials were my best bet for longer wear. A Michelin man teetered in the wind, held down by a pair of cables attached to the main building. I went in and walked to what looked most like a reception desk. A young woman in a navy polka dot dress smiled. She looked cemented in place, smile and all. "How can I help you?"

"I left a message for Mrs. Huddleston yesterday. About a business opportunity? I was hoping for a word with her."

The smile remained. "I'm so sorry," she said. "Mrs. Huddleston isn't in right now." There was something off about her face, but the smile was so riveted that it was hard to notice anything else.

"If she'll be in soon, I'm happy to wait."

"Oh, no," she said. "I can't tell you when she'll be in. I just don't know." I realized what was off. She was not moving her lips as she talked. She sounded perfectly fine. She was almost like a ventriloquist in her speaking. You could see her teeth a little. The smile was set. And her lips barely moved.

"How do you do that?" I asked.

"Do what?"

I couldn't tell if she was joking, or if I might be about to offend her. "Nothing. Never mind that. You have no idea when she'll be in?"

"No. Or even if she will."

"I thought she ran the place." I knew she owned it. The impression I'd been given is that she took over from the old man and it was her going concern. "That's what I thought, anyway."

"Oh, she does," the smile said. "She's absolutely the best. Everybody here just loves her."

"But you don't know when she'll be in? To run the place?"

The smile remained, but the volume decreased. "That's the secret sauce. She's so good that she doesn't even have to be here. We all know how to do our jobs. And she trusts us to do them." Her volume resumed. "You're welcome to wait. There are chairs and a coffee pot over there." She pointed to a corner by a water fountain. There were stacks of magazines, presumably all about tires.

I said I would wait. I poured a Styrofoam cup full of thick coffee and took a sip. There wasn't a time stamp but it had been heated past its "sell by" date. I put it down among the magazines and took a seat. I should be able to recognize her when she walked in, I reasoned. Such a paragon of business would be easy to spot.

I have to admit that the place did seem to run with precision. Most tire monkeys are covered with the things that adhere to tires. The young men who came in and out, dropping off invoices and maintenance forms at billing were all neat in their navy workpants and black steel-toed shoes. Their dark green "Huddleston Tire" shirts tucked in and emblazoned with the company's blue logo, which was also on their navy caps. The young men and women working at desks and behind counters all effected airs of easy professionalism. Even the customers seemed immune from distress, moving in and out with their own regularity.

I admired the ecosystem in front of me for a while, then picked up a magazine about Michelin in France. I was engrossed in a map of the Auvergne region of France when I became aware of a shadow over me.

It was the smile.

"I've heard from Mrs. Huddleston. She is not coming in today. She has business in Memphis today." The smile didn't waver.

"Did you tell her there was someone here to see her?"

"Oh, yes. I did."

I reflected on Mercer's definition of stalling. "And did she say she'd meet me?"

The smile remained, but the eyebrows arched, just a little. "Oh, I didn't try to make an appointment for you. I don't even know your name."

"It's Jackson Trade." I gave her my card. "How do you do that?"

"Do what?"

"Your mouth. It doesn't move when you talk."

The smile shortened a bit, but it was still there. As she talked, her lips still barely moved. "Oh," she said. "I had a root canal, and somehow the needle gave me lockjaw. They say it will eventually go away as long as I do my therapy."

"I'm sorry. None of my business."

"It's ok." The smile broadened again. "You could come back tomorrow. I think she'll be back from Memphis."

I told her I might just do that. I didn't know that I would. I didn't know that I could tell the difference between stalling and lockjaw.

I got back in the Impala and drove back to my side of town. I stopped at the bank and cashed a check for fifty bucks, then took the car back to my place. Along the way, I thought that maybe it would be useful to drive the Torino over to the Ford dealership, just to see if there was anything I could pry out of them.

The wind had stopped blowing but the sun had disappeared, with the result that the temperature was stuck unseasonably chilly. I put on a heavier coat and began the walk to Blair again. I stopped at the Steak and Eggs on West End, by the mortuary school, and had a quick bacon and egg plate. By the time I set out in earnest, it was close to three.

When I turned up Blair Boulevard, I immediately noticed there were a lot more cars parked on the street. People were streaming into a single house. I stopped a couple on the sidewalk. "Death in the family," the man said.

People were bringing in food. Some were just bringing themselves. Everybody says that funerals are for the living. I don't know about that. It's pretty clear who the casseroles are for.

I walked past where I thought the car should have been. With all the parking on the street, it was a little harder to judge. I walked by the same spot three times before I found the little blue house it had been parked in front of. It was a half dozen doors down from the bereaved, and the car that was there was now a fifteen-year-old black Pontiac. Not a tan Torino. Not by a long shot.

I walked up the little set of steps and followed the sidewalk to the front door of the blue house. When I knocked, I got an immediate "wait a sec," so I did. A fat, bald man opened the door but left the storm door shut. "Yeah?"

"There was a tan car there for the last several days."

"Yeah? What about it?"

"It's not there now." The wind had picked up again and was blowing through my best winter coat like I didn't have one on. "Do you know when it left?"

"You didn't take it, then?" He had pushed a terrier of some kind out of the way with his foot and looked around me. "You're right. It's not there." He reached down and picked up the dog. "Would have figured you took it. You've been out there in it."

"Yes, I was there earlier today."

"And a couple of days ago too." He put the dog down and it raised up on the screen doors frame, pawing at the door and whining. "Don't mind Homer. He thinks he likes all company."

"You saw me, but you didn't see anyone else?"

"Listen, feller, I saw you twice. But it's not like I sit here watching. I haven't seen anyone else. Didn't even notice it was gone until now." A second terrier came flying from the back of the house, barking. "Dang it, Jethro," the man said.

"Homer and Jethro?"

"That's right. You old enough to know Homer and Jethro?"

"I live in Nashville, sir. You don't have to be old enough to know them. You just know them."

That seemed to relax him a little bit. "Well, I can't tell you what happened to that car. I reckon it was yours?" I let that pass as if the answer was yes. "I don't know what's becoming of the world. Used to be that this was a safe part of town. Car stealing. That little girl over on Acklen. That old woman that was killed."

"I thought she was on the north side," I said.

"Don't much matter. World's going to hell, and Hillsboro Village along with it. Had a law-and-order president, and they run him out. Now you got this Ford and that Carter. I don't think either one of them can get this mess straightened out." He was raring to go, and Homer, or maybe it was Jethro, was starting to howl. "Sorry, feller. I don't know nothing about your car. Good luck to you." And he shut the door without a further word. Jethro, or maybe it was Homer, still had something to say, but you could hear them moving away from the door as he said it.

I tried the houses on either side, but no one was home at either. I stuffed my hands in my jeans pockets and walked as quickly as I could back toward Hannigan's.

I had reached a dead end. I had a car key to a car that had disappeared. I had a benefactor, or something, who finally had a name but was nowhere to be found. I had a dead girl killed by a dead roommate, both of whom may have been gay. Or not. I had a father in Indiana paying me to construct a profile of who his dead daughter had become.

What I wanted to say was that she had become what Betty, the apartment super, had said. She had rendered herself invisible. I had sat in her car and felt not emptiness, but absence, as if even her spirit was sucked out of it. The apartment they shared was mostly cleaned, and the order there was not order, but something more like absence, absence of the small chaos that even the most ordered lives tolerate.

They tolerate it because they must. That's the way the world works. I could have said to Homer and Jethro's owner that a car theft, even a murder, isn't a rending of the social fabric. It's the price we pay, the chaos we tolerate, in order to live our lives. We're messy creatures. Even the best of us have secrets the world could not bear. The worst of us, well, we're scarcely worth the trouble sometimes.

By the time I got to Hannigan's I was fully in a funk. Charlie smiled and waved, then saw whatever he saw on my face and just poured me a bourbon and sat it on the bar.

Yes, that's probably the right answer for now.

There's something that you don't want to feel. There's a whole moment when you really don't want anyone to intrude on your being. If I had to try to define it, I'd say that it is a moment where you would kick the hell out of anyone who wanted to talk to you. That's probably the look I gave Charlie. The interesting thing is that he'd seen it enough to recognize it, and he just let it go.

Three drinks later and an order of French fries hadn't put me in a better mood. I'd put ten dollars in the pinball machine and lost it all. I'd tilted the damn thing twice. There was nothing going on that said, sure, Jackson, have a good night. Have a good day. Have a good life.

In other words, screw me.

About nine o'clock Art Blake came in. He sat with me in my booth. "What the hell's wrong with you, Jackson?"

"Meaning what, Dean Blake?" Meaning I'm ready to fight about it.

"You're drunk," he said. "You're mad about something and you're drunk." I remember the look. It was condescending. Even the handlebar mustache seemed like it judged me.

"I'm very likely drunk," I said. "I'm most certainly unemployed. Unmarried. Unsuccessful. Where do you want me to stop the chronicle of my failures? Served my country, served my time? Managed not to get killed. Fat lot of good."

"How about you just slow down?"

"Seriously? I'm saying that my life is completely screwed up, and all you got is slow down?"

"Slowing down might be a good idea."

"Just how? Just how would acting like I give a shit change anything?"

I said this quietly, as had Blake. This wasn't an argument. This wasn't something that would end up on the front page of the paper. This was personal. This was about us.

"Do you care about your career?" he asked.

It was not a good question. I had had a career. I did the best I could. Then he fired me. No career. No paycheck. No future. Everything I thought was in my future was yanked out. So how should I answer? "I don't have a career. You saw to that."

"Leave me out of it, just for a moment. Do you have any idea how to resurrect your career?"

"I don't have a career to resurrect." I put my hands below the table because they were shaking. "If you wanted me to have a career, you could have done things differently. Now all that is down the drain. You see what I've been having to do to make a little money? I'm walking around town all day, talking to people about a dead girl. It might even be a little interesting, if there was anything to uncover. There's nothing to find out. Nothing. And even if there was, this is a one trick pony. And it won't do the trick but once." I could feel the color rising in my face. I knew I was too drunk to have this conversation. I got up to leave. "There's nothing you can do to help me. I don't think there's anything anyone can do."

"Go home, Jackson. Sleep it off."

"You know what, Art?" I was about to let loose. I was about to blame him for every single thing that was going wrong. But that wasn't correct. He had only been the executioner. I was the one who did the crime. "Forget it, man. I'll see you. Sometime."

I pushed the door open and went out into the night.

Right and then straight was home. That's where I should have gone.

I went left.

Because left is the direction of the High Life.

When I got there, no one was in the front room except the bartender. All the action was in the back room where the pool tables were. I got a Pabst longneck and went into the back. It was not my crowd. In fact, I didn't recognize any of them.

It was a motley crowd of a half dozen. Two stocky biker types with long hair and beards, wallets secured with silver chains. A couple of cowboy types with boots and hats. One guy who looked like he could be an ex-defensive end, but not at Vanderbilt. He was too big. And a short guy wearing Duck Head khakis and a pink Izod polo shirt. He was face down on the one table in the back.

The bikers appeared to be playing alternate shot with the cowboys. Everybody was about two beers past competence, so there was a good bit of scratch-and-reshoot. I was having just a little bit of trouble keeping balanced on the stool that had been imported from the bar area.

The taller cowboy pointed his cue at me. "Hey, hippie. You wanting next game? You could shoot with Harlan here," he said, pointing to the giant next to him, the defensive end. "Harlan's been waiting for a couple hours to get on the table."

I'm a decent size. Six foot two and two hundred pounds, easily as big as any of these guys and bigger than the bikers and the preppy. But the giant easily went three hundred without looking fat. I guessed he was six-eight, but I could have missed that by an inch on the short side. He had massive arms and a Fu Manchu mustache. He looked at me and grinned. "Yeah. We got next game."

"I'm not that good," I said. "I'd hate to be a disappointment."

"Only way you can be disappointing is if Harlan don't get to play." The cowboy sank his next shot. "Like I say, he's been waiting."

It took a little too long for them to finish up, but in the end the cowboys won. Harlan had already chalked up his cue and was ready to break as I took a cue from one of the bikers. The giant sighted and then struck the cue ball with a punching stroke that scattered balls everywhere. Three went in, two stripes and a solid. And the game was off.

As messy and drunkenly as the previous game had been, this one was brief and precise. Harlan had surprising touch for a man his size. He drew the cue ball back in place when he needed to or stopped it on a dime when it sank a ball into a pocket. He made use of a side bank when his target was obstructed, and he sank the eight ball for the win with a bank off the far rail and a roll the length of the table into the corner pocket.

I didn't have to take a shot. Nobody did. Harlan ran the table. "That's what I'm talking about," I said and finished my beer. "Nothing for me to mess up."

"Go get a round of beers," said one cowboy to another." Bring one for the hippie too."

Two more games proceeded in the same fashion. Harlan once ending a game by taking the cue ball of the side rail and sinking the one ball in the side and the eight, after it, in the corner, just as he had called. It was an exhibition. I clapped my hands. "Bravo, maestro. Good shooting."

I put my stick on the wall mount. "Time for me to go to bed, boys. Been fun watching." I should have said, I was mad when I came in, but watching someone do something well put me in a better mood. Drunk, yes, but in a better mood.

For the second time in a night, I pushed a bar door open and walked out into a cold night. This time, turning left meant turning for home. This time, I did.

It was time. It was one in the morning. Everybody closes at two. But on a Wednesday night, there's nobody much on the street. A quiet walk, even in the cold air, might clear my head a little. It might even sober me up some.

I passed the long wall that separates Centennial Park from the sidewalk. The Parthenon was up lit so that it looked surreal, like the storybook Parthenon had been beamed down by aliens. Maybe that was the look they were going for.

At the dark edge of the park, I heard shoes land on the sidewalk. Before I could turn, I heard a grunt, followed by the thump of something hard hitting my side. I went down, and a sharp boot found my face. I tried to speak but caught another kick in my gut. I tasted blood, beer, and vomit, and then felt another kick to my head.

I groaned. Were there two of them? Three? I tried to raise up on my arm. Something hard and wooden cracked my head. Stay down, I thought. Be still.

Something else hit me. Where? Was it my head? I couldn't tell. I couldn't see.

Just like in combat. Stay down. Don't move.

Chapter Twenty

There was pain. That was clear.

And there was darkness. I couldn't see.

I couldn't feel my legs beneath me. I couldn't move. Was I paralyzed?

Silence. Shouldn't there be the sound of traffic?

I tried to call out. Nothing came.

I should be feeling cold. Where is the wind? If I'm lying on the wet sidewalk, shouldn't I be chilled?

Ah. There were voices. Far away.

I moved my mouth. The words didn't form. I made noises like someone without language.

Where were they? Could they see me?

Why was it so dark?

Someone was rolling me over, leaning over me. I couldn't see. Was I blind?

Another person stuck something in my eye. A finger? No, sharper. I moaned.

I began to float. I thought I heard an airplane. Was it an airplane? No. A train?

More voices. Music. What was that music? Outlaw.

I screamed.

Hands everywhere. Not friendly ones.

Pain.

Sleep.

Chapter Twenty-One

I awoke, but I wasn't sure where I was. All around me there was noise, some of it human and some of it, if I'm honest, was of unknown origin. Steady. Regular. Constant and in the background.

My head hurt the way it might hurt if your brain was too big for your head. Pressure. Pounding. Wanting to get out.

There was a pain in my side that intensified when I breathed. I tried regulating my breath. It didn't help much.

My left leg was numb.

Voices.

Art's voice. "What do we know?"

Another. Unknown voice. "We'll see when he comes to."

Mercer. "Stupid son of a bitch."

"I resemble that remark," I said. I tried opening my eyes. The light was bright. I kept them shut.

I heard footsteps. Metro footsteps, I was willing to bet. "Mr. Trade? You awake?"

"Alive," I said. "Awake and alive."

"I'm Detective Belden, Metro Police. If you're able, I'd like to ask a couple of questions."

I lay flat. The bright lights of the hospital room were all turned on, and they pinned me to the bed like a captured fly.

I squinted. "Anybody want to flick a light off? Nothing here to see that you can't see with less light." The light flicked off.

I answered his questions. I was alone. I didn't see anything. I couldn't identify anyone. I don't know how many there were. They didn't say anything. I didn't have any idea who would do such a thing. That's what I told him. By the time he asked three different ways, and I told him the same thing each time, he left.

"That," said Mercer, "was singularly unhelpful."

"Glad to be of service," I said. "Could you give me a glass of water? All that talking dried me out."

Mercer poured a glass from the bedside pitcher. "Could be that you're hungover?"

He handed me the glass and I drank it down. "Who can tell? I hurt in places that hurt when I'm hungover. I'm hurting in places I'm pretty sure have nothing to do with a hangover." I looked toward the corner of the room where Dean Blake was standing. "Hi, Art."

"Jackson." He didn't say anything else. I took it as acknowledgement that he saw me and had nothing else to say.

"What's the verdict?" I said to Mercer. "I get to leave soon?"

Mercer plopped down in the chair next to the bed. "We've been here a while, Jackson." He looked at his watch. "It's ten a.m. now. They found you about two. I've been here since they called me, got here about two-thirty. Dean's been here since three."

"Sorry to ruin your evening," I said. "My evening's been shot too, but that's not on you." I hit the button on the bed, making the part under my head rise. I winced. "My guess is that I've got a broken rib or two."

"That's right, Doctor Trade. Very good. Two of them. And a broken nose. Likely concussion too."

"My leg's numb."

"Can't help you there," said Mercer. "No broken bones there, as far as I know. But we didn't see a doctor. This is com-

ing from the charge nurse, which may be more authoritative."
He smiled. "I wouldn't mess with her, by the way. I think she
could do the same kind of damage to you."

"Does Nurse Rached say when I get out?"

"Nurse Wise," said a voice near the doorway. There stood
a woman in white, about five-two, with the nurse cap of
Vanderbilt Hospital. "If you like, you can leave now. I have no
interest in people who will not do as they are told." The voice
was firm, but there was a touch of the playful in it. No, that's
not right. Playful isn't quite right. Teasing. The kind of teasing
an older sister might administer before pulling the football,
Lucy-style, from Charlie Brown's reach.

"If you're telling me I can go, Nurse Wise, hand me down
my walking cane."

"I'd be more interested in seeing her give you a cane across
the knuckles," said Art. "What does the doctor say, ma'am?"

"The doctor says he can go when he feels well enough to get
out of the bed. He also says that he should take his time." She
walked over to the bed rail. "I doubt you'll listen to anybody.
Drunks who get in fights after midnight don't usually listen.
But here's my two cents. Stay in the hospital for the night. We'll
check on you, make sure that you're not so concussed that
you're in any danger. We can make sure the bandage is good
on the ribs tomorrow morning." She looked at Mercer. "If you
have any sway with him, tell him to sit tight until morning."

Mercer put two fingers to his forehead and saluted. "I will
do my best, Nurse Wise."

The nurse looked back to me. "Think it over. You leave, and
you're on your own."

She turned and marched out the door, her shoes making
small squeaks as she did.

"Let's get out of here," I said. "Where are my clothes?"

Mercer got up from the chair. "You want to try?" he said to
Art.

"Guys. Please." I knew that I didn't need to be in the hospital. I was pretty sure I couldn't afford what it had cost already. I didn't need a night's bunk when I had a free bed over a garage.

"You know what you are, Jackson?" Blake leaned against the bed rail. "You are an ass." I started to protest, but he held his index finger in the air. "No. Hear me out. You are an ass. You are a Vanderbilt graduate, and you are an ass. You were an influential person, rare for your age, and you are an ass. You have many talents, and you act as if you have none, because you are an ass." The index finger stayed perpendicular to the floor. "And now, you have been thrashed, by persons unknown, but most likely because, in one way or another, or in every way, you are an ass." He took the finger down. "Do you dispute any of this?"

I kept quiet. Any argument I had with his analysis was a difference in style, not in substance.

"I didn't think so. I told you last night that you need to get this figured out, Jackson. Neither Mercer nor I have any idea why you are a target. Do you?"

I shook my head. It was a route I'd walked, drunk, half-sober, and sober for seven years. "Two times in three days."

"What?" Blake looked from Mercer to me and back. "This isn't the first?"

Mercer raised his eyebrows. "I seem to remember asking you about two men and a pickup truck. You said there was nothing to do with you. Right?"

"Yeah," I said. He had me. I forgot that we'd had that conversation and I'd denied there was a fight. "Anyway, two guys jumped me further up West End two nights ago."

"It went better than last night, I take it?"

"Well, define better." My ribs stabbed me. "Let's just say I'm pretty sure the first two weren't in any shape to do what was done last night." I motioned to Mercer. "Can I have more water?"

"Let's just say that they weren't. Who have you ticked off enough that they can just run out a second set of thugs to rough you up?" Blake took the water glass and handed it to me. "That sounds like you've got yourself involved with somebody pretty unsavory."

"You got me, Art," I said. "I'm just nosing around about the Pittsfield girl. You know that." I drained the glass again. "The best reason to leave now is so I can have a cigarette. Unless you can smoke in here."

"No smokes, no jokes," said Mercer. "I had to go outside to sneak one."

"You must have tripped some wire," Art said. "Who have you been talking to?"

"Some students. A bookstore owner. A lawyer. A girl at a tire place. The boy's brother. The girl's first roommate. Not exactly a crime syndicate."

"I agree," said Mercer, as he took the glass away from me. "That doesn't sound like a violent bunch."

"What I think is that the newspapers are right. Nashville's changing. It's on edge. People that used to keep it under wraps feel free to walk the streets and look for trouble." I closed my eyes. "It's been that way downtown for a while now. It's finally making its way west. Before you know it, there'll be home invasions in Belle Meade."

"That sounds just great, Jackson," said Mercer. "Nashville's turning into New York City."

"Nashville's always been this way. It's just coming out now." I said this with a splitting headache and a busted rib that wouldn't let me breathe. "And it's just now getting around to me."

Chapter Twenty-Two

I was released from the hospital the next morning, after making the right decision to stay the night. It was a decision made easier by the fact that Blake had sent my clothes out with the Head Resident of Oxford House, just down the street, and said to bring them back clean in the morning. It wasn't like I could go walking out into the night with that backless gown they give you.

My clothes were there, and so was Mercer, in the morning. He dropped me at my apartment with the admonition, "Stay close, ok? Get some rest. Heal up."

I picked up the phone and dialed the number Betty had given me the week before. When she answered, I said, "Betty? It's Jackson Trade."

"Hey there, Jackson. What's the good news?"

"Wondering if you had some time today."

"Absolutely. Give me an hour? I need to clean up."

"See you then."

I made some instant Folgers and read the Tennessean I'd picked up from the Bucket's driveway. The FBI was taking files for a grand jury on people who apparently received executive clemency from the Governor. Jimmy Carter was taking congratulations all around, including from Ford. The Mayor was getting a swine flu shot at the Courthouse. That seemed like the right idea, if the idea was to inoculate himself against the pigs in politics.

Vanderbilt had lost to Ole Miss 20-3 on Saturday, and the coach was talking already about the good progress they were making toward next season. I'm not sure exactly what it is about Vandy football, but it has the curious effect of causing people to give up in the middle of the season and begin talking about basketball. Unless you are the football coach. Actually, the coach had VU at 7-4 last year. But they had reverted to type. The rest of the sports page was about Wayne Garland, the Oriole pitcher, coming home to Wayne Garland Day. That's Nashville sports. The good stuff is all borrowed from other places.

I left the newspaper and locked the door. For once, it was a nice day. Seventy-five and a light breeze. Easy enough to walk, if I didn't breathe too hard.

She was quick to come to the door. She had on hip-hugging jeans and a white tee shirt topped by a blue plaid flannel shirt, unbuttoned and flowing. She was barefoot and her toenails were painted bright red. She had big gold hoop earrings on, matched by a necklace of gold hoops that reached to her waist. She smelled nice.

"You don't look so good, Jackson," she said. "Are you ok?"

"I have had a little bit of a rough time." I leaned toward her as she gave me a light kiss on the cheek.

"Well, come on in."

She led me into her apartment. It was unlike Josie and Mark's upstairs. Where theirs had been neat and spare, hers was opulent, almost decadent. The couch was a forest green velour and padded so that you could sink deep into it. Where their walls were off white, hers were wallpapered, and the wallpaper was what I'd call Victorian, a riot of green tendrils and yellow blooms on a pale yellow background. If the apartment upstairs was all Euro modern, Betty's abode was steamy Mississippi delta.

"What the hell happened to you?"

I sat, or sank, on the couch. The hardwood floors were meticulously shiny, and the white shag throw rug made them look even cleaner. I could not have lived in that place, but it was an interesting place all the same. "I ran into some people who took an instant dislike to me."

"I know it's early, but would you like a drink?"

"Not now. Maybe later." The couch was trying to eat me alive. I pushed up, with some effort, to perch on the edge of the cushion. "I wanted to ask you about Josie."

"I told you what I know." She sat down on the middle cushion of the couch and put her hand on my knee. "Are you sure you're ok?"

"Did she ever have any guests? I know," I said as she started to shake her head, "I know what you told me before. I'm asking a very specific question. Was there ever an older woman who visited?"

"Like, how old?"

"I'm not sure. Forties. Maybe fifties. She probably wouldn't have looked like your ordinary housewife. Probably more like a successful businesswoman." Because that's what Marie was. I assumed she looked the part.

"No," she said. "That doesn't ring a bell."

"Ok. It was worth asking."

She leaned back against the couch, her leg touching mine. I looked at her. Brown eyes. Brown hair. A freckle or two. If you described her that way, you'd probably walk on past. But there was something about the way her eyes and her mouth went together, just so. It was attractive. One click either way, and they would be absolutely seductive.

"I'm glad you thought to come by. Even if you're not in the best of shape." She smiled as she leaned back into the couch. "I thought you might, though."

"I would lean back too, but I don't think I would be able to get back up." I pointed to my midsection. "Broken ribs."

"You probably just need somebody to take care of you for a bit," she said. "I'd volunteer, but I would probably do more harm than good." She winked. "Get yourself better, though, and I'll do more good than harm."

"You're direct, Miss Betty." I pushed all the way up, got to my feet, and offered a hand to her. She took it, and we found ourselves body to body. I could feel myself wanting to do more than stand there. I took a step back. "And, like you say, I'm in no shape to do much but walk. Walking over was about the best I could do this morning."

We walked to the door. As I leaned down, she gave me a kiss, which I returned. "You come back when your ribs are better." Where my hand had enveloped hers, our hands reversed, hers around mine. "You'll do that, won't you?"

"Take care, Betty."

"Don't you worry, Jackson Trade. I will. I will most certainly take care."

I went to Mack's for lunch. Chicken fried steak with gravy, mashed potatoes, and green beans for a dollar fifty. Refills on vegetables and coffee. I don't know why everyone doesn't go to Mack's for lunch, and for dinner. And every day.

From there, I went to the Joint Universities Library on 21st. I needed to do some research.

I walked into the entrance on Library Lawn, between the D-School and the Math Building, and through the main space. Up the stairs, down the back stairs, and into the microfilm area. I showed an old ID, and the young woman let me into the space.

I found the Tennessean of the right year, pulled the spool and found an empty microfilm reader. I threaded it and started the process of reading the old newspaper. It's not like you can do this without getting interested in some other story. Everything, even something just a few years old, starts to look interesting.

Finally, I found the obituary for Mr. Huddleston. He was an impressive man, if by impressive you meant came from nothing to make a lot of money. In tires. He had died of a stroke. His wife was Marie, and they were childless. Four years earlier he had passed day to day management to his wife.

Nothing.

I don't know what makes the mind do what the mind does. Maybe there's something that you see, while you're scanning, that makes you think of something else. Maybe there's just something that makes your mind race. At any rate, I went back and got another spool.

This one was for four years prior. It was the year that Marie took over management of the business.

It was also the year that Paul Simpson graduated from Horace Williams College.

To be honest, I hadn't expected much. I didn't expect that there was anything there. I guess I wanted to find out how good a ball player Paul was He had a scholarship. He said he was pretty good. Was he?

What I found was interesting

I found a game where Paul Simpson fouled out after scoring seventeen against Belmont. I found a game where he fouled out after scoring seven against Trevecca. I found a game where he fouled out after not scoring against Tennessee Temple. Every game I found, Paul Simpson had fouled out.

I went back and got the previous year's spool. There wasn't a single game that Paul Simpson didn't play in. There wasn't a single game where he didn't foul out.

That was not a normal thing.

If I had fouled out twice in a row, there would have been a major meeting of the minds. Which is to say, I would have got my stuff straight or I would have been on the bench.

By my arithmetic, Paul Simpson had averaged less than ten points a game, and had fouled out of every game he'd been a part of.

I put a dime in the phone outside the JUL and asked for directory assistance. After a protracted dance, I got the athletic department at Horace Williams. I asked for somebody on the basketball staff. I got a guy named Tommy, who said he was the assistant coach.

"I'm writing a story for the Banner about the team that won the conference championships back in the late 60's. I see that this Simpson guy fouled out a lot. What was up with that?"

"Geez. Really? You're writing about a great team, and you single out Simpson?"

"It's just a little strange, Coach. You've got all this success and this guy Simpson sticks out like somebody's sore thumb."

"Look. This is off the record, right?""

Sure.

"He had mommy issues. I mean, his mother was killed right before he came here. He was always trying to live it down. Or he was trying to live it up. I don't know. He was just a wild man on the court, though. Good player. Bad attitude."

"Good grief. Why keep playing him?"

There was a long pause. "We're a Christian school. We try to do right by all our kids, ok?"

"Are you saying Vanderbilt doesn't? Roy Skinner would be interested in hearing that." Skinner was the head coach, and he was known as a player's coach, the kind who'd do anything for his guys.

"I don't mean that," Tommy said. "It's hard to explain if you're not here. We play an ok brand of basketball. I mean, Tennessee State would whip us most days. We probably wouldn't score much against Vandy. But we're ok."

"I have to admit I don't follow Horace Williams much."

"No reason to. But we have some young men here who just need a chance. They probably aren't even in college if they're not playing ball."

"That was Simpson?"

"Pretty much. Not the brightest guy. Not the friendliest guy. But a guy who needed basketball if he was going to finish college. Look, a lot of those games, we put him on the best player the other team had. Sometimes it didn't take the first half before he'd have four fouls. And sometimes, you know what? It frustrated the other guy so much that it just took him out of his game."

"Did it ever get out of control?"

"Sure. It was always just a push or a shove from being a brawl." He paused again, as if searching for a memory. "I guess, when I think about it, we weren't doing him all that much of a favor. Probably should have sat his butt on the bench, try to teach him a lesson."

"That's usually what happens," I said. I found myself wondering if the aggressive behavior went beyond the basketball court. So I asked.

"Nothing unusual. The regular scrapes that boys get themselves into. He came to practice one time with a fat lip." He laughed. "We razzed him a little. All he said was, you should see the other guy."

It was an interesting side to the fire and brimstone preacher I'd met. "You know he is a minister now?"

"Paul Simpson? He's a minister?" I imagined I could hear his head shaking. "I guess all kinds of things happen that you can't see coming."

I spent the rest of the morning and part of the afternoon lost in the library. As an undergraduate, I'd always found peace there, though sometimes I was there because I wouldn't have any peace until a research paper was done. I pulled a set of Horace Williams yearbooks and took them to the Reserve Reading Room, an august wood and brass affair that always looked, I imagined, the way the Library of Congress would look. The light was soft and the quiet was tangible, as if you could touch it in the air.

I found Paul Simpson's freshman photo. You could see the man inside the boy, but the boy would have to lose some of his baby fat and most of his fear. You could see it in his eyes, a sort of persistent fear that would pass for mild distress if you didn't know him. But it was there, and I almost felt sorry for the young man who peered back at the camera, distrustful of its gaze.

By his junior year, the fear had been replaced with a look of anger. This was a young man whom I could easily believe was capable of hacking his way through a half of basketball. His hair had grown longer, though still parted on the side and giving him a look of general unkemptness. It's not that a lot of guys didn't go that route. It's just that it was not a good look on any of them.

By his senior year, the picture had hardened. His hair was still longer, and he had grown a beard. The anger had turned into something of a sneer. His lip was curled just a bit, as if he had suddenly thought of something disgusting to say to the person taking the picture. I wondered if he was aware that he had taken on that look. I wondered if it was so omnipresent that he was not even aware he had it on his face.

I put the yearbooks on the return cart and went back to Microforms. I rolled through several months of Tennesseans and Banners from three years before his arrival in Nashville. I didn't really expect to find his mother's obituary but, as they say, you'll never find if you never look.

At about 2:15, I found it. I had not expected much of an obituary, an obscure minister's wife in a small town an hour from Nashville. But there it was. And it was not an obituary. It was a news story, albeit on page sixteen.

Mrs. Laverne Simpson, wife of Reverend Paul Simpson of Waverly, Tennessee, was found dead on Thursday, August 2, 1969. She died by hanging. There was some extraneous matter about the house, and other language about the Reverend's grief, the boys' dispositions, and the neighbors' care.

Some six days later was a small blurb that somehow managed to imply without saying that her death was self-inflicted, while giving the funeral arrangements. Besides the husband and the boys, only a brother survived her. Elrod Kinsey, with an east Nashville address.

Somehow, that's what made Mark who he was. I don't mean that's what made him gay. I mean that's what made him domestic, sensitive, and shy. Probably. That's what made Paul an angry, fouling machine. Probably. Who could know? But who could doubt?

Maybe that's what Mark had meant when he was screaming in Branscomb. Not just that Josie was "motherfucking dead," but that his own "Mother, fucking dead." Maybe even Josie and Laverne Simpson got mixed up in his brain some way.

Who could know? It was a mess either way.

I left the library and walked across campus towards Hannigan's. But it was the wrong place for now. I headed over to the Dead Ringer on Elliston, had a quick plate of nachos and several bourbons. Then, I started up the street. I had a couple at the Top Hat. I had some beer at Linda's. I lost at money pins at the High Life and had a few more to celebrate.

By midnight I'd had more than enough. I was numb. Nothing hurt. Not my head. Not my ribs. I was sitting at the bar, talking to a guy who was drunker than I was. I knew it because he was having a lot more trouble staying on the bar stool than I was.

"How do you figure people get so messed up?" he said. "Look at those guys back there arguing over a pool game. A pool game." He nodded. "If they don't watch it, they'll be trading punches back there."

"I was reading something about that today. Some guy said it's a mommy issue."

"I don't know what the hell that is," he said.

"I think it means that something bad happened when he's a kid. Unresolved stuff. Anger. Feeling of helplessness. You find ways to cope, and sometimes they're not very good ways."

"Sure, sure. Like there's some psychological excuse for every damn thing. You think whoever did what they did to that little Baldwin girl has an excuse? Not likely one a jury will care for."

The Baldwin case had not receded from the public's view over the past few days. Dan Miller and Will Carlisle were all over it on WSM, and Chris Clark was practically throwing every ten minutes to Jessica Settles's live remote on WLAC. The talk boys on AM radio couldn't get enough either. "If the media has its way, there'll just be a hanging."

"Everybody's saying it's a kid in the neighborhood," he said. "I bet his life ain't worth living. Probably wants to just get away. But that'll be hard if you're a kid with no way to travel."

"Huh?" I said.

"Ain't likely a kid has a getaway car, right?"

"True enough."

The car. Where had Josie's car got to anyway? I half thought that Marie Huddleston had repossessed her property, but why would she have done that? She wouldn't have known, in all likelihood, where it was. It certainly didn't make sense that it was a mile from Josie's apartment.

But if not Marie, then who would have taken it? I supposed it could be likely that someone hotwired it, but Blair Boulevard didn't seem the usual target for car thieves.

"Yep, no getaway car for that boy," he said. "Too bad, too. He'd get out on the run, get caught. Then you might have that hanging, if people got to him before the police."

Why was the car on Blair? Why wasn't it there now? Who moved it? Twice? And why?

This is what happens when you're drunk. You ask questions you don't have answers for. If you're smart, you stop asking before you begin making up answers.

"I tell you what," he said, "if I'm that boy I find me a set of car keys and if I have any sense at all, I make a run for it. I take my chances. That's what I'd do."

What if somebody was taking his chance?

In fact, what if the two murders, Josie's and the girl's, were linked? The linkage was provided by the car, halfway between the two murder scenes.

And now the car was gone.

"Hey, bud. You're zoning out. You want another beer?"

I stood up, unsteady. "I think I'd better see myself home." the room turned a little, then settled down. "I appreciate the conversation, my friend. I really do."

I walked down West End and turned my path into the park. Suddenly, I felt very tired. For that reason, I guess, I thought the most logical thing to do was to lie down.

I lay in the middle of the large space in Centennial Park. I once played touch football here. Those were good days. Except that I took off my Elgin watch. And somebody stole it.

I don't know how my life became what it has. When I came here, there was so much promise that no matter what happened, there was going to be a way to prevail. Yes, there was, no doubt, going to be trouble, but there was never going to be the kind of trouble that would keep me from being who I wanted to be.

I was going to be something.

Not really. I had made a hash of my life. I was lucky to have a roof over my head.

And Josie Pittsfield, who really had found a way to prevail, who really had put herself in a position to succeed, was dead.

And Brenda Baldwin, who didn't even know yet that she had to prevail, was dead.

And I was alive. And utterly unsuccessful.

What the hell kind of deal was that?

I could feel the wet of the ground soaking into my denim jacket. I didn't care. I knew that I could cry out into the night, and nobody would come to rescue me. I wanted to sink into the ground.

And what if I did? On the other side of the park, there were couples coupling. Or tripling. Hell, who knew what was going on over there?

On the Parthenon steps, tourists were taking pictures. They were marveling on the exactness of the replica.

It's just a building. Just something that Nashville put up. It's not like this is Greece. None of it is real.

I felt my voice singing. "Good hearted woman. Good timing man." It was off key. I tried again. "Wicked ways that she don't understand."

Why was I even singing?

Can my friends from last night find me here? Is there some kind of homing device that they can use? Do they already know where I am?

My life is pretty messed up if they can. If they do.

I lay in the middle of the large space in Centennial Park, about a hundred yards from where they beat the hell out of me. That was a bad day. Yesterday was a very bad day.

"Please tell me you won't try that voice over on Music Row."

It was Mercer's voice. Where did it come from? "Where you at, Donnie?" I continued to lie on the soaked ground, sinking into it.

The toe of his boot nudged my foot. "How many you had?"

"Too many, if the local constabulary is out looking for me." I tried to raise up on my elbow, but my ribs wouldn't let me. "Forgive me, Officer, if I don't get up." I laughed, and my ribs hurt again.

"You're in a pretty bad place, my friend."

I couldn't really locate him. Or rather, I knew he was somewhere near my feet, but I couldn't get my head up enough to see him. "I'm in Centennial Park, if you must know. In Nashville, in Tennessee, in the US of A. Western Hemisphere. Planet Earth. Do you need latitude and longitude?" He kicked my foot. "Hey."

"Smart ass." I heard the squishing sound of boots walking toward my head. He squatted beside me. "Why are you doing this? You got beat up pretty good last night, not far from here. Are you really this stupid?"

I could have told him that stupid was my middle name. Or that I was just waiting for the tourists on the Parthenon steps to come take pictures of me. Or even that I was going to camp out tonight, since it was such a fine night. I didn't. "I don't much care, Don."

"Jesus." He turned his head and spit tobacco juice.

"I played pool earlier that night, Don. Got pulled into a game of doubles with a couple of wannabe cowboys and this giant of a man. Harlan, his name was. You never saw a man shoot pool like him. I mean, he was masterful. He made every shot, three straight games. Ran the table by himself, every damn time. He was like a machine, Don. A make every shot pool machine." I lay on my back. There were no stars.

"I've seen guys like that. I saw them in the Army every weekend. That's just what they did. That's all some of them were good at."

"I have no idea what else Harlan was good at or not good at. He was such a wizard with a pool cue, I didn't have to shoot. And that was a good thing, because the cue I had was warped so bad that you could see it. All you had to do was look down the stick and you could see it was warped a good half inch. If I'd have taken a shot, it would have been beyond bad. It would have been as crooked as the stick was."

"So what? If you were at the High Life, you probably had one of the good cues. Anyway, you didn't have to find out. What's his name, Harlan, took care of it."

"I'm being metaphorical here, Donnie. That cue is my life. It's the stick I play the game of life with." I managed to pull myself up on an elbow, with just a little pain. "I want to run the table, man. I want to impress. At least I want to make a shot or two, hold up my end of the game. But all I have is a crooked stick."

"Get up," he said. He laid his hand on my shoulder, then put the other under my arm to steady me. When I was standing, he put both hands on my shoulders and looked at me. "You keep going this way, you're going to kill yourself. Or get yourself killed. I don't know which. But I know that you can't keep this up." He turned me toward the sidewalk and went alongside. "If you don't like your stick, Jackson, then straighten it out."

"Not to be contrary, but you really can't straighten a pool cue once it's warped." It was meant to be witty, but it came out flat. It wasn't witty. It wasn't funny, even if it was true.

"Then get a new stick. Get a new one. Nobody's stopping you. Except you."

We walked along in silence. The wet pavement met the streetlights with a glare. It occurred to me that Mercer was walking me past the spot where I'd been jumped. "You don't have to do this," I said.

"There are things we do that we have to. And then there are things we want to do. I want to walk you as far as your street. That ok?"

"Sure."

We got to the end of my street soon enough. "You feeling ok, Jackson? Anything hurt?"

My ribs were stiff. My head didn't hurt, but it didn't feel altogether right either. "I'm fine. I just need to get a good night's sleep."

He shook my hand. "Do that, then. And get up in the morning ready to find a new stick." He held onto my hand just a little longer. "Do that for me?"

I nodded. If I was going to find a way through all this, I had to find a new way. I knew I did.

I woke up late for me. The sun was already halfway through the sky, and the temperature seemed warmer than it should have been. I rolled over, waiting for my ribs to hurt. They weren't great, but they were ok.

I unbandaged my ribs. I took a gentle shower. I bandaged them up again, got dressed, then went out toward breakfast. One that would stick to my ribs, as they say.

I thought I could make it as far as Campus Grill, but the fact of the matter was that I was lucky to make it to IHOP. So I admitted defeat and ordered a Western omelet and the blueberry stack. It was more than anyone needed, but I probably wasn't the best judge of that.

Mercer was right. I needed something new. I needed to adjust whatever you called my attitude. But what was my problem? Lost a marriage. Check. Lost a job. Check. Lost my way. Definitely check.

I've heard people say you don't know what you don't know. That the process of growing up or growing older involves meeting new and unexpected tasks, then learning, then applying that knowledge to the next unexpected thing. Ad infinitum. World without end. Amen.

What if that's not entirely true? What if you're better off not knowing what you don't know, because what you knew about one thing could fool you into thinking you know something you don't. What if it's better to be in a perpetual funk, half aware that you don't know what you're doing and half not giving a shit? What if the thing you count on is native, raw curiosity?

That's where I was. I knew that my life was just basically screwed up. I knew that there's a lot I can't know. But, damn it, I know more than most people. And I'm pretty sure that, if you ask me a question, I can get you an answer that's more than enough.

Let that be the new cue stick, I thought.

Let the game be on.

Chapter
Twenty-Three

What's that joke about psychiatrists and the light bulb? How many it takes to change a light bulb? It takes just one, but the light bulb has to really want to change.

Fair enough. I figured that I could worry about really wanting to change once I got some answers in Hillsboro Village.

I was feeling well enough after the big breakfast to walk back and get my Impala. I drove it over to Blair Boulevard. This time, I went door to door. Most people weren't even aware that a beige Ford Torino had been parked on the street for a week or more. Why should they be? Most people went about their day to day, never paying much attention to anything outside their line of sight.

A few people at houses closer to where it had been parked had vague recollections of it but couldn't tell me when it had been there or when it had left. I left Homer and Jethro and their owner alone, although his driveway was empty so perhaps he wasn't home. A lot of folks weren't.

I realized about halfway through the operation that I was performing the foot bound equivalent of spinning rolls of microfilm through a library machine. I was scanning information that was given me, most of it of absolutely no use, in the vague hope that something interesting would turn up.

I was two-thirds of the way down the street when a kid on a bike pulled up next to me. "You a salesman, Mister?"

A reasonable assumption, I guess, given I was going door to door. "No. Just asking questions about a car that disappeared from this street."

"The beige one?" he said.

"Ford Torino? Yes, that's the one. You saw it, did you?"

He was a skinny kid, red hair, probably about twelve years old. Why he wasn't in school was anybody's guess, but he looked less like a truant than a kid who had been sick enough in the morning, before his parents left for work and got well pretty quickly after they left. "Sure. It was here about a week."

"You see anybody drive it?"

"Some guy." To a twelve-year-old, all adults are probably indistinguishable.

"This guy live in the neighborhood?"

"Nah, I don't think so. I never saw him before." He shifted feet, one on a pedal, the other on the sidewalk. "Nope, I don't think he was from around here."

"What makes you say that?"

"I saw him park it, then he walked down the street, over there," he said pointing to the west.

"So you think he didn't park his car on his own street?" I puzzled over that for a second. "That doesn't make sense."

"Lots of people have been parking over here and walking over there," he said. "News guys, television guys. There's no place to park on Acklen, what with all the fuss over that girl."

"You think this guy was with the news?"

"I don't think that. Why would he leave the car for a week? It's not like he's staying with the family."

"Very observant," I said. "Who do you think he was, then?"

"Just some guy, I guess. There's been a lot of extra people around."

"Nosy person? Busybody? That kind of thing?"

"Maybe," he said, getting ready to ride off. "Who cares any-way? He isn't here now."

As he rode off, I allowed myself a smile. Yes, he isn't here now, but now I know it wasn't Marie Huddleston. Whatever her role in all this, she wasn't the one who brought the car here or took it away. That was certainly someone else.

I went back to the Impala and drove it to Acklen Avenue. There was a makeshift command center that had been con-structed in the first hours of Brenda Baldwin's disappearance, and nobody had bothered to take it down yet. Its tarp walls were rustling in the afternoon breeze.

Along the street at intervals were vans bearing the initials of the television and radio stations that continued to wait, like predators, in case a break in the story happened. Certainly, though, any break wouldn't happen here. But then, any break would call for a reaction from the family. And although they hadn't been talking to the press, there was always a first time, and the assembled media wanted to be there when it hap-pened.

I nosed the Impala as close to the Baldwin house as I could without drawing attention to myself, and I waited along with the others.

There was nothing to see. A neighbor woman arrived with what appeared to be a casserole dish and handed it inside to a faceless set of hands. Television people got out occasionally to have a smoke. The day began to turn.

I wasn't sure what I was trying to accomplish here. My legs had gone stiff. My ribs ached. The headache that had never quite left was considering getting worse. I was a little chilled. A bourbon at Top Hat would take the chill off, and it was a scant few blocks away.

As I was reaching toward the key to turn in the ignition, a car arrived. It pulled into the Baldwin's short driveway. Late model Plymouth Valiant, maybe a 1974. Dark blue. It was a nice enough car, but nothing you'd notice. It wasn't as if a

Barracuda had pulled in. In fact, it was just a Dodge Dart with a different badge on it.

Just your average family sedan.

The figure that emerged was not your average figure, though. It was Paul Simpson. He went to the door, the storm door opened, and he went inside the house.

I literally shook my head, like a cartoon character does to clear his head. The preacher is a part of another story, a story about a dead brother, which is a story about a dead girl. This story is about a dead girl. A different dead girl. I don't know why he's in this story.

I got out of my car and walked toward the Channel 4 van. They'd changed their color scheme. Something about branding. But the big 4 on the side gave it all away. I knocked on the window, wondering if any of the anchor talent was aboard.

All it took was the window coming down and I knew I wasn't looking at on-air talent. A bearded man, with a baseball cap and a gold tooth, opened the window. "Yeah?"

"Hey, man. Bobby Moore with WRVU News." I figured that the college radio station was both well enough known and easily enough dismissible. "That dude that just walked in. Who the hell is he? I never saw him before."

The bearded man was about fifty. He had the look of hard news, the guy who did the hard work. "Preacher at their church. You know that the mama isn't talking to any press?" I nodded. I didn't know that, but why quibble? "She's religious, and that's her preacher man. He's the key to this, news-wise. Just between you and me?" I nodded again. "Get him to tell what she is saying, and you have the scoop on this whole thing."

"I don't get it. Why is what she's saying the key?"

"Man, aren't you paying attention? Law enforcement is talking about this neighbor kid. But everybody else is wondering what the mama is hiding. She's the one who says the girl left at the time she left. She's the one who said it's about Girl Scout cookies. The mama's the key, man."

"Really?" I hadn't heard any of this. But I didn't doubt it. The drumbeat of suspicion hits closest to home first. "The preacher is a source?"

"Not what I said, man. Preacher is just doing his preacher thing. But he may, at some point, have some news to deal. We're just waiting."

I can't say that the conversation let me know anything important. What I can say is that Channel 4 gave me an insight into what the news media was doing. There was a dead child. There was a suspect. There was a mother who wasn't cooperating with the news gathering group. And so, the mother was suspect in some way. Even if the boy was the main suspect, the mother was under the spotlight.

"Has the preacher been out a lot?"

"Every day, brother," said the bearded man. "He's shepherding his flock, I reckon."

I admit I don't know much about how you'd do that. Thinking of a congregation as sheep that need to be herded, well, that's just a concept that insults people. Or insults sheep. I don't know which. But I do know that it was a jolt to see Mark's brother turn out to be the Baldwin family's personal spiritual advisor.

It made me want to see the brother preach.

Chapter Twenty-Four

I had to cool my heels for a few days, and it was a good thing. I went to the grocery, then stayed in the apartment eating food that I cooked. I went light on the bourbon. And my head and ribs began to feel, if not healed, then considerably better. When I no longer yelled in pain when I sneezed, I figured I was getting as good as I would be.

On Saturday, I stayed in and listened to Vanderbilt lose to Kentucky. How can you get beat at football by a basketball school?

On Sunday, I put on a tie and drove out White Bridge Road.

The White Bridge Free Church stood alone in a field with a parking lot in front of it. Once, probably, it had belonged to some other congregation. Its age would seem to have preceded the Free Church, which by its sign signaled an establishing in 1967. This building seemed a hundred years older than that, though its sides bore fresh white paint, which served to accentuate its green doors and the red cross above them. The entry way led to a larger area, the main part of the building, and that part had yet another, larger red cross painted onto it. To the right was the parsonage, a brick ranch, where I'd interviewed Paul Simpson before. Some ways behind the church was a barn, which led me to think that the property had been, at one time, a farm, with a church added on.

I sat in the Impala as the congregants arrived. A number were there already when I arrived at 10:30, presumably the Sunday School participants. The Baldwins came late but still in plenty of time for the 11:00 service. I waited until I could hear the opening bars of music before I went in myself.

Inside, the church was plain. There was a large wooden cross nailed to the back of the building, behind the pulpit, which was centered behind a chancel rail. The cross loomed over a small choir of fifteen, mostly female, voices. The choir leader, who seemed to be doubling as the song leader, turned from the choir to the congregation alternately, holding his hymnal in one hand and waving his free arm in time with the music, as if to encourage ever greater volumes of sound.

Sitting to the left in a small armchair was Simpson. His head was down, and he swayed in time with the music.

I sat down in the back row, partly concealed in darkness since the overhead lights didn't penetrate to the back of the church. I had the left back row to myself. A lone usher sat in the right back pew.

They were singing a song I was not familiar with, though the theme was familiar enough. I'm a sinner, and the grace of God is sufficient. There was some pastoral imagery and a general sense of the love and power of the Almighty. It seems to have a tonic effect on the congregation, as each subsequent verse propelled them into greater voice and more movement.

It was hard not to be a little caught up in it.

It was startling when the music abruptly ended. I seemed to be the only one surprised. But it felt like a jolt.

There followed a set of announcements from the choir leader, and then Paul Simpson rose.

"Let the children come forward," he said. His was a voice that could be loud even in repose. When the six children were assembled, he dropped it a register. The effect was meant to be kindly, but to me it had a note of condescension, as if he was lowering himself to speak to them. He knelt in front of them, the communion rail separating them.

"Children, do you know what sin is?" There was a general, shy nodding of heads. "Cathy, can you tell us?"

A brown-haired girl, about seven years old, was his object. "It's when people do things they're not supposed to."

"That's right. Do you ever do things you're not supposed to?"

She dropped her head. "Sometimes." He waited for her, and she finished her sentence. "Sometimes I don't do what my mama tells me to do."

"Or your daddy?" She nodded. "That's all people, children. People don't do what their Father tells them to do. He couldn't be more clear, and we just don't obey." He shifted his weight. "What does your daddy do when you don't do what he says?"

Cathy looked back toward the pews. "He whips me."

"Punishment is what we expect, and it's what we deserve. But do you doubt that your daddy loves you?"

"No, sir, Brother Paul."

"And that's the way it is with our heavenly Father, children. We deserve punishment, but He loves us, and He sent his son to save us. Isn't that a glorious thing?"

The children seemed less convinced that it was glorious than the preacher, but that's probably just because they weren't sure what glorious really had to do with this story about getting whippings.

"Try to do what you're told, children. Always listen to your parents. Know that their love is constant. And know that God's love is better even than that, and that it's perfect. God wants what's best for you. That's why you must do what He says."

He prayed briefly over the children, and they were ushered back to their seats.

"Brothers and sisters, as is our custom, let us read together our scripture today. We read today the words of the apostle Paul, in his admonition to the people of Galatia."

Simpson began: "Paul, an apostle--sent not from men nor by a man, but by Jesus Christ and God the Father, who raised him from the dead."

The congregation answered, "and all the brothers and sisters with me."

Simpson continued, "To the churches in Galatia: Grace and peace to you from God our Father and the Lord Jesus Christ."

And the response came, "Who gave himself for our sins to rescue us from the present evil age, according to the will of our God and Father, to whom be glory for ever and ever. Amen."

Simpson read next: "I am astonished that you are so quickly deserting the one who called you to live in the grace of Christ and are turning to a different gospel."

And the people answered, "Which is really no gospel at all. Evidently some people are throwing you into confusion and are trying to pervert the gospel of Christ.

Simpson looked up and paused. Then he said, "But even if someone, or an angel from heaven, should preach a gospel other than the one we preached to you, let them be under God's curse!"

The answer came, "As we have already said, so now I say again: If anybody is preaching to you a gospel other than what you accepted, let them be under God's curse!"

The minister looked skyward, "Am I now trying to win the approval of human beings, or of God? Or am I trying to please people? If I were still trying to please people, I would not be a servant of Christ." He raised up his arms and the Bible. "If you have ears, O my people, then hear."

Amen, then. And amen.

"The apostle Paul," he began, "is not amused. You can tell. He's usually more about, "how y'all doing?" He's usually more about settling into it. That way, you make it easy to get into a conversation. But this time, this way, he's getting right to the point. The Galicians have made him mad. They've not been behaving."

"Yes, brother." The congregation was answering.

"We are saved through grace, not works, says Paul. You knew this. You knew when I left you. And then you forgot." Here he paused. He looked across the congregation from the pulpit. "Are any of you willing to say that you are like the Galacians? That you sometimes forget, between Sunday and Sunday, that I told you? You are not saved through works. You are saved alone through faith."

"Yes, Lord." He had them moving in their seats.

"Understand. A group came into Galicia. This is the story of this text. They came to cast aspersions on Paul. They said that the law of Moses must be followed. They said that Paul was not a real apostle. They called him fake. They said that he was wrong." He was almost wheezing. He was making his speaking rhythmic and he was using his breathing to cause percussion. "Perhaps you do the same." Wheeze. "Perhaps you find yourself," Wheeze, "willing to think it's going to be easy. Perhaps you think," wheeze, "that is won't be hard," wheeze, "to follow what you know is right."

"Tell it, brother," shouted a red-haired man in suspenders.

He looked rueful. His hands were spread upon the pulpit and he looked downward. Then he leveled his gaze. "These men, like so many men today, say that the truth-tellers, the people like Paul, the pastors like me, that they are just people pleasers. They say that we do not preach the gospel because it is the gospel, because it is the law. They say that we ignore the teaching of the prophets. But listen to me." And here he leaned up on the pulpit, as if to take the congregation into his confidence.

"Amen," came the scattered answer from several directions.

"If I was trying to please men instead of God, would I have just pronounced as cursed anyone who taught a gospel message other than the one that I taught them? Look at the evidence. I am not trying to please any man; I am serving Christ and seeking God's approval. That's what Paul says."

"Come on, now. Bring it," shouted the red-haired man again.

"And if I was fixed on what men want, and not what God wants, would I preach a message of grace?"

"Lord, no," came the answer, this time from most of the congregation.

"How quickly we forsake the message of Christ."

"Amen." The volume was rising.

"How fast we are willing to walk away from grace."

"Oh Lord." The congregation was teeming with emotion.

"Hear me, O Israel. If you are willing to believe any teaching that goes against this, you are going to be eternally damned. You are dead to God. Only through grace. Only through grace. Only," and he took a full breath, "through grace are we saved." He looked wrung out. He slumped onto the pulpit. "Brothers and sisters, we do not serve man. We look only for the approval of God. Paul tells us. If there is a gospel being preached other than this? May it be cursed." He looked far away. "May it be cursed."

There was a long silence in the sanctuary. I thought it hard to end a sermon on a curse, but that was where Simpson was going to leave it. Nothing but a curse, I guess, could illuminate this particular theology. From the Apostle Paul to Brother Paul.

I've heard it before, and not just in a church. It says, if you don't believe what I say, then you can go to hell.

The rest of the service was about like I'd expect. There was a good bit of praying and a little bit more singing. There was a section that you'd describe as the sacraments, if you were Catholic, though they were honored more in the abstract than in the particular. The benediction was notable for its brevity and its force.

"Now we leave. We will do God's work. No matter the cost."

All right then.

I slipped outside before the recessional that would have made me shake Simpson's hand. I went back to the Impala and watched in the cool morning as everyone passed before the gaze and handshake of the preacher.

There wasn't much there to notice. Most grasped his hand with enthusiasm, or at least a movement that suggested enthusiasm. When the Baldwin parents emerged, the father got a handshake, and the mother got a short, perfunctory hug. It didn't tell me anything.

All things considered, it wasn't a surprising performance. The kind of church it was, and the personality, as far as I'd seen it, of the pastor should have made me believe that it would be the kind where "saved by faith, not by works" would be the order of the day. I also knew enough about theology to know that the dividing line had always been thus. Could you earn your way into heaven? Probably not. But could you do any damn thing you wanted and still get in? Well, there was the dividing line.

I've always suspected that those who think you are saved by grace alone come equipped with a little sensor that causes them to be aware of how little others are able to be saved by grace. As in, your behavior tells me that you don't get it. And if you don't get it, God won't let you have it.

It's a little circular. On the one hand, you don't need anything but grace. On the other hand, your behavior tells me you won't accept it.

In my experience, that gives them license to do whatever they want against those who won't accept grace.

I watched the last car pull away. I saw Simpson go toward the parsonage and get his car out of the garage. He got in with the woman I'd seen the time before, and they backed out, then pointed the car toward the city.

I slumped down as they passed.

After ten minutes, I got out of the car and did what I needed to do.

Chapter Twenty-Five

First, I rang the doorbell. No reason to commit breaking and entering when someone was in the house. There was no answer.

I had come prepared to break in the parsonage but, in the end, he left the side door to the garage open. From there, it was a short walk to the mud room door, also open. I knew the way from there.

The room hadn't changed much in the few days since I'd interviewed Simpson. A wool throw rested on the chair where I'd sat, near the fire. I bent to breathe it in. Yes, the woman's scent. Or, at least, some woman's scent. The house was cool. Probably they had turned the heat down before church and, knowing that they'd be at least until after lunch before coming back, they took the frugal option of leaving it off.

It was a bit chilly. But I didn't come for comfort. I came to see what I could see.

I began with the desk. The drawer was locked, so I grabbed a couple of paperclips from the desk caddy.

I straightened the paperclips, and with one, I felt for the lock's pins. I couldn't feel the pins, so I pushed one paperclip inside the lock. I raked the sides of the lock with the paperclip to find the pins. Got 'em. I held the pins with one paper clip.

I took the other paperclip and inserted it, so that it was parallel with the other paperclip. I pushed just enough to put pressure on the lock cylinder, being careful to move the clip upward against the pins.

I turned the pins in the lock with the paperclip. There was a small satisfying click as the lock cylinder began to move. I let the paperclip move along with the cylinder until it stopped.

Success.

Inside the center drawer was the usual array of desk paraphernalia. Pencils and pens. A large eraser. One of those small, one-hand staplers. Sheets of paper that looked to be mostly invoices.

To the left was a three-drawer stack. The top one was more desk supplies, a ruler, and cellophane tape. The second was church stationery and envelopes. The third was a stack of old bills and papers marked paid.

The preacher needed to be a little more organized with his business affairs, I'd say.

On the right side were two deeper drawers. Filing drawers with hanging files. The top drawer seemed to hold sermons for the past several years, handwritten notes and typed scripts. You had to be prolific, I guessed, to get up and perform original material every week.

I rifled through the file folders. As erratic as his bookkeeping seemed to be, his organization of his essential work material was excellent. Behind the folders with the chronological sermons was a set of folders that appeared to separate his themes. Sin. Repentance. Gospel fallacies. The Savior. That one was written in all capitals and underlined three times. It was a full quiver of arrows.

The hanging folders in the lower drawer were less well populated. Some contained correspondence to church organizations and people who seemed to be part of his network. There was an especially thick folder with letters that covered a four-year span to and from a man named Carson. Clearly it was someone with whom he'd had a college friendship with, and clearly they'd grown apart. The relationship seemed founded on arguing Biblical points.

Mostly, it was wasted time. Or blood sport. Who could tell? The last letter was dated in 1974, so they must have lost interest.

The last few folders seemed to be empty, but they were pushed askew in an unnatural way. I pulled them forward and found an open box of Thin Mints.

As I reached for them, I heard a sharp bang, like a door. I froze. There was no other sound. I looked around the room. There was not a good hiding place.

I moved quickly to the side of the entry door. If someone came in, I would have the jump on them.

I stood for a while. My wristwatch said ten minutes. My body said more. But there was no further sound throughout the house. Maybe something that was propped up just fell.

I went back to the drawer and slid it back out. The cookie box bore the stamp of this year. I reached inside with my index and middle finger and withdrew a silver dollar with just a hint of chocolate on its rim. It was an odd place to find it. I put it back, replaced the box, and shut the drawer.

I moved around the room, looking at books on bookcases, checking under tables, even picking up lamps and seeing if anything was underneath. If there was anything to see in Simpson's study, I wasn't finding it.

I looked both ways leaving the study, then moved quietly along the carpeted hallway toward the back of the house. My senses were on high alert, but there was nothing to hear or see. Whatever made the noise may not have been human-caused.

When I came to the garage door, it occurred to me that someone could have come in the same way I did. I opened the door to the garage quickly and sprang down the steps to make it harder to hit, shoot, or knife me. But I came to rest in the middle of an empty garage. I got myself back up, shut the door to the house, and sprinted toward the unlocked garage door.

As I did, the garage opener hummed, and the door lurched into motion. I slid out the door, and shut it, just before Simpson's sedan pulled into the garage.

I kept close to the house, then ducked behind a hedge until I got near the road. By the time I reached the Impala, the lights were on in the house.

I was ready to start the car when the garage door opened again, and Simpson backed the car out once again. This time, he backed out quickly and sped away, again toward West End Avenue. The Impala wasn't quite as responsive, and it was a minute before the engine engaged. I u-turned in the street and drove in his direction.

I didn't have a plan. I didn't have a clue. I didn't have a direction. But I was moving.

Chapter Twenty-Six

There are thirty-three traffic lights between the Free Church and 31st Avenue South. I know, because I caught red on twenty of them, and I must have made the yellow lights last on another dozen. I was already behind when I started following Simpson, and by the time I got to the outskirts of the Village, I had lost all track of him.

If there was something he could tell me by where he was going, I wasn't going to find out.

I took a walk over to the VU police house to see if Mercer was working the day shift. The student who was covering the dispatch desk was a squirrely looking guy I knew from around campus when I was Assistant Dean. Willie had evolved over his four years in college, from a kid with a prep school accent to a drawling, Southern-fried redneck. At least he talked that way. He was a constant feature at police headquarters now, having progressed from student foot patrol to Sunday dispatch.

They put him there because nothing much happened on Sunday afternoons and because they had to put him somewhere. Otherwise, they'd never get rid of him.

"LT is out on patrol, sir," he said, all but rising and saluting. Like me, Mercer had been infantry in Vietnam, and I knew that anyone calling him LT would have made his Army Sergeant blood boil.

Willie had managed somewhere to find a blue shirt that looked enough like police issue to convince on first sight and had wheedled the Chief into giving him a magnetic name plate like the full-time staff. It shone in the florescent light, and Willie had ironed the shirt sleeves into precision. You couldn't fault the guy for trying, I guess.

"You mind getting him on the radio? See if he'll meet me for a ride around?"

Willie's face told me that the doubted that was regulation, but he did as I asked. Mercer's voice came back on the box. "Tell Jackson to meet me in the Branscomb entry in five minutes."

"10-4, LT."

"Don't call me LT, Willie."

"10-4, sir."

Five minutes is what it takes to walk from the little house to the front of Branscomb, and Mercer was waiting when I got there.

"Hey, LT. What's happening?"

"Don't start that shit with me," he said as I shut the door. "He's going to drive us all nuts, you know? His junior G-man act is getting old."

He pulled out, turned left at the Kappa Sigma house and headed toward West End. He turned right on West End and headed toward 21st.

"Have you decided to behave yourself?"

"That's interesting," I said, lighting up a cigarette and cracking open the window.

"Please don't throw anything from a police vehicle," he said. "I really don't want to run you in for littering."

"Just ashes, officer." I flicked the butt for effect. "I have been keeping myself quiet, as you suggested I should."

"I've been thinking about your problem. Is there a chance that the person you've ticked off is this Marie person? If she's a lesbian and nobody knows, you might be a threat."

"I don't know that she is." He pulled into the parking lot between the library and the Divinity School. "I don't know that it's a threat if she is. For all I know, if she's a lesbian, she's out."

"Ain't nobody out in Nashville, Jackson. They just peek out of the closet once in a while."

"It's not Simpson. He's angry enough to beat on anybody, but I'm not a threat to him either. I just want to know about his brother." I finished the cigarette and tossed it out the window."

"For God's sake, Jackson. Didn't I just tell you . . ."

"I thought you meant when we were moving. We parked now. We're on campus."

"Same damn thing."

"You need to be clearer, then. By the way, I went to hear him preach today."

Mercer turned fully to face me in the car. "You did what?"

"I went to his church."

"You never go to church, my man. You are the unrepentant Jackson Trade. What the hell possessed you to do that?"

"I've been looking for Josie Pittsfield's car. It was parked over on Acklen, then it disappeared."

"Sugar Momma came and got it?"

I shook my head. "I don't know. Maybe. How would she know where to find it? But I got to thinking. Maybe there's a reason it's parked over there."

Now Mercer lit a cigarette and cracked the window. "Like what?"

"Like maybe there a reason two murders happened within a mile of each other and there's a car parked halfway."

"Mark Simpson was dead before the Baldwin girl was found. That won't fly." He flicked an ash out the window.

"Watch out that you don't litter, officer."

He puckered his face and tilted his head. "Just tell your damn story."

"What if Simpson isn't the murderer, though?"

"The case is closed, my friend. And if Metro is right, the Baldwin case is closing. Neighbor boy did it." He threw the butt out the window. "None of this has anything to do with why you're in church on a perfectly good Sunday morning."

"I told you. I've been over in the neighborhood. Asking questions. Observing. And I observed an odd thing."

"Your point, please?"

"Paul Simpson is a friend of the Baldwin family. He is, in fact, their pastor."

"I read that the Baldwin girl's mother is a little bit of a Jesus freak."

"I don't know about the freak part, but they are definitely born-again folk. And Simpson is a fire and brimstone kind of guy."

"Well, everybody's got to be something. It's interesting that he's their preacher, but what does that tell you?"

"It tells me that there's a Simpson in both stories."

He rolled up his window. "It tells me you're excited by a coincidence. Nashville's still a small town. Look two steps back and Junior G-Man probably has a connection to both stories."

"Only in his dreams, LT." I leaned far enough away that Mercer's swipe missed me. "Now if you told me that he was having me followed and beaten? That would be a really, really small town."

"Look, Jackson," Mercer said, putting a serious face on, "It may be a really good idea for you to watch yourself. I mean it. There's a chance both times it was just guys out, wanting to beat up a drunk for fun. The fact is that both times it was you," he paused.

"I know. It makes it seem like they want to beat up a specific drunk. I got it."

I opened the door and got out. "Call me, Jackson. And keep your head down."

I waved goodbye. Keeping my head down was exactly the wrong thing to do.

Chapter Twenty-Seven

Rather than heading toward campus, I struck off in the opposite direction, two blocks down Scarritt Place to the little College eponymous with the street, or vice versa. Scarritt College had been founded in Missouri as a progressive and color-blind, or as color-blind as you could make it, institute dedicated to the preparation of church workers. Transplanted to Nashville, it had been rechristened Scarritt College for Christian Workers and a beautiful little campus of Late Gothic buildings had sprung up in the block bounded by Edgehill and Grand north and south, and 18th and 19th Avenues on the east and west.

As an undergraduate I had found the little College a world apart from Vanderbilt, despite being less than a quarter mile away. On VU's campus I could hardly go five minutes without seeing someone I knew, and could rarely go anywhere, except in the dead of night, without seeing lots of people I didn't know. Scarritt, on the other hand, was a place where I could go an hour without seeing more than the random graduate student heading into one of the six stone buildings that made the campus distinctive.

I first began going there as a sophomore who was looking for a deserted place where he could study outside. All that spring I lay on my stomach and read, took notes, studied. Once I was chased inside by a pop up storm and ended up inside Bennett Hall. There was no one there when I went in, and never anyone there when I went subsequently. Inside was a beautiful parlor, with rich wood furnishings and a large fireplace at each end. Once I found this, Scarritt College became my rain or shine studying place, unless I needed the Joint University Library for something.

I can tell you that I came for more than the studying and the desertedness. Yes, the fact that Bennett was connected to Scarritt Hall by a cloister gave it the feeling of an abbey, and my monkish tilt, which some might call antisocial but I preferred to think of as solitary, made the College seem an oasis that had been constructed just for me. In the same way that the gymnasium at West End Methodist made me stop and breathe, these two blocks of pastoral did the same thing.

There was an iron bench with wood slats for a seat that I headed toward. It was usually sunlit, and a warm place to be. When I got there, an elderly man sat on one end. When I hesitated, he motioned with his hand for me to sit. "Plenty of room," he said.

He was in his seventies, I'd guess, and his gray hair had thinned to reveal pink skin in most places, the hair now an incomplete covering for his head. His bifocals were thick, and his eyes had the look that old people's eyes get when their eyesight is weak, as if they'd stopped trying very hard because trying very hard didn't work. He wore a tweed jacket but didn't look much like an academic.

"Do you teach here?" I asked.

He smiled. "I do not teach here. Nor anywhere, anymore." Before I could ask, he said, "I taught at Peabody."

George Peabody College, the education college across 21st from Vanderbilt, had long been derided at VU as the home of Peabody Freebodies. It wasn't a description of the female Peabody student body, as much as it was a way to scorn what were, in many cases, people who were not in a Vanderbilt student's social class.

That would not have been true of me. I didn't belong there either.

"I used to come here to think," he said, "when I was still teaching. It's close by, and it is always so peaceful. I come to get in touch with my thoughts."

"Funny how that works. Me too."

"Is that because you are religious, son?"

I sat with my hands in my lap, palms facing each other. I looked out across the little courtyard. "I was raised to be religious. But I'm not. I lost it somewhere." I leaned back and looked at the sky. It was a clear blue, but a blue too late for November, a blue that belonged in January maybe, when winter was fully on you. "You see enough stuff, you don't really see where religion fits. Except maybe as a story you tell yourself to feel better." I turned to face him. "Sorry. That may be a little rude. Are you religious?"

"Jack Lincoln," he said, offering his hand.

"Jackson Trade."

"I'm a John, not a Jackson," he said. "Pleasure to meet you. Yes, I'm religious, after a fashion. At least, I taught religion. If you teach it enough, you begin to see the problems. But it doesn't mean that I'm not still religious."

"If you see the problems, how can you still be a believer?"

He leaned an arm on the back of the bench and looked through the thick lenses at me. "It's not so much being a believer. It's believing that the gaps and the problems are just a part of it." He squinted, as if working to see me. "I'm in my church right here. I don't worry too much about whether it's organized to send me a message right now. I'm just here in case it does. And if it does, I don't worry too much whether I understand it or not."

"That doesn't sound like much of a religion. With all due respect, Jack."

He shrugged. "What's religion anyway, Jackson? Just a bunch of people trying to know the truth, believing that the truth will set them free, as the saying goes. Baptists, Catholics, Jews. All of them listening for a lesson, waiting on a sign, living their lives the way they think they're supposed to."

"Or living their lives the way they want to, no matter what the lesson says."

"There's that. But those are the pretenders. They are in disguise. The real believers, whether we think they're right or not, are faithful."

"And you're faithful to this courtyard?"

He spread his arms upward. "The Church of the Courtyard," he said. "Well, that's as good as any, I guess. Over there," he motioned with his head, "is Wightman Chapel. Originally Methodist, still is nominally Methodist, but what gets preached in there is about as ecumenical as it gets. Love your neighbor, do good, be humble, pray for others."

I remembered Simpson's sermon earlier. "Works, but not faith?"

He shook his head. "That's an old red herring. Still gets people confused, though. Faith begets works. Maybe works begets faith. But just saying faith is all of it? That's bad theology."

"I don't get it."

"If you know the Scripture, all the things Jesus commands are things you do. Acts, Jackson. Not beliefs. Yes, the ultimate lesson is that you can't be good enough that you won't need grace too. But there's not much there to suggest you can do whatever you want and then just grab the big brass grace ring on the last ride." He took off his glasses and rubbed his eyes. "Christians are supposed to do good." He repeated it. "Do."

"You still consider yourself a Christian, Jack?"

"Not much of one." He moved his body forward, then braced on the bench arm and stood. I hadn't noticed a cane hooked to the arm, and he took it, standing straighter. "I would believe in the truth. So, I listen for it. If you can say that thinking is prayer, then I pray for it. As I get older, though, I have more certainty about only one thing."

"What's that?"

"I am more certain that I know less, for sure, than I ever did."

"That seems kind of sad to me."

He tapped the cane gently against my leg. "Unless it's the case that nothing is certain at all. If that's true, then I'm getting closer to the truth." He winked. "Enjoy the Church of the Courtyard, young man. I leave its sanctuary to you."

The old man took a hundred small steps down the sidewalk, then turned in the direction of the parking lot. I lost sight of him as he went past the edge of Bennett Hall.

If he was right, given that I was absolutely sure of nothing, I was getting closer to the truth.

Maybe I just needed to listen.

Chapter Twenty-Eight

By the time I had walked home, the light was beginning to fade. The sunlight that had made Scarritt so seductive disappeared not long after the old man, Jack, had left. It continued to be unseasonable. Too cold a temperature and, in Green Hills, too hot a neighborhood.

Mercer was right. In many ways, Nashville in 1976 was still a small town. Or rather, each section of the city was its own small town. East Nashville had its own vibe and its own temper, as did the north side of town. Belle Meade, of course was richer and snootier than you, so neither you nor it cared. Hillsboro Village, though, was an enclave of small town, almost Mayberry-like. If it had had a sheriff, it would have been Andy Taylor.

But the rape and murder of the Baldwin girl had set the neighborhood on edge. When she was missing, the edge was a sort of "us against the world" posture. Now that she had been found, and found in the neighborhood itself, the posture had become a kind of unfocused rage.

It had been bad enough when the evil came from outside. Now that it appeared to come from inside, there was a fear and an anger that displayed itself every night on the news, in increasingly pained and ugly ways.

The radio jocks were the worst. They were going for day-time ratings now that the FM stations were beginning to bleed off their listeners. The Banner and The Tennessean were better, but their editorial pages sometimes veered into what could be called provocative pieces, in the sense that the overblown rhetoric hardly gave anyone in Hillsboro Village, or Nashville for that matter, any comfort.

Somehow, it was the television stations, and especially WSM and WLAC, which did the best. Their ability to take a sound truck and tower to a remote location and report directly from there had two effects. For one, it made the scene immediate and real, in a way that an anchor behind a desk just could not. But maybe more important, it forced fact on the storytelling. Yes, it may well be that the detective, or the neighbor, is just flat wrong. But a good journalist could, by asking the right questions, lead you to make your own determination.

And if many Nashvillians had determined that the citizens of Hillsboro Village were about at their wits' end, they'd have been right.

I turned on the set expecting to see a rehash of the week's interviews, the kind of crosscut of stories that weekends are good for. Instead, I heard staccato symphonic music, and heard the voice of Dan Miller, the weeknight anchor. "Break-ing News," he said. Must be, I thought, if the main guy comes in on Sunday night.

"A body has been found tonight in the Harpeth River, west of Nashville off Highway 100. The body has been positively identified as that of sixteen-year-old Darrell Lee of Green Hills. Metro police have confirmed that the youth was the primary suspect in the abduction, rape, and murder of Belinda Baldwin."

Miller threw his broadcast to a field reporter who was un-known to me. She was apparently standing near the river. The scene was very dark and grainy.

"We are standing here with Deputy Chief Mike Beverley. Chief, can you tell us what you've found?"

The Deputy Chief wore a pained face, somewhere between fatigue and disgust. He was bareheaded and wearing only a long-sleeved shirt. If he'd been in the river, he'd be wet. And he'd be cold. So pained was about as good as his look was going to get.

He looked down at a paper and read. "At 5:05 we received a call from two kayakers who were paddling from Franklin. They saw a body face down in the river. They came to shore, and one of them ran to a neighboring house to call us. We were dispatched to here and found the boy, the Lee boy, apparently dead."

"Do you know the cause of death?"

He looked the young woman in the face, ignoring the camera, if indeed he saw it at all. "We do not have that information yet. I can say that there were no visible marks on the body, so we assume that he drowned."

"And can you confirm that this was the prime suspect in the Baldwin case?"

"I can say that he was a person of interest in that case. I can't say more than that." But you could see the answer on his face. He was sure of what he knew.

She looked into the camera. "Back to you in the studio, Dan."

Miller had a somber looking man who I recognized as the Chief of Police next to him at the anchor desk. After introducing him Miller asked, "What else can you tell us, Chief?"

What followed was a standard retelling of elements that told every kind of detail and meant virtually nothing. It was the sort of recitation that impresses people with its apparent comprehensiveness. In the end, though, a full set of irrelevant detail is still irrelevant. I suppose it was merciful in the sense that it was only a few minutes, and then they went to commercial.

When they returned, the studio threw back out to the Harpeth River crew, now joined by Andy Rye. I knew Rye as a police reporter. He had worked for both papers at one time or another, and I'd come across him at Mack's a time or two at dinner. He was a straight shooter who asked good questions and usually got answers that were better than everyone else's.

"Dan, the police have combed the riverbank here on the Harpeth River. For orientation, we are just past Percy Warner Park at the Highway 100 put in. It's a fairly steep pathway down to the river from the highway, and the river here, after a summer of above average rainfall, is deeper than usual."

"Police combing the riverbank found the boy's shoes and his jacket. Relatives have told us that Darrell Lee could not swim, and the supposition is that he went into the river with the intention of ending his life."

"Dan, we know from anonymous reports that the young man was a suspect in the rape and murder of Belinda Baldwin, the Hillsboro Village girl who disappeared while delivering Girl Scout cookies. This young man had been repeatedly questioned on the matter."

"I can report, Dan, that police found further down the bank a half-eaten box of Girl Scout cookies, inside which was a silver dollar. This last is important because Belinda Baldwin had a lucky silver dollar which she carried as a good luck charm every time she made a delivery. It was given her by an aunt, who bought her first box of cookies with it."

"Police are trying to confirm if this is the same silver dollar."

"Dan, the police are clearing out here. They have finished their work. And I'm Andy Rye, Channel 4 News."

When you don't know anything for sure, that's one thing. When you know something for sure, and you can't tell anyone, that's something else.

Andy Rye just gave me the key to a locked door. Two locked doors, actually. The key was the silver dollar. Everybody knew that Belinda Baldwin never left on a cookie run without it. Everybody but me, apparently.

But I knew for sure that it was in Paul Simpson's locked desk. And I knew that it was now in the possession of the police, who thought it proved that Darrell Lee had killed Belinda Baldwin, then himself.

Except the key to that locked door was founded on my breaking and entering. I had enough trouble on my resume without getting rousted for that, no matter how much good it might do.

It was clear enough to me that the preacher was the operator here, whether he had done the deeds or not. But since he was holding the silver dollar, it made sense to believe that he was the killer of the girl and the boy. Or that he knew who was.

But Belinda Baldwin had been cut as well. If he was going to throw the police on Darrell Lee's trail, why wasn't the knife found as well? Wouldn't Metro be asking this question?

It was a question that I needed to answer.

I dressed warmly and put on my waterproof boots. The sky was still cloudless, and the heat had begun to drain from Nashville. I backed the Impala out of the driveway and headed down West End to where it turned into Highway 100. I drove until I got to the south end of the park, pulled onto Old Hickory Boulevard, and parked the car in some trees.

From there, I walked down Vaughn Road until I came to the Harpeth River. I was about two miles upriver from where the boy was found. I planned to walk along the river until I came to the scene.

Andy Rye had said the police were gone, but that was an assertion rather than a fact. And it was a statement that could be meant to bring someone out of the woodwork, or out of the woods literally, if the police thought something was amiss.

I thought something was amiss since there wasn't mention of a knife. Who knows what Metro would think was amiss?

When I was in combat, I took point more and more until I was almost always point. Out in the boonies, you have your point guy, you have a slack guy, and a compass guy. And while it's true that the enemy would be advised to let the point pass in order to get a clean look at the whole unit, the fact is that walking point carried with it a responsibility to see things, hear things, and sense things that kept the unit alive. Never mind the traps and triggers that could blow you up fast.

I walked point plenty. Too much for my own comfort but I trusted me to do it more than anybody in my unit. That means I know how to walk with my eyes open. You know what? I can almost do it with my eyes closed. I did it enough in the dark to know.

And I was approaching the Harpeth the same way. Not because there were enemy. But because I just didn't know what was there. And instead of an M-16 and a machete, I had a flashlight to keep hooded.

I had on dark clothes and my waterproofed boots made soft sounds as I went. I made good time for about the first 200 yards, then hit a portion where the vegetation had grown completely over the bank. Even with the summer rains, the river was walkable there. Anyone kayaking would have portaged through there. But after about a half mile, the river rose, and I half floated, half dogpaddled until the bank came back into view.

I hadn't anticipated being soaked through, and the wind cut through me. I shivered. It seemed to me you should be able to get wet in late November in middle Tennessee without catching your death.

Of course, that's exactly what Darrell Lee had done.

Just as the bank came easily into view and I started walking on ground again, I caught sight of a light up from the shore. I sank to my belly and waited. Male voices were talking. I moved closer, creeping over a log, and hugging the slight rise above the shore.

"Jesus, Mickey," one voice said, "how is it that you got four and I got two?"

"You don't drink fast enough," said the other.

I kept crawling just below the rise. Teenagers drinking beer at a picnic shelter shouldn't be hard to skirt.

The water next to me exploded.

"Come on, Mickey. If you're too drunk to skip a stone then you're just too damn drunk."

"Maybe I was trying to hit something."

I checked the light. It was not a bright night, but there was some light. Had this guy seen me?

"Watch this."

I heard the whir of a rock pass over my head and glide onto the water, skimming about forty yards all the way across the river.

"Hah. Top that, buddy boy."

"Son of a bitch," said the other, presumably Mickey.

I lay on my belly for the better part of a half hour while they drank their last beers and more or less unsatisfactorily tried to match the perfect skimmer. By the time they left, I was chilled to the bone.

As I heard their car start, I resumed my trek along the river. The Harpeth is not a major waterway by any stretch, but what it lacks in majesty it more than makes up in variability. It winds and rises, winds and falls, and generally surprises with its changes. Unless you know it, and I've only been down one stretch of it once, you can get fooled by it.

The Harpeth is basically a river in the middle of Nashville, but the homes are not near and the Warner Parks set it off from civilization. Even on a summer's day, you won't catch much more traffic than the occasional fisherman. Upriver, the current can get a little fast, but down on the stretch I was walking, it's as much portage as paddle, except when the rains have really set in.

Tonight, once I got past Mickey and his beer drinking companion, it was a pretty easy walk, except for the cold. I moved the way I remembered moving. Without a unit behind me to protect, I focused on me, on what I could hear and see, what I could smell and sense. The river was cold, but it was clean. The riverbank was cluttered in spots, but it was cluttered with natural things. There was nothing out of place on the Harpeth.

I felt the thing that made me a good point man to begin with. I felt the way I always did when I was outside. Growing up as a kid, being outside was a natural thing. It wasn't just about hunting and fishing. If you grow up feeling comfortable outside, then you listen and hear. You smell and you know.

It's like Jack and the Church of the Courtyard. It's there, but only if you're still enough to get it.

The water made a soft, lapping sound and I made no sound at all. I was walking point. I had a flashlight. I hooded it and was invisible.

At the biggest bend in this stretch of the Harpeth, where another little stream fed in, I saw the strobe of a police car. I crab walked to a makeshift pier that was built over the water and lay down close to the pilings. Whoever was there couldn't see me, but I couldn't see them either. And the strobe lit up the bank so that I was pinned down. No matter where I moved, the light would catch me.

This is the problem with being a sneak. Unless you've announced yourself in some way, no one is out to find you. Something they have naturally done has compromised your ability to do what you want to do. The only solution is to find a way to encourage them to do something that will set you free. Or to change your own situation so that you're not compromised.

I didn't think I could do anything to make them, whoever they were, do anything. I could backtrack and go up toward the highway, but that didn't seem to offer much in the way of the positive. I would go up, then go back down on the other side of them, with no guarantee of making any progress. Or, shivering, I could backtrack, swim across the river, and approach from the other side.

As usual, the less comfortable option was the right one.

I moved sixty yards or so back, took a deep breath, and swam the river again, this time across. You can swim quietly, but it requires you to endure longer times as your body engages the water. And this makes you colder.

I felt like my blood must be ten degrees colder. My ribs ached in the cold. I knew that my hands were numb, and I couldn't feel my feet. I climbed the bank, got behind the tree line, and made my way forward.

When I got to the place where the police were, I found they had pulled a car over and were now performing a field sobriety test. The young man being administered was failing his test. I wondered if it was Mickey.

I knew a little something about failing tests, even without getting pulled for a DUI.

I pushed forward on the south bank. When I came to the fork where the Little Harpeth meets the Harpeth, I climbed back down to the riverbank. Unlike upriver, this was deeper water. Even in a dry season there wouldn't be portage here, and the wash was a little swifter. Trees hung over the water, giving it a darker, less certain feel.

I quieted my mind and closed my eyes, listening.

In summertime this place would be alive with sound. Crickets, night birds, and all sort of other indigenous sounds would make the place appear teeming with life. Now, in the too cool November, crickets had gone silent. There was the quick soft flog of the Little Harpeth as it met its sister water, a little like a small waterfall. The occasional gurgle of water submerged by water punctuated the white noise of the river. As a boy, I had camped near a river like this, made drowsy by its constant soothing.

People go to the ocean because they are drawn to the rocking and crashing of the waves. A different kind is drawn to the river, where it nestles against the bank and invites you to join it. The ocean is vast and obscures all that is nearby with its sound and motion. The river denies that it is separate from its surroundings, and winds away from the place you are. I'm not talking about great rivers like the Mississippi. I mean the smaller ones, the tributaries of the tributaries, whose scale is human.

A breeze kicked up, reminding me that I was colder than I wanted to be. I didn't sense anyone here. The excitement at dusk had dissipated into the night air. Only the irregular hoot of a distant owl disturbed the near-winter quiet. The river and I had the place to ourselves.

Opening my eyes, I peered toward the opposite shore, or shores as it was. I was standing at the break, where the two rivers, both called Harpeth, met. To the east, toward Nashville, was a bank that mimicked the same overhanging trees where I stood. To the west, amid a clearing, were a series of steep steps made of railroad ties that disappeared up toward Highway 100. That was the canoe access point, and that's where Metro had found the shoes and the silver dollar.

Once again, I zipped my flashlight into my jacket pocket and made another night swim. This time I had to fight with the current a bit. I angled east, then let it carry me downstream, westerly. In this way, I was across the river and on the bank in about half the time it would have taken me, and with less effort, than if I had tried to swim across.

My broken ribs were aching from the effort, though. The river soothed, but it made its demands if you wanted something other than what it had to give. I kneeled on the shore until my breathing returned to normal.

I unzipped my coat and got the flashlight beam trained on the bank. There were boot prints everywhere. Had Metro noticed Simpson's along with the boy's? Maybe not. It had been wet, and the river was up. Even in November, there would have been canoe and kayak enthusiasts out.

I walked the shoreline, keeping the beam trained just ahead of my feet. The water lapped against the shore, occasionally splashing, making small bursts of spray no taller than a few inches. The quiet made it easy to focus. But there was nothing to see.

How would he have done it? Had he ordered Darrell Lee to take off his shoes? Had he incapacitated him some way, and carried him out into the middle? Once he had done whatever he did, had he placed the cookies and the silver dollar carefully, out in the open, easy to see? Probably not. He couldn't be sure that the boy would be found quickly. What if someone came before the police?

Too many questions. Only one certainty. Simpson was responsible for this. And because he was, he was responsible for the Baldwin girl too.

I kept at my slow task. The wind gusted, then picked up, and I felt icy fingers wrapping around me. My ribs ached. It was a good thing I could breathe shallow breaths. That's all I could manage. The bones of my fingers felt like unresponsive rods inside my skin.

Being out here was beginning to look like a stupid idea.

I had worked my way from the access point down river about a hundred yards. Then I retraced my steps and began working my way north toward the highway. The shoreline was clear for about thirty feet, then began to be covered by low hanging branches that jutted out over the river. I clanked my head twice on branches before I decided I was better off walking hunched over.

With the tree cover, there was also much more leaf cover on the shore. It was the sort of leaf cover that, being constantly wet, will test your footwork. I moved at my snail's pace for fifteen minutes, until I broke into a clear space that extended upriver. Going a little faster now, I covered enough distance that I felt sure Simpson couldn't have thought to hide a knife, or anything, that far way.

I walked back the way I had come. If there was anything to find, it was in the tree-covered part of the shore. Once there, I resumed my search, this time on my knees, inch by inch.

The human body responds to extremes in interesting ways. I knew enough about hypothermia to know that I was just uncomfortable, albeit very uncomfortable, but not in danger. The pain in my ribs, and the cold in my joints caused in me a well-practiced effect of compartmentalizing the pain and focusing on the task at hand. If anything, the discomfort made me sharpen my focus. It was a way of ignoring the throbbing that was everywhere.

Just ahead, halfway up the bank, my light caught a sliver of something. Before the clearing at the access point, the glint of something was angled in such a way that could not have seen it walking from the other direction, and that I would not have seen now if I hadn't been on my knees, below it, looking slightly upward.

I crawled toward it. A stained wooden handle, with a blade sunk into the wet earth, stood there as if it had been thrown. I pulled it out of the ground. It was a 6-inch blade, what we called a butcher knife when I was growing up. I ran my finger along its edge, and found it was plenty sharp. The handle was worn away a bit, but it had not been in the elements long. It was just wet, rather than wet and slimy.

It had to be the knife Simpson used on the Baldwin girl. And unless I missed my guess, on Josie Pittsfield.

I put the knife between my belt and my soaked pants and covered it with my coat. The wind was dying down a little, but it was too late to save my frozen body. I hiked up the railroad ties, got to the highway, and began walking the couple of miles back to my car.

When I got home, I took a long, hot shower, then nursed a bourbon until my body was thawed. I fell asleep under two quilts and didn't dream at all.

Chapter
Twenty-Nine

I woke with a nasty headache that was matched by a painful knifing sensation in my ribs. I lay in bed and checked other parts of my body. My fingers worked, though with difficulty, and my ankles were sore, but functional. I could feel the cooler air of the apartment against my face and felt the pleasant weight of the quilts on the rest of my body. My wet clothes from the night before lay in a pile near the bathroom door, as if I needed a reminder of why I hurt.

Getting out of bed wasn't what I wanted to do.

I lay in bed until the call of nature could not be ignored. I pulled a quilt around me and made it to the bathroom, then quickly dressed in jeans, a flannel shirt, and a hooded sweatshirt. Once I got socks on, and coffee made, I felt better.

I sat looking at the knife. Though he had cleaned it, there were specks on the handle that I surmised were, or could be, blood. The knife was completely unremarkable, other than the fact that it was old, well-used, and well cared for.

It also made me want to make a call and, when I got the answer I hoped for, I threw on a coat and took a walk.

When I knocked on her door, she was a minute getting to it. "Just a second, ok?"

Betty opened the door wearing jeans and heels, with a short-waisted white jacket with a fake fur collar. "Miss Betty," I said.

"Hey, hun. You look a little better than last time, but not by much."

I followed her into her apartment. She sat on the sofa and patted it. "Come and sit. Tell Betty about it."

"Actually, I'm here because I'd like to see Josie's apartment again. You said it was still empty."

She rolled her eyes. "Yes, it's empty. Everybody in town knows what happened there. I haven't even had any calls to look at it."

"All her stuff still there too?"

She nodded. "Can't give that away either. It would have been so much easier if her father had taken all that stuff when he was here."

"Tough to do when you don't know there's an apartment. An apartment full of stuff he didn't buy."

"If you say so." She made a pouty face and patted the sofa again. "Can't you sit and talk for a little bit?"

"Maybe after I look at the apartment." I patted the knife in my coat pocket. "I have to test a theory."

She sighed a little dramatically and got to her feet. We climbed the stairs, and I made sure to be a step or two behind her. I didn't want to go at her pace, and I didn't mind the view.

Inside, Josie's apartment was as it had been. Betty had been at work cleaning the stains out of the flooring, and she'd done a good job. But otherwise, the apartment looked as I'd left it the night I broke in.

"Might be easier to rent unfurnished," I said.

"Might be. Might not. Owner says leave it here for now. College students sometimes come in and say, what the hell, I'll take it with the furniture. Beats what they have. We'll see."

I walked over to the kitchen counter and pulled the knife block over to me. It was well-used, and the two empty slots that I'd seen the very first time now felt like a puzzle piece falling into place. "Think they picked this up at a flea market? It's a pretty good set, and it's older than either her or Mark."

"I guess," she said. "it's missing a steak knife, and another piece."

I pulled the knife out of my pocket. "Like maybe this one?"

Her mouth made an O. "Jackson," she said, making the last syllable last for a while. "What the devil?"

I took the knife and positioned it above the largest slot in the block. It slid in, like butter, all the way to the handle. "Welcome home, big fella."

Betty came to the counter and stood by me. "Is that?" She didn't finish the sentence. She didn't need to.

"Yes."

"How did," she started.

"I get it?" I finished. "Too long a story. But it's why I don't look as good today as I should." I pulled the knife out of its slot."

"Now what are you going to do? You're taking it to the police, right?"

"I'm not. The police don't have a place for this piece of information."

"But it's a murder weapon."

"And they have the murderer. And the murderer is dead."

She eyed me, and not in the way that says seduction. "You're not telling me something," she said.

"That's right. The less you know, the better."

She had put her hands on her hips as if to scold, or to tell me off, but she stopped.

"Give me a day or two," I said. "I have to take care of a few things, and then we'll see."

"We'll see what?" She didn't have a smile on her face, but she had a smallish sparkle in her eyes.

"We will grab a bite, maybe go see some music somewhere. Sound like a deal?"

This time, she did smile. "If you are asking me out on a proper date, then yes. That is a deal, mister. Do your thing. Get feeling better. Then come get me." She turned and walked toward the door. "Come on. Get out. If you're not going to spill the beans, get going."

We walked down the stairs to the entryway. "Thanks, Betty. I couldn't have done this without you."

"That's a lie, but you're sweet." She leaned up against me. I could feel her on my ribs. Strangely, that pressure didn't hurt at all. "Give me a kiss," she said. I complied with a quick peck on her cheek. "You'll have to get better at that too, but there's time."

"We'll see," I said, grinning.

She swatted my backside as I passed her. "Call me."

The weather had finally warmed in this abnormal autumn. It was almost noon, and the sun was out, the breeze was still, and the temperature was flirting with 70. I took off my coat, folded it around the knife, and walked home.

It's odd on a college campus how warm days bring out young men in shorts, where only a day ago they were walking around campus is coats and scarves. Especially in the South, where warm temperature can last until Thanksgiving, any early cold will upset the season rhythm. I'm guilty myself, but I never was part of the crowd that wore shorts until wearing shorts was just ludicrous.

Now, though, with a break in the cold, I walked my shortcut across campus and found person after person wearing shorts with a sweatshirt, half with the sweatshirt sleeves tied around their waist or neck. Even the women sported the attire, everyone looking as if they had escaped from a walk-in freezer, but with summer tans intact.

Carrying a coat, wearing jeans and a flannel shirt, I looked like what I'd become--a stranger on campus, maybe an interloper.

I now had knowledge that no one else, save Paul Simpson, had. It was knowledge that they didn't know they wanted, and maybe they didn't. Some of it was knowledge I'd gained illegally.

Metro had closed the book on Josie's murder. Mark did it. Mark killed himself. The knife might be an inconvenient fact, but there's no real accounting for it.

Metro was closing the book on Belinda Baldwin. They had made Darrell Lee for it. Darrell had turned up dead with the cookie box and the silver dollar. If they had found the knife, it would have been a convenient fact, but they didn't really need it.

I knew that Paul Simpson had the cookie box and the silver dollar because I broke into his parsonage. That was a really inconvenient fact for me, but even more for him.

I knew that the knife came from Josie and Mark's kitchen, which likely made it Josie's murder weapon.

It was also inconvenient that these two instances had come together. It was convenient that only Paul Simpson knew until now how they were linked.

Somehow, I had to make it terribly inconvenient for him that I knew too.

The driver's seat of the Impala was still wet from the night before. In the sunlit heat of the car, the seat had taken on the smell of wet cigarettes and old French fries. I found some plastic sheeting in the Bucket's garage and put it over the front seat. It didn't help the smell, but it kept my jeans and shirt dry.

I drove out to White Bridge Road and parked down the road in the Minit-Mart lot. I brought binoculars so that I could keep an eye on the parsonage and the church. I had a plan working in my mind, but I had made a guess that had to be right for it to work.

The woman left first, backing an Oldsmobile station wagon the size of the Queen Mary out of the parking lot. She had to wait for a good while for traffic to clear enough for her to back into the road. It had the turning radius of the Queen Mary too, but she finally navigated it in the direction of town and left.

Fifteen minutes passed before Simpson himself appeared. His Mercury was in the driveway facing the road. Unlike the woman, he started the car and drove straight into the road, going fast enough for the wheels to leave a little squeak as he turned.

I walked to the parsonage and rang the front doorbell. No answer. I rang it several more times. No one answered.

But it wasn't the parsonage I wanted to burgle. I walked behind the church, hopped the rail fence, and walked toward the barn.

There was one piece of evidence missing, and the barn was the one place it could be.

It was an old barn, made in a distinctive style. It had a high-pitched roof and a large mouth opening at the top, so that hay could be tossed up and stacked in the loft. Its steep pitch was covered with tin that long ago had been painted red, and then baked by years of summer sun, so that it now showed silver through the red. To each side on the lower level would be stalls for livestock, either feeder calves or horses, perhaps, each one led in through the center opening. In many barns of this type, the center opening was wide open, which gave a cooling breezeway during the summer months but could be brutal in winter. This barn had the other option, a double door, with crosshatched beams, secured by a beam across them both.

I walked to the rear of the barn, the side that did not face the road. There I found a similar arrangement as the front, except that the beam to secure the doors rested against the barn. Something had lately disturbed the grass in front of the doors. That was a good sign.

I dragged one of the big doors open, scraping the ground through a worn path, until it opened wide. I repeated the action with the other door.

I looked inside. The afternoon sun was shooting in little darts through the gaps in the facing on the other side of the barn. But there it was, just as I thought it must be, sitting in between the stalls on either side.

I had found the Torino.

I took the key I'd left on my key ring and fired up the engine. Carefully I rolled it forward, making sure not to brush against the stalls or the door frame. It was a relatively tight fit, but it was a fit. Once it was outside, I shut the barn doors, opened the barn lot gate, and idled the car down past the gate.

I made sure I fastened the gate tight. I laughed to myself. This was a clear case of shutting the gate after the horse has escaped.

By the time I got back into town, I drove around back of the VU police station and parked the Torino in the lot. I put the knife in the trunk and shut it tight. No need to worry. Josie had the right parking sticker for that lot. I locked the car.

Inside, I found Mercer bent over some papers. He looked up, spun his pen, and pointed it at me. "You look too damn pleased with yourself. Do I want to know?"

"I just need a ride, sir. My car is at a Minit-Mart on White Bridge Road."

Chapter Thirty

I drove west out I-40 until I got to the Bucksnort exit. The Simpson family had lived there, somewhere near the Humphries County line. I didn't know what I wanted, but I knew I wanted to ask around.

The wide spot in the road known as Bucksnort wasn't at the exit. To get there you had to follow a narrow two-lane road that narrowed further to a gravel road, then sprang into a wider road, still gravel, covered by the branches of trees. Half a mile further on, the trees relented, and I emerged onto a blacktop surface, unmarked by lines.

This was Bucksnort, an incorporated town that was unlikely to last, given its placement. On one side of the blacktop was an Esso service station, on the other a building that purported to be a diner. It looked a lot more like a honky-tonk, the brown clapboard and narrow windows promising a dark interior better suited to long drinking than to a meat-and-three.

I parked, got out, and went inside.

The opening of the door flooded the place with sunlight. A window air conditioner was cranked to its lowest setting and the fan was on full tilt. Even so, the place hung with the heaviness of humidity. I shut the door and let my eyes adjust.

There were indeed five tables that would seat four diners each. But there was also a wooden bar that stretched the length of the building. It had two taps, Miller and Miller Lite, and a small selection of liquor on the counter behind. A man sat behind the bar, as far as I could tell the sole proprietor and maybe the sole occupant, maybe for days.

He had glanced up when I entered but had returned to whatever he was reading. As I approached him, he looked up again. He appeared to be mid-forties but used up. He had on a short sleeve chambray shirt and a red bandana tied as a headband. His skin was leathery and dark, more like someone who spent his days outside in the blistering sun than someone sitting in a dark, humid dive. He put down the paperback he was reading and squinted one eye at me.

"You lost?"

"Nah." I looked up at the liquor. "Hard to find VOB in the well anymore. Pour me two fingers, neat."

He looked at me without changing expression, then slowly moved toward where the Very Old Barton bottle stood, looking back toward me twice. He poured a couple of ounces into a highball glass. "Water?"

"Nope. Just the bourbon."

He brought the glass to the bar and set it in front of me. He moved the book to the side. It was O'Brien's *If I Die in a Combat Zone*. "You served?" I asked. The expression never changed. A few seconds passed, more than should have. "Me, 69 and 70. Alpha Company. 54th Infantry."

He nodded. "101st Airborne. Long range recon."

"LURP." Tough cookie. Probably more at home in the dark. I held out my right hand. "Jackson Trade."

He shook my hand. "Phil Shelton." He sat down across the bar from me. "You sure you're not lost, Jackson Trade?"

"I'm trying to figure something out."

"Ain't we all?"

"You hear about this kid from up this way? He killed a girl in Nashville."

"You drove here, right? You see any TV towers?"

"I know you can get Nashville news in Hickman County."

"Sure. If you want to and if you can put up with the reception." He tapped the book. "Easier for me just to read."

"Fair enough," I said. "Kid's name was Mark Simpson. Ever hear of him?"

He scratched the side of his mouth and got up. He reached under the bar and pulled out a glass, then poured off a Miller Lite. He sat back down across from me and leaned his elbows against the bar. His eyes were tired, enveloped by small folds that made him look older than he probably was. They had been half-open before. Now, however, they were open, as if he was concentrating hard. "You say Mark Simpson killed somebody? Mark Simpson?"

"That's what they say."

He exhaled and looked down. His brown hair had given way to a bald spot in the back. "You know much about this area?"

"To tell the truth, I just know the exit sign on the interstate. Funny name, Bucksnort. Everybody knows it. But I doubt anyone has a reason to get off and come back this way."

"People get off if they're going to Waverly, though if you ask me that's not a reason to get off the highway." He took a sip of his beer. "Back in the 50s, this was a transfer point, back before the interstate. Moonshine from east Tennessee got here and got divvied up for Memphis, Birmingham, even some points north. The law knew about it, but this is a well-sheltered area and there's several ways out, so it was safe. All this was before the interstate was much of a thing."

"I didn't know that." But I could believe it, after the gravel road trip I'd had.

"So, there were people in the transport business. We had a motel here, a little one that catered to people coming and going with moonshine. Gas station's still here. And this establishment, which my mama and daddy ran until they passed."

"And that's the story of Bucksnort."

"Pretty much. There's farmers around, of course. And as you get closer to Waverly there are little businesses scattered, engine repair and the like. You know how it goes."

I did. It was like the little spot in the road where I grew up.

"And where there are people in Tennessee, there will be a Baptist Church. And that's Briar Creek Baptist Church. Little white church, just down the road, right where it joins onto Highway 13."

"That's where Brother Simpson pastors?"

"You know it."

We sat in silence, me with my bourbon and him with his beer. He got up, picked the bottle of Barton and set it beside me. I poured out a touch more.

"She was smarter than him," he said. "The wife. She was a town girl, from Waverly. Father was a state representative for a while, then he came back and got elected judge. Had a heart attack and died in his robes." He was talking and looking toward the wall, like he was telling a story to himself. "Anyway, she married the preacher, and he got her pregnant pretty much right away. That's the older boy."

"Paul," I said.

"Yes. Road to Damascus Paul."

"Kind of a weighty responsibility, I'd say."

"Well, this Paul didn't have to have a conversion experience. Right away the preacher took him on. Used the mother as a nursemaid, but otherwise he molded that boy the way he wanted him to be. I don't know if he made a preacher, but that was what he was meant to do."

"Actually," I said, "he did become a preacher."

He sipped at the beer, still looking away. "No surprise. That's what he was bred to do. Kind of like a prize hog."

"You went to this church?"

He laughed, a quick, nearly soundless burst of air. "God, no. We were in the liquor business. They didn't want us there, and we didn't want to go."

"Then how do you know all this?"

"You from a small place, Trade?" When I smiled, he said, "Everybody here knows everything."

"What else do you know?"

"I know the wife got less and less. The preacher was mean to her in public. I don't doubt he beat her with his one good arm."

"He only had one arm?"

"Farming accident when he was a boy. Withered up left arm. But I imagine he whaled on her with the right arm and called it the will of God."

"Sounds like a real peach."

"Yeah, he was a case. But so was the son. He bossed the woman too. Told her to sit down. Told her to shut up. I don't think I've ever seen anything like it."

"I heard she killed herself."

"Wouldn't you? Well, maybe you wouldn't. But nobody was surprised when she did."

"Where does Mark come into this story?"

"He came in years after the first boy, Paul. The preacher already had his boy, and he left this one alone. He was a skinny kid, always looked like he'd missed a meal or two. Maybe they didn't feed him. Hell, that wouldn't surprise anybody either."

All this time he'd been sipping at the beer, almost in rhythm, taking a pause and a sip, then resuming. Now he waited. I waited too.

"Yes, she killed herself. Hanged herself from a beam with an extension cord. I heard it was the older boy who found her. Hell of a thing."

"They sound like a lovely family." I finished my bourbon. The sour heat of cheap bourbon burned the back of my throat. Or maybe that was the sarcasm that burned it.

"You know what, Trade? They were lovely enough that nobody around here stopped him from acting like he did. Nobody quit his church. Nobody said a word." He finally looked at me again. "I hadn't thought about them in years, though the old man still has the church. But you said Mark, the younger one, killed somebody?"

"Killed his roommate. Butchered, more like it."

He whistled. "Damn. The skinny bastard? I would have bet on the other brother." He finished the beer and put the glass in a sink behind the bar. "Shows what I know."

I climbed back in the Impala, raised it to life, and pulled onto the road, still heading away from the interstate. It was pretty enough country, though overgrown and messy. Everywhere the vegetation threatened to get angry for good and overtake the road. I had the feeling it was only the dust raised up from behind the car that beat the vegetation back.

I came to the end of the road, where it joined Highway 13, a two-lane state road. On the left was the church, as advertised. There was a four-step stair with a weathered, unpainted rail, as well as a beat-up ramp that looked too steep to do any good. The door was a simple double-sided affair, and you could see down the side that there were three windows at intervals, all three were double-hung with a cross above in cheap stained glass, and one had a window air conditioner, framed by a metal cage to foil anybody who decided he needed to take it off their hands. The sanctuary didn't look very big, but I doubted that unit could cool it off.

Side by side with it, facing the highway, was a small white frame house that could only be the parsonage. I parked the car in front and walked to the door. I knocked, and a fierce little man with wire-framed glasses answered. He wore dress pants that weren't that dressy anymore and a white shirt. He opened the door but left the screen door latched.

"Yes?"

"You Brother Simpson?"

He kept his hand on the door, ready to slam it shut. "I am." That was all I was getting until he decided he wanted to give me more.

"My name is Jackson Trade. I'm from Nashville. I'm here about Mark."

"Mark is dead."

"I know that, sir. I'm here because I've been hired to find out more about the details of his last days."

He looked doubtful. "Hired by who?"

"The dead girl's mother and father."

"Knowing more about Mark won't bring their daughter back."

"Not arguing that point, sir. They're trying to understand what happened to their daughter. Not only how she died. That is clear. They are trying to figure out who she was before she was killed."

"That answer isn't in Hickman County. Now, if you'll excuse me." He began to shut the door.

"I can't help but believe some of it is here. In your wife's suicide."

The door stopped moving and his face tightened. "This has nothing to do with my wife."

"In a funny way, maybe it does." The hand that wasn't on the door clenched. "I'd appreciate just ten minutes of your time, sir. I don't mean to bring up old memories, but I think I can help." He didn't move, either toward opening or shutting the door. "If it was Paul, you'd want somebody to help. That's all I'm doing here."

At the mention of his older son, he looked quickly at me. He unlatched the screen door. "Ten minutes. That's all I'm giving you."

The living room was furnished in the same way, I assume, it had been since forever. There were touches here and there that suggested a woman had lived here. A doily here, a lace-covered pillow there. It had an oddly Victorian feel to it, but it had been occupied for so long only by men that it had converted itself into a drab folly, as if it wanted to suggest comfort but couldn't bring itself there. There was a couch that looked uncomfortable, and two straight back chairs that would have been better suited to a dining room. The one nod to comfort was a La-Z-Boy recliner which faced the television set. That's where the preacher settled himself. I picked up a straight-backed chair and placed it so that he and I were face to face.

"Paul told you about Mark, I guess." He nodded, his face set in what I imagine was his idea of stern tolerance. "Were you surprised?"

"I can't say I was. I can't say I wasn't. Mark was not normal. He was never normal."

"How do you mean? Not normal in what way?"

"I suppose you know that he declared himself a homosexual? That is not normal."

"But you loved him."

"As God the Father loves all his children, then yes, I loved him. But I did not approve of him."

"But you approved of him before that, right?"

"Mark was never normal, Mr. Trade. Not before his mother's death. And certainly not after it."

I sat on the edge of the chair, looking into his eyes. They were hard, the eyes of someone who did not love easily and probably didn't love much at all. "But you'll agree that the suicide of your mother is a hard thing to bear."

He snorted. "Life is hard to bear. This is a trial. It's not supposed to be easy. You would have seen, if you'd been here, that Paul weathered this storm in his life and prevailed. For Heaven's sake, it was Paul who found her, swaying from the beam. Did he take it into his head to moan and cry? He did not." The look on his face was clear. "Mark was weak, like his mother."

"Help me understand your wife, his mother. If he's like her, then that will help me."

"It won't help."

He was a mean old man. You could feel the hate coming off him like heat off a road on a sunny day. But all the energy that made his heat was coming from inside him. He was burning up with anger.

"Tell me about her."

He gritted his teeth and spoke. "She was prideful. She thought too highly of her intellect. After we married, she was disagreeable. It is not a woman's place to be disagreeable. It's not her place to contradict."

"What was she disagreeable about? Was it about Paul's up-bringing?"

"What would you know about that?"

"Just that I heard you had charge of Paul from a young age. That must have been hard on his mother."

"Boys should be brought up strong. Brought up strong in Scripture. She was wrong-headed on this. She wanted to bring him up weak-minded like her. Entertaining different sides of every question. Listen," he wagged a finger at me, "nobody's able to consider every side of a matter. God has spoken on everything that man will encounter. There's nothing more to say about it. And for our sins, His grace is sufficient."

"And Mark? You didn't also take charge of Mark's upbring-ing?"

He flushed. "That is my failing. I had become too busy. And the boy was, in a way, unexpected."

"An accident."

"No. God does not permit accidents. But he came to us un-awares, and I was not in the same place in life as before. Thus, she raised him. She ruined him. He could not be salvaged. Though as God is my witness, I tried. The ladies of the church tried as well. But he could not be brought into line. She had already ruined him."

"When you say ruined, what do you mean?"

He leaned forward and sat on the edge of the recliner. He lowered his voice, but it was not a lowering that suggested collegiality. It was a lowering that sounded threatening.

"She taught him to be weak. Weakness is to turn from God and God's word. It takes strength to follow the right path. She taught him to ignore the path, to do easy things instead. I could not turn him from his ways. It was that simple."

He stood up. "That's all the time I can give you."

I rose too. As we walked to the door, I asked him, "When Paul found your wife, where was Mark?"

"Mark was in the house somewhere. I know he couldn't have heard anything, and Paul told me he took care to keep his brother outside the room until everything was cleared."

"But he knew."

"While she was killing herself? I sincerely hope not." He reached the door and stood aside. "What are you getting at?"

"I just wonder. Mark hanged himself in jail."

"Well, I wouldn't put much stock in that. As I said, he was weak. Like his mother. If not by hanging, then by any other means." He shut the screen door and latched it.

Through the screen, I asked, "Why do you think your sons didn't get along?"

"I have one son now. I get along with him just fine." He shut the door firmly, and I heard the lock turn.

I looked at the map in the Impala. There were three ways to get from Bucksnort to Centerville, the county seat, and all of them looked like they'd take longer than it was worth. I finally settled on one and spent the next thirty minutes moving under forty miles per hour behind an old man in an aged Plymouth. At least the delay gave me a chance to think.

Brother Simpson was angry, and I suspected he'd been angry for a long time. Angry about his wife's being smarter than him. Angry that she wouldn't mind him. Probably angry that she'd killed herself and made him look bad. He didn't seem the sort of person who could bear the disapproval of people well, and a preacher's wife committing suicide wasn't a good look for him. Never mind that it wasn't an ideal result for her.

I couldn't help thinking that the withered arm was an apt thing. The old phrase "busier than a one-armed paperhanger" came to mind. If that's what happened with a paperhanger, what happened to a man of God who was trying to lift up an entire congregation? With a wife that wouldn't go along? At least, that's the way he would have seen it.

In his version, he had to take the boy under his broken wing. And he had turned him into a version of himself, one with two good arms and an anger that committed fouls at fearsome rates. It seemed clear that Paul didn't have "mommy issues," but he may have had a "daddy issue" or two.

No wonder the woman in the parsonage, his wife, presumably, was utterly silent. He'd found the right woman just as his father had not.

I pulled into the parking lot of the Hickman County Courthouse. I didn't know if I could get what I wanted, but I knew I had to try.

The Courthouse looked more like a schoolhouse than anything else. Made of yellow brick, the first floor appeared to be all offices, and the upper floor looked to be courtrooms, two to each side of the center, and a stairway in the center that had a large window on the second-floor level. Hickman is a small county, so even this much courthouse might be overkill.

I climbed the steps and entered the building. A sign pointing up the stairs signaled both courtrooms and jury rooms were on the second floor. To the right were clerk of court, the tax assessor, and the district attorney's office. To the left were the county judge, the county auditor, and the office I wanted, the county sheriff.

I entered through a glass door with the name of the sheriff, Cletus Hayes. Behind an oak railing sat an older woman, methodically pecking at an old Royal typewriter. She glanced sideways at me as she continued her steady, slow typing. "Help you?"

"I wonder if I could see Sheriff Hayes." No reason I shouldn't come right out and say it. Anybody presumably could and, since it's an elected position, presumably he wouldn't mind.

She turned in her chair, leaving her fingers on the keys. "Clete." I wouldn't say that she yelled it. It was more like a loud bark. One syllable, crisp, with a sharp point at the end. When he didn't answer, she did it again.

What emerged through the inner office was still half asleep and didn't look too happy about it. Clete Hayes was younger than I expected, a barely out of shape former athlete, and he gave the impression that he could still run somebody down on foot if it came to that. But he looked like you'd need to give him a day's notice to get motivated. His uniform shirt was wrinkled, and the clip-on tie had barely hung on to the collar, which was unbuttoned.

He looked at the woman and barked back, "What?"

She pointed a bony finger at me. "Somebody to see you." Then she went back to typing.

Though still sleepy, Hayes gave me a once over, then jerked a thumb over his shoulder. "In here," he said, and went back through the door he'd come through.

I walked into about what I'd imagine a sheriff's office would look like. A green metal desk, with two metal chairs uphol-stered in a tired gray vinyl. Two green metal file cabinets on one wall, all lit by florescent tubes in the ceiling. A couch that didn't match anything, here or probably in the world at large, occupied the back wall, and both pillows were at one end. I bet if I looked hard, Hayes's cheek print was on one of them.

He sat behind his desk and motioned toward the other metal chair. "How can I help?"

"Sorry to interrupt your nap."

He sneered. "Sleep is a passing thing when you're out half the night on stake out."

"Hickman having a crime wave?"

"Hog thieves." He drummed his fingers. "How can I help you?" he repeated.

"Do you know the preacher over at Briar Creek? Simpson?"

"What's Brother Paul got into?" The drumming stopped.

"You do know him?"

"Part of my family goes to Briar Creek."

That was an interesting way to put it. "But not you?"

"I don't hold with the Baptists. But I've got cousins who do." He picked up a file folder and flicked it. "What's he got into?"

"Not him. His son."

"Paul or Mark?"

"You haven't heard, then. Mark killed his roommate. In Nashville. Couple of weeks ago."

Clete Hayes didn't look so sleepy anymore. "You don't say."

"I do say. And he killed himself right after." Hayes tipped his chair back on its hind legs. Before he could say anything, I added, "Hanged himself. Just like his mother did."

He remained tipped back, then leaned up to make the chair go forward. It hit the linoleum floor with a thud. "Mark. I'll be damned. If you told me Paul, his brother, I wouldn't have been that surprised. Paul was always a hothead, like his daddy. But Mark." He looked me hard in the eyes. His were a little bloodshot, but they were an ice blue that made you think he would be good in a fight. "I wouldn't have thought Mark had that in him."

"Nobody did. Although his father didn't seem all that surprised."

Hayes made a noise somewhere between a raspberry and a rip.

"That old man is capable of it. Bad arm and all." He settled back into his chair and made a steeple with his fingers. "So, Mister. . . ?"

"Trade. I'm trying to help the murdered girl's parents out. They aren't asking for justice. Since Mark killed himself, they have all they're getting. But they want to know more about why. I'm trying to get into Mark's psyche."

"And you figure, since his mama did it the same way, there's a clue there?"

"Something like that. Mind if I smoke?" He pushed an ashtray toward me, and I shook one out and lit it. "I went to see the old man. He wasn't any help."

"No surprise there."

"So, I came here. I assume that this office responded?"

"I would think so," he said. "Before my time."

"You would have been pretty young." I pointed at the metal file cabinets. "But those cabinets have old stuff in them, I bet."

"What are you looking for, Trade? There's not going to be anything in a file that can tell you what you don't already know. She killed herself. If you had to live with Old Man Simpson, you might have done it too."

I tapped the cigarette on the edge of the ashtray, kicking off a quarter inch of ash. "I don't know what I'm looking for. I've just learned that, the longer I look at the obvious, the more I see that wasn't there before." I pulled in a lung of smoke and pointed at the file cabinets. "Mind if I stare at the obvious?"

He sat without moving, looking at me, maybe looking for the obvious he couldn't see in me. Finally, he got up, walked across to the door, and said to the woman, "Erma, we're going to be a minute. If anybody comes in, unless they're bleeding or on fire, tell them to wait." Then he shut the door, walked to the file cabinet on the left, third drawer, and soon came out with a thin file folder.

"This is all we have."

Just as I had with Josie's file back in Mercer's office, I read the report. It was straightforward. Call received. Woman hanged. Dead by asphyxiation. Son found her. Nobody was surprised. She'd been miserable for a long time. Coroner suspected it took her five minutes to suffocate. People always thought it'd be instant death, from a snapped neck. Almost always they suffocate.

Also, like Josie's file, photographs were included. One showed her hanging. One showed her after she was cut down. One showed the extension cord. Unlike Josie's there was not any blood. Not that it mattered. She was dead anyway.

I stared at the photos. I looked again at the one of her hanging. She had stepped off a chair that was placed, in the photograph, just to her right. The picture was taken from her left. That was where the noose was formed. I looked at the one of her laid out. I squinted to see. "Sheriff, you got a magnifying glass?"

Hayes rooted around in a couple of drawers, then finally came up with a small glass. I put it over the second picture. There, in the photo, was something obvious that no one had seen.

"What is it?" Hayes had moved to my side. "Got something?"

I left the glass over the picture. "Tell me what you see."

He steadied the lens and looked. Then he looked some more. "I don't see anything."

"Look at the ligature marks on her neck."

He took the lens again and spent more time over the photo. "I see the marks. What about them?"

"If you commit suicide by hanging, the rope, or in this case, the extension cord, will leave a triangular mark. If you are strangled, the ligature mark is straight." I realized I'd let the cigarette burn out in the ashtray, so I pushed it in. "Hers is straight, Sheriff."

He took a deep breath and looked again. Finally, after a couple of minutes, he said, "I can't say that I see it, Trade. The picture isn't that good. Besides, there's nothing in the report that says anybody though it was anything but suicide."

"Think about it, Sheriff. You get a call for a suicide. It looks like a suicide. Nobody is surprised it's a suicide. Don't you get just a little focused on the suicide?"

"Sure. I understand."

"I'm just telling you that the marks don't look the way they should. And if it's not a suicide, Sheriff, it's a picture framed on purpose to look like one."

And I knew who owned the frame.

Chapter Thirty-One

I booked a 9:00 flight to Indianapolis on Eastern. It was the closest to a direct flight I could get on short notice, and the layover in Louisville wasn't as bad as it could be. By the time I touched down in Indianapolis, I'd had two bourbons and was hungry enough to eat whatever was in the airport.

Fortunately, the first cab in line took me to a deli he claimed was the city's best. It wasn't bad.

When I'd cleared up the hunger issue, it was almost 2. I put a dime in the phone and called Landon Pittsfield. "I'd like to talk to you," I said. "In person."

"I can't come to Nashville. Things are really busy here right now."

"I'm here. In Indy. I can be there in no time at all."

"Oh." There was a noticeable hesitation. "Let me clear my schedule for later this afternoon. Say around 4?"

I said that was fine. I could find other things to do. I can kill time. I do it well.

His office was above the showroom. Pittsfield Pontiac Buick was a going concern, as they say. There was a fleet of salespeople, two of whom tried to interest me in the latest version of the Riviera. I don't know what about me looked like I'd be hot for that car, but hey, they work on commission. Might as well start high, I guess. I was shown past banks of finance agents and accountants to a gleaming, chrome-lit

office with a bank of windows. It was something almost out of
The Jetsons. Very modern. Very unlike Landon Pittsfield.

"I think I've found out as much as I can about Josie." I lit
a cigarette and realized I should have asked first. He went
around to his desk and pulled an ashtray out of a drawer. He
set it in front of me on the clear glass coffee table. "Thanks."

We sat there in silence as I smoked. Finally, he said, "Is it
bad?"

I should have said, define bad, when you've lost your only
child to a killer. Brenda Baldwin's parents knew. The Pitts-
fields knew. They knew how bad it could be in a way that I
couldn't. All I knew was that nothing I discovered could bring
them back. Which meant that my job right now was about
stitching up what wounds I could and getting the hell out.

"I can provide some corrective to the story that's being told.
I don't know if that's good or bad."

He turned his wedding ring over and over on his third finger,
as if the repetitive act could steel him against whatever I had
to say. "Ok. Go ahead."

I took a last drag on the Marlboro. "First things first. Josie
moved into the apartment two weeks after arriving at Vanderbilt. Her name was on the lease. She had references that said
she had a job. That wasn't true. She was a fulltime student. She
used her Branscomb room, the same as she used her Tolman
room later, as a kind of campus stop. But she lived in the
apartment on Lombardy."

He had his elbows on his knees, hunched forward, eyes
down. Everything about him said that he was determined to
take whatever came.

"Everyone thought that she must have a man paying for that
apartment. That's the obvious thing. And from there, because
she was pretty and had an easy way about her, there was the
further point that she was a mistress, or maybe an escort."

"Was she?" He didn't look up. The voice seemed to come
from the floor.

When I said no, you could see some tension fall. "No, and she wasn't being kept by a man either." I watched to see if this would make him look up. It didn't. "She was being kept by a woman."

Landon Pittsfield raised his eyes to the ceiling but never looked at me. "How do you know that?"

"I connected some dots. The apartment. A car she bought for her. The trips they took. I believe your daughter was gay."

"So, she rented her an apartment? Did she seduce Josie?"

I could have told him that it was more likely Josie who seduced Marie Huddleston, but I let the opportunity pass. "To be honest, I think it was more about helping Josie out. This woman had been married, was a widow, without children. There was probably a certain amount of nurture there."

Pittsfield did not meet my eyes. "What else? Did this lesbian widow enjoy breaking my family?"

"I think you have it wrong, Mr. Pittsfield. I don't think I'd put it that way." I lit another cigarette. "I don't suppose you have anything to drink around here?"

For the first time, he looked directly into my eyes. Without a word, he got up, went to a file cabinet, and extracted a bottle of Jack Daniels, almost full. Holding it up, he said, "This do?" When I nodded, he got a water glass from the sideboard and brought both to my chair. "There's no ice. Maybe in the staff lounge refrigerator."

I took the bottle and glass. "This is fine" I poured myself half a glass and drank it. It burned. But it felt like it cleaned out something that was keeping me from finishing the story.

"They traveled, as you know by now, to New York City and Miami Beach. This woman was able to take her places, show her things, that opened up her world. As did Vanderbilt, of course. From all reports, your daughter became an accomplished, mature young woman. She would have no doubt gone far. Done quite amazing things."

"Except the Simpson boy moved in and then killed her."

I drank the second half. "That's what everyone says. Whether I buy it or not, it's not what you asked me to find out."

He had resumed his former posture, but this made him sit straight up. "Explain," he said.

"Mark Simpson was gay. In this way, he was something like Josie. He had a pretty hard time of it, both in terms of coming out and then in terms of being out. I can't judge. I'm not a gay man and I didn't know him. But I think it's safe to say that he never was comfortable with his identity until he moved in with your daughter."

"I don't understand."

"I believe they managed, somehow, to be the solution to each other's puzzles. Mark was calmly and quietly domestic. He liked making a home. His mother died when he was young, and his growing up was largely managed, and none too organically. I believe that his upbringing became pretty sterile and without love."

"Are you saying Josie loved him?"

"Trust me. Lesbians are quite capable of loving others without its leading to sex. They're just like other people in that way. I believe that Josie offered him something that he needed and had not had."

"And what did he do for her?"

"Her first roommate, a girl named Elyse Hyde, said it this way. When she moved out, Josie was crushed. Not because she loved Elyse, though that might have come in time. But because Elyse represented the possibility of comfort, of normality. Mark, in a very domestic way, became the partner that Josie had never had. Not as lovers, more like brother and sister. A brother who accepted his sister as she was."

"But the blood." He shook his head, disbelieving. "The blood. He literally had blood on his hands."

"The public defender assigned to him answered that question. He held her. She had died, and he lay on the floor and held her. Because," I added before he could ask, "He wanted her to feel, to know, that he loved her." I put out my cigarette. "It's something I don't think he had the chance to do when he found his own mother dead. I think he needed to do it."

I stood up and walked to the bookcase. Like the rest of the office, it was a chrome and glass affair, the sort, I guess, that the marketing department believed was the essence of the Buick brand. There were a few photographs. One was Josie, probably her high school studio shot for the yearbook. She looked young, but bright. She had more than a little sparkle for the camera. He watched me as I picked up another, a family shot. Josie, him, a shorter, darker complexioned woman. "Your wife?" He nodded. Of course, it was. "Josie favored her?"

"No," he said. "She looked like my side of the family."

I put the frame back on the bookcase. I looked at Josie in both pictures. In one, she looked confidently out toward the future. In the other, she seemed hemmed in between two adults. "You knew she was gay." It wasn't a question. I poured another half glass of Jack.

"My wife," he said. "She was the one who said the word first. What did I know?" He had given up now. "She said, several years ago that Josie wasn't the way other girls were. It wasn't that she was gay. It was that she was different. In a good way. She had her act together. She wasn't boy crazy. She was working toward a goal."

"Then you encouraged her?"

"Can't say that. We didn't encourage it. We tried to encourage a boyfriend. A boy friend. Anything." He got up, moved to his desk. It was the sort of move that said he was about to move to a conclusion. He was feeling like he needed a closing statement. "Where do we leave this?"

I sipped a bit of the Jack. "You had a gay daughter. She was someone to be proud of. Everyone who knew her thought she was fabulous. But I suspect, however you did it, that you and your wife told her that you were disappointed in her.

She didn't behave the way you thought was proper. You left her wondering how to be the person she should have ben. Someone came into her life at the right time. She gave her confidence. She made her feel love and acceptance. It may have been a pretty narrow thing, or it may have been the love of her life. But it made a difference to Josie."

"You're saying we screwed up, and someone made it right."

"I'm saying that your daughter was a good person. And she was on her way to being a great person."

"Then, why is she dead?"

There were truths I couldn't tell him. "I don't know. Like I said, I don't know if he killed her." He looked at me with widened eyes. "I really don't. They were brother and sister in a lot of ways, and that can lead to all sorts of things. But I know that, even if he had killed her, it would not have been because he didn't love her."

"He was homosexual. How could he be in love with her?

"Not in love. But he could easily have loved her. They had security. They had domesticity. There's no reason to doubt that they gave each other what they needed.

And that was it. I'd told him what I'd known. His daughter was not a hooker, was not a bad person. She was gay, and she was on her way to being something special. I believed that. I didn't say what I also knew: that Mark Simpson was absolutely not her killer. That wasn't what he asked me to find out.

We ended up at the Eastern Airlines gate an hour ahead of the flight back to Nashville. I went to the men's room and, when I returned, he was holding out a check. "This is for you."

It was for another $500.

"You don't owe me this," I said.

"It's worth it to know about my daughter. Keep it."

I kept it. It's not like I get a paycheck doing anything else.

Chapter Thirty-Two

I was as good as my word.

I couldn't really take a date out in the Impala, so I walked over and picked up the Torino from the B Lot. When I held the door open for Betty, she gave me a look but didn't say anything.

Neither of us knew how seriously to take this idea of a date. She was dressed in jeans and cowboy boots, with a white blouse covered by a red leather jacket. She had on simple earrings and a gold chain necklace. Understated. Conventional. Looking very good, but not to the nines.

I did what I could with what I had. Dark dress pants, blue shirt, and the navy sport coat that pre-dated Lynn. It didn't get much work, so it was still fine.

I took her to O'Charleys. We split a salad, then had our entries. She had a couple of glasses of wine. I had two bourbons, then switched to wine with dinner. Since I had plenty of money in my pocket for once, we both ordered filet. Our conversation was light. It was just a little too light.

"This really feels too much like a first date," she said. "It's not like we haven't talked before." She said this while swirling the last of the bread in the last of the spinach dip.

"I was thinking the same thing. What do you want to talk about instead?"

"Let's start with the car." She raised her eyebrows and then laughed at my expression. "You can't tell me about that, even?"

"Let me tell you about a guy in my unit in Vietnam."

Now it was my turn to laugh at her expression. "I didn't know," she said.

"But not here. Too public." I signaled the waitress. "Back to your place?"

"You're driving the car. Even if it's not your car."

We got back in a few minutes after leaving the restaurant. I told her that the décor suited her. She put on a cassette in her Pioneer stereo and made drinks for us while Al Green played.

"How long have you been here? It's a nice place, but not the job you expect."

"For me, you mean. Yeah, that's true. But I told you once I'm handy. And I'm trying to be a songwriter." She looked over toward the stereo. "You'd think a girl wanting to be a Nashville songwriter wouldn't be listening to Al Green."

"Funny How Time Slips Away?"

"Good one," she said. "Yes, Al sings Willie songs. But you know what I mean."

"You ever married?"

"Wow. We're off the first date conversation now, aren't we?" She held her drink up in salute. "Yeah. Almost two years. Divorced for four."

"I'm doing the math."

"Thirty-two."

"Twenty-six here."

"Rob the cradle. That's my thing."

"Ain't no magic number," I said. We sat for a minute silently. She had brought the Jim Beam into the living room, and I leaned over, my ice still intact, and refreshed my drink. I left the armchair and sat next to her on the couch. Suddenly, without coaxing, I started laying it all out. Maybe it was the bourbon. Maybe it was just a relieving of stress. She hadn't asked again, and now I was telling her. Not everything, but the part about Josie and Mark, the part she had helped with at the beginning, but couldn't have known.

"How'd the father take it?"

"Well enough that we ate steak tonight. I wanted him to know that they'd raised a great young woman. I wanted them to know that she was going to be successful. But I also wanted him to know that somehow, they'd driven her off. And that she'd been going to make it despite that."

"You wanted him to feel shame?"

"No, not at all. I wanted him to have the answer to the real question he had. Who was she? They had lost her, Betty. He wanted to have her back. To have the knowledge of her. To feel like he knew her. That's what my job was. The murder. The knife. That wasn't the job."

"Well, but he already knew that, right?"

"He knew what he was told."

Her expression grew worried. "There's something else?"

I got up and poured a couple more drinks, found a couple of cubes of ice in the freezer. I handed hers to her when I got back.

"Thanks. You'll need to be extra nice to me. I'm right at my limit."

"I probably am too. I'm telling you way more than I should."

"That's because you trust me," she said. She curled her feet underneath her, still discretely apart from me on the couch. She sipped her drink, and dipped her chin, looking up at me. It could have been that she was trying to look trustworthy. I took it as a questioning look, though. A "what are you up to?" look. "Back to the father."

"He hired me to find out things. He didn't hire me to correct wrong impressions that didn't have anything to do with why he hired me."

"He wanted to know."

"We all want to know something. Do you know why you are divorced?"

"God, yes," she said. "I married the wrong person. It took me two years to get out of it. And you?"

"I know what caused the divorce, the proximal cause. She cheated. I caught her. There was no going back."

"Well, there you go," she said. "You were married to the wrong person too."

"I know the proximal cause, but I don't know why. I don't know why she cheated. I don't know that I have any right to the answer to that question. I don't know if it has an answer. From that, I infer that we don't get all the answers. Mr. Pittsfield got the ones he paid for. Not the others."

"You're trying to work something out, mister." She wasn't flirting now. She wasn't being coy. "How can I help you?"

"I told you I could tell you about this guy in Vietnam. I need to tell you this story, for some reason."

"Is this a flashback kind of thing. Some kind of traumatic stress? Cause I can listen but I don't know if I can help."

"No. Nothing like that. So, back here in the world, as we called it, things got tense about the war. In just a couple of years, the public decided that they couldn't stomach the war. Those were the couple of years that I was in. Drafted. Did a two-year hitch. Training, then a year in country, then some bullshit assignment until my time was up. That's the way the game rolled.

"My unit is out in the bush. I walked point a lot. That's the man at the head of the unit on patrol."

"Sounds dangerous," she said.

"Could be. You could trip a bomb. You could get a sniper. Smart VC let you walk the unit all the way into the trap. Your job was to see the trap."

Betty shuddered.

"And in the middle of all that danger, all that violence, a lot of the social crap back home, the race divisions, the social classes, even just the hatred of the war--all that got into the armed forces. You had insubordination. You had guys who wouldn't report. And you had lots of guys who hated, and I mean absolutely hated, the officers.

"And it was easy enough to understand why. Officers were out in the field for six months, for starters, where we did a year. And officer rotation meant that you got an idiot second lieutenant fresh from ROTC come into command after a six-month training barking orders at senior enlisted who had been in the field and really knew what they were doing. Enlisted like me, like us all, joined the unit at different times. There wasn't much of what they call unit cohesion. There was just a lot of guys trying to stay alive for a year.

"All of that made some things pretty squirrely. You'd have guys get to within six weeks of their exit date refuse to do anything. I ain't getting killed this close to going home. You'd have guys purposely overrule the kid lieutenant. Some guys just stayed stoned. And that was probably preferable to them running around agitated all the time. At least they were mellow. At least they could be a little focused."

"My God," she said. "It sounds awful."

"I'm halfway through my tour. Our unit was out in the boonies, working a joint operation. We were on one island while the other unit was on an adjacent island searching for an enemy supply center. Sure enough, we discovered an abandoned position, which we proceed to destroy. After that, as we began to move out for a river crossing to get to the other island, we came under pretty intense fire. We managed to get covered, but we lost a couple of men. The senior NCO and a green lieutenant both took it in the back."

"Sounds like you were surrounded," Betty said. "Coming at you from all angles. It's a wonder any of you survived."

"Yeah, that's the story, all right. Except the guys in the rear of them didn't take any hits at all. Our cover wasn't perfect, but it was good. The only guys who got hit were the senior guys."

"You think they got hit by friendly fire."

"Nothing friendly about it. I think a guy in our unit did it. A guy named Giles."

"But why?"

"Back in the war, there was a thing called fragging. Some higher up screws you over, or just pisses you off, you roll a grenade where he's sleeping."

"You're kidding."

"You could look it up. It got so bad toward the end of the war that the higher ups made rules restricting weapons and grenades."

"But why this Giles guy? What was his deal?"

"Giles was three weeks out. He was, as they said, a very short guy. He was doing absolutely nothing. And if you have one guy who refuses to do anything, out in the bush, he can be dangerous to everyone. He just thought it was our job to make sure he made it back to the world. Sergeant chewed him out half a dozen times. The baby LT ordered him to pick up the slack on patrol."

"That isn't enough to kill somebody."

"Maybe not you. Maybe not me. But somebody already mad at the world, and ready to go home? Look. He was a danger to the unit. And we'd just lost two men who shouldn't have been worried about their rear.

"So the two guys I worked most with when I walked point, Dewey Preston and a guy we called Bob-Bob because his name was Robert Roberts, we hatched a plan. Once a month, for four or five days, units got to stand down, usually at a place behind the forward area. Dewey and Bob-Bob would score a cache of grenades from the munitions area and leave behind Giles' ID, then put the grenades in Giles' locker. I would be with Giles the whole time, his air-tight alibi.

"Our plan went as scheduled. A full bird Colonel came roaring down on Giles with a squad of MPs. You see, fragging was much worse in the rear areas before the weaponry got locked down, and officers like colonels were good targets. Giles just pointed calmly to me. I was airtight. He had no idea how his identification got there.

"I still remember the look on his face when I said, Corporal Giles must be mistaken. I haven't been with him at all since we came in from the field."

"Amazing."

"He just looked at me. As they put him in handcuffs, I walked close enough to say, "You'll need to watch your back in lockup, Giles. You never know who's behind you.

"He drew ten in the stockade stateside. About two years in, I heard that a guy tougher than he was put a knife in him."

She had finished her drink as I talked, and now I finished mine in one long drink. "Why did you need to tell me that story, Jackson?"

"The bit with Josie's father. I know things that he would like to know, but he didn't ask. Giles knew the thing he wanted to know, who set him up, but he didn't know why. Oh, he knew the proximal cause, but why me? Maybe he didn't have the right to know."

"But you told him. He killed your colleagues, so you set him up."

"I was pretty sure. If I'd been completely sure, maybe Dewey or Bob-Bob would have punched his ticket in a fire-fight on his last day in country. I wasn't completely sure. I was sure enough to do what I did."

"And are you sure enough for what comes next? Is that what this story is about?"

"Can't say, Betty. Don't know."

She lay her head in my lap and curled up. "You have plied me with liquor, mister. And now I'm ready for bed."

I put my hand on her cheek and stroked it. "I've plied me with liquor too, and now I'm plowed."

"You can stay."

"I'll go. But not right now." I leaned over and put the empty glass on a coaster. "You go to sleep. I'll just sit here quietly."

"And do what?" she said. She was falling asleep. Her voice was a little hoarse.

"And try to figure out how sure I am about what comes next."

She was breathing in a deep sleep when I lifted her head and replaced it on the sofa. I put a pillow underneath her head and got a comforter from the back of the armchair to cover her.

I drove the mile back to campus carefully in case any Metro cops were inclined to stop a beige Torino with a driver slightly over the limit. And then I went home.

I thought the conversation would keep me up. But I went right to sleep.

Chapter Thirty-Three

"I don't understand, Mr. Trade. What sort of question is that?"

It was the third time I'd been in Paul Simpson's study. This time I rang the doorbell, and someone answered. "I think you do, Simpson. It's the sort any minister worth his salt could answer."

"Cain and Abel were brothers. Cain was the older and was a farmer. Abel was a shepherd. They had a falling out. Cain killed him." He raised his eyebrows and shrugged. "Good enough?"

I sat in the same armchair, near the fire, as before. "He murdered his brother, then lied about it to God, and was therefore cursed."

"That's right."

"And with the curse on him, the earth was no longer able to bear for him, and so he wandered the earth a fugitive, alone."

"Clearly you know more scripture than it would appear."

"And he received a mark from God, and that mark meant that no one could kill him. Either so he would know what suffering was, or so that he would never find out what it meant to be murdered."

"Did you come here just to impress me with exegesis?"

"No, I came to ask a question about two other brothers. You and Mark. Why did you let him kill himself?"

"We have been over this territory, Trade. My brother killed himself. That's a sin in some quarters. It's nothing compared to the sin of homosexuality."

"I think the sin of murder trumps them all."

"Well, yes. He was a murderer too."

"I don't mean him. I mean you."

"What on earth are you raving about?"

"I think you know."

"Mark committed a murder. A terrible, horrible act. He mutilated the body. He went screaming into the streets. I pray for his soul. But God cries out for vengeance. His will be done."

"Don't preach to me. I'm not an audience. I'm something else." I watched his face as his mind turned black. "I'm the guy who knows the same things you know. And we're the only two who know them. And one of those things is that Mark didn't kill Josie Pittsfield. He killed himself, but he didn't kill her."

He sat across from me. He turned red, as if he was burning inside. He let out a long breath. "What things do you know that make you believe that?"

I began to tell him all the things I'd found out about Josie and Mark, things about their life together, about Josie's studies and Mark's work. I painted the same picture of Josie that I painted for her father. He looked away in disgust, but I told him that Mark had tried for a while to live a gay club lifestyle, but it didn't suit him. What suited him was living with Josie.

"All well and good," he said. "But what makes you believe that he didn't come home in some fit of passion and kill her. Couples do that all the time. It's in the papers every day."

"Except he didn't kill her. You killed her. You made her perform oral sex on you, and then you killed her."

"That's completely preposterous. How can you even say that?" He rose to his feet and shook his fist. "Get out of my house. Get out and don't come back."

"Sit down, preacher."

"I mean it. Get out of my house. You have no right to say anything like that."

"I have the knife."

"What?" He stopped gesturing, and the color drained from his face. Then all the tension left his body. I thought for a moment he might fall, but he steadied himself, and sat back down. "Then you," he stopped.

"I know everything. I know about Belinda Baldwin. I know about Darrell Lee. I know about everything." I leaned my elbows on my knees. "What I don't know is why."

He collapsed against the back of the chair and looked at the ceiling. "I don't understand how you could have the knife. Or even why you would know to look for it. How did you even connect that evil woman and the girl?"

"I have the Torino too."

"Oh, God." He didn't say the deity's name. He agonized it. "There was a second key."

"The world is going to hell. I don't mean that the way you would. I really mean it. Satan has this world in his grip. And sex is the worst of it. Even little children."

"Even Belinda Baldwin?"

"She should have known better. Good family. She was raised right."

"Tell me about Josie."

"Her." He sneered. "A lesbian. Too good a word. Too genteel. She was a faggot. Do you know where we get that word?"

"It's not a genteel word. I can tell you that."

"Faggot is a bundle of kindling. To make a fire. They burn witches. They should burn queers too. Faggots for all."

"Did you go there to kill her?"

"Not at first. I went to tell her to leave Mark alone."

"How did we get to the oral sex and killing."

"She laughed at me. Prissy Vanderbilt lesbian. Too smart for me. Yes, sir. Too smart for a lowly preacher."

"Then what happened?"

"I made her know what women are supposed to do. She was foul mouthed about it, but she did it. I got the knife and I made sure she did it right. Do you know what she said when it was over?"

I had no idea. I wondered what was so bad to get her killed.

"She asked how such a big prick could have such a little one."

"You killed her because he made fun of your size?"

He buried his head in his hands.

"And the Baldwin girl?"

"A little hussy. Where do they learn it, Trade? Or are they just born evil? She was always coming on to the Lee boy. He was a good boy too. But you could see it in her. She was going to bring him low. I know how that feels. I know how an evil female can tempt you to do things you know are not right. I know how they work."

"I took the Pittsfield girl's car. Nobody knew it in the neighborhood. Just in case. I got Belinda into it. I took her back to the house and gave her what she thought she wanted. Turns out she didn't want that."

"And you killed her?"

"That was an accident. She was screaming. I put my hand over her mouth. When I was done, she wasn't breathing. I must have suffocated her."

"But you brought her back to Green Hills. You were already thinking of framing the Lee boy."

"No." He yelled it. "I couldn't leave her here. I had to get rid of the car. I put her in the Alexander's outbuilding. They are members here. I knew they were out of town. If anyone found her, they would be gone."

Simpson wandered to his desk and sat hard on the chair. "I don't understand," he said, "how you put this all together."

I wanted to tell him that all I did was listen and watch. All I did was wait. But the self-pity was too much for me. All is said was, "Do you think you're that much of a genius?"

"Not at all. But once I knew what I wanted to do, I made sure that other people got the blame. Mark made the Pittsfield girl easy. But the Baldwin girl? That just fell into my lap. It was too easy to pin it on the boy."

Somehow, I wasn't surprised. "You're a piece of work, Simpson. You're supposed to shepherd a flock. Not kill some and deceive the others."

"Don't moralize to me. You're not qualified. Only my God can hold me to account."

"You don't think he will?"

"For doing His work? Not at all."

"For raping them?"

"What is rape? Absence of consent? Sinners lose that right if they are unrepentant. Do criminals have to consent to serve their sentence?" He was explaining it to himself, not to me. "How did you know?"

"I know you've been a violent man for a long time. I mean, I've never known anyone who fouled out of just about every game he played in." He looked up, shook his head. "That's right. I know about that too. I also know that your mother was killed. " He gave a start and stared straight at me. "I've seen the pictures. The marks on the neck aren't right for a suicide. Your father has a bad arm. Your brother was little. Seems to me the only suspect for that is you."

He continued to stare. "Congratulations."

"You made a basic mistake, using Josie's car. If it had stayed where it was, I wouldn't have been interested in it. But it was where it was not supposed to be. And that started it all."

"But the knife."

"The knife came last. I had already talked with you, about your brother, when I discovered your connection to the Baldwin family. You can imagine, can't you, how that, coupled with the Torino in the same neighborhood, would start things rolling."

He groaned.

"That's ultimately what made me find the silver dollar."

"But," he said, then stopped. "How do you know about that?"

"This is not the second time I've been in this room. It's the third. I saw the cookie box, and the silver dollar, in that file drawer there."

He put his head in his hands. "But it was locked."

"Locks are unfaithful things. I didn't know the significance of it. Not until I saw the report of the Lee boy's death. Metro's pretty good at getting the story out, if they think they've got the story."

"And you found the knife. The police didn't. I saw that on the news."

"That's right. They didn't. In the dark, you must have chucked it further than you meant to. I made a pass down the shore before I saw it coming back. But you're right. Metro would have connected it to Belinda Baldwin. They wouldn't have connected it to a closed case."

"But you did."

"I did. I had noticed missing knives in the block they had in their kitchen. I took it over there, and I put it in its rightful position. Perfect fit."

He had his head bowed, as if in prayer. I don't believe in prayer, and I don't think at that moment he did either. If he ever really did. His breathing was regular but shallow. He made no other sound. At last, he looked up. "What are you going to do?"

"It all depends on what you do." I let that lie for a moment. "I know things I can't quite explain. I broke in here, for instance. You know that's a no-no. And I'm holding evidence I should give to the police. I should have told them days ago what I thought. Maybe Darrell Lee would still be alive. If that's true, that's partly on me.

"So here's what I'm going to do. I'm going to give you a chance to make it right. You can't bring back any of them. But you can own it. You'll get the electric chair, but maybe it'll be a while before they kill you. There won't any mark of Cain on you. The state will kill you, eventually."

"I can't do that. I can't have that."

"Like I say, it all depends. If you don't do that, I'll turn the car and the knife over to Metro. I'll take my lumps if I have to and tell them everything I know. I even know the date on the silver dollar, so there'll be no doubt that I was here, just like I say I was. And I can tell them for sure that they had a DUI pulled on Highway 100 just above the picnic shelter the night I found the knife. That will be proof I was where I say I was."

"You're not leaving me any choice."

"I am giving you a choice of how to do it. If your God gives grace, you can start to earn it by owning what you did. Nobody's good enough for your God, so you have to ask for grace anyway. You might as well earn the gift, right?"

"Nobody earns grace. It is given."

"Fine. Think of it this way. Assume the position to receive the gift." Just the way you made Josie, and Belinda, I added silently. Just the way you made your mother.

I got up to go. "This is your choice, preacher. You can do it either way. But either way, you're going to jail, and you're going to pay."

On the way out, the woman stared at me as if I'd already killed him. "What went on in there?" she asked.

"I believe Brother Simpson is contemplating the way of all flesh." When she said nothing, I added, "The mortality that defines us all." I waved as I went out the door. "Have a blessed day, sister."

Chapter Thirty-Four

I settled into the corner booth, near the door, under the television. I sat at the outer part of the circular bench, where I could keep an eye on the set.

"Really, Jackson?" Charlie said. "You're going to take up the six-top all by yourself? Come on, man. What if a big group comes in?"

"I'll get up if they do. And if they want me to." Charlie knew all this. He just wanted to bust my chops a little. "Besides, I'm paid up."

There wasn't much to do except wait to see whether Paul Simpson was going to turn himself in or not. If I had to guess, he wouldn't. If I had to guess, he'd try to make a run for it. I didn't much care. Either way he was going to get caught, and he'd never see the outside again.

I had started the afternoon at the Dead Ringer, then made my way to Hannigan's for dinner and a couple of beers. Now I was letting Dan Miller get the news out at 6. His first story was about the mayor. Since the mayor wasn't in the story I was interested in, and since the story I was interested in would have led every newscast, I signaled Charlie for another beer.

A female voice said, "That sounds good. Would you bring me one as well?"

She was short, and I put her nearer fifty than sixty, but her hair was stylishly silver and suggested a knowledge of what looked good on her. She wore a pink pantsuit with pearls. "I'm told you are Jackson Trade."

"That's right, ma'am." I stood and shook her hand. You never know if work is coming for you. I hadn't seen Lanford Pittsfield coming. "And your name is?"

"I am Marie Huddleston. I believe you've been looking for me." When I looked surprised, she added, "Yes, I had to do a little asking around, but you're not that hard to find out about. Or to locate."

Indeed.

We sat and talked for the better part of an hour before we got to the meat of the story, or at least the story at hand. I told her what I had surmised, and what I had told Josie's father.

"You have the essential points approximately correct."

"I have a talent for connecting dots. I just didn't have all the dots."

She smiled. "I was born in 1920, Mr. Trade. I have dots that go very far back."

She was charming. I could see how she might appear a mentor for a young woman trying to find herself. "Did I get the part about your relationship with Josie, how did you say it, approximately correct?"

She twirled what looked like a diamond wedding ring on her finger. When she saw me looking at it, she said, "Yes, it's my wedding ring. I have continued to wear it after the death of my husband. I suppose you have the option to take it off. I never did."

"I don't know the protocol. I know that I took mine off when I divorced. Clearly that's different."

"Clearly," she said, missing my humor. "I was a dutiful wife. I suppose I could have done otherwise, but my generation, well, the options were not then as they are now."

I waited for more. "But after Mr. Huddleston's death?"

"I am a Vanderbilt graduate. You will have learned that, perhaps? Hugh was as well. We were not classmates--he was two years ahead--but we were part of the same social set. And we found ourselves together all the time. One thing," she said and sighed, "led to another, and there we were, one day, saying our vows in front of five hundred people at Immanuel Baptist Church."

"Ah, in Belle Meade." I wondered if the rich one was her. He started with nothing.

"No. This was before the move. We were married at the original location, at 17th and West End."

I thought there was a Shell station there now. The Baptists fled downtown for Belle Meade when all the other stuff came flooding in, I guess.

"At any rate," she said, "it was not a loveless marriage, but it was a childless one. I tried for a while to make myself enjoy the process of creating children, but it was not a natural one for me and, to be quite honest, was not the first interest of my husband. The business was always first, though he was, after his own fashion, kind and good to me."

"It seems like a brother and sister relationship, if you don't mind my saying."

"I cannot in good conscience disagree, Mr. Trade. We certainly cared for each other, and we loved one another, but it was not a physical intimacy. Those attempts, unfortunately, went rather awkwardly early in our marriage. Later, we simply didn't try."

It seemed a sad kind of deal, but she talked about it as if it were an adequate bargain. "But it was different with Josie?"

She blushed a little, and the pink on her skin caught the pink on the pantsuit almost perfectly. "Not at first. Your conjecture about our meeting was very nearly correct. It was not at Orientation, though, that we met. It was a few weeks into fall term, her first year. The girls' RA staff had a program, something like Vanderbilt Women in Business. We were to come there and regale the freshman women about all the great things they could expect when they graduated. I think there were four of us on the panel. Josie came up and introduced herself"

"She wanted to know more," Marie continued, "and we met for coffee the next day. Such a lovely, self-assured young woman."

"Everyone seems to have thought so."

"She had an aura about her. Not as if she were at all a teenager, but more like . . ."

"More like someone who already know who she was. And where she was going."

"Exactly. My, Mr. Trade, you have connected the dots well. I believe you have outlined her quite well."

"But not your relationship."

"Ah. That." She had been folding and unfolding a paper napkin. Now, she balled it up in her hand tightly, as if to keep it from getting away. "We were not lovers at first. Indeed, I put her in the apartment because her roommate had somehow discovered that Josie was not heterosexual, I believe from a diary or some such, and Josie did not feel safe. She feared that the girl might 'out' her."

"Did she?"

"I beg your pardon?" She looked momentarily confused. "Oh, did the other girl tell her secret? I don't know. Josie never mentioned it." She shut her eyes, as if trying to remember. "I said that we were not lovers at first. I installed her in the apartment, and because she didn't have a car, I was a bit of a chauffeur, taking her to campus and back."

"It's not that far, you know."

"Yes, and she's young. I know all that. But I loved being around her. And in relatively short order, we were together every day for some part of the day."

"You were falling in love with her."

"I know. If I were a fifty-year-old man, there would be cries of inappropriate behavior."

"Or envy."

"With men, I suppose that's so. I wasn't really worried about that. I just knew that I felt incredibly alive around her. I wanted to be with her all the time. Mr. Trade, you do not seem judgmental about this at all."

"Why would I be?"

"People are. Men, I believe, in particular, are threatened by it."

"Maybe. But you've already told me a lot."

"I was about to tell you this, and I realized that I've not been forthcoming about this to anyone. Not even Josie, though she must have known. And with her gone, well, it's too late to tell her. May I tell you?"

"Of course."

"The first time I kissed her, we were returning from the symphony. We were both enraptured by the concert. I don't know that she ever derived as much pleasure from Beethoven as I did, but she seemed to have enjoyed it immensely. At any rate we were talking and laughing and reliving the best parts when she turned quite suddenly. We were at her apartment door, so I was taken aback. She put her hands on either side of my face, looked me straight in the eye and then kissed me. It was a long, lingering kiss."

She stopped with her eyes closed again. This time she seemed to be reliving it

"I hope you understand, Mr. Trade. I am a widow. I am more than twice her age. And her kiss unlocked a part of my heart for which I had lost the key. Perhaps I didn't know that part existed anymore. I very nearly fell to my knees. I very nearly wept, and once I was home, alone in my home, I did. I wept tears of joy."

"Why didn't she move in with you? Or you move here?"

"You must remember, Mr. Trade. I am a successful busi-nesswoman. I have many contacts in Nashville and in other places. And she wanted to be near Vanderbilt. And, if I am honest, she most likely had other lovers that I never knew about."

"I don't believe she did."

"That's a fond thought. But I am resigned if she did. It was enough, Mr. Trade, to be loved by her."

"And to take her to New York and to Miami."

She blinked. "Well, there are two dots I'm surprised you found. We were quite careful."

"She sent postcards to her family. And there's the Ford you bought her."

"We're never as good at deceit as we believe, are we?" She opened her hand, and let the napkin fall out. "She would have been finishing soon, and I knew that she would take flight. I was reconciled to losing her to the world. We had been seeing less and less of each other."

"And then this happened."

"Yes. And then this awful thing happened." She chewed the inside of her lip, as if trying to find words there.

"I'm sorry," I said, "that you lost someone you loved."

"I was worried at first when they told me you'd come around. I couldn't imagine what good speaking with you could do. Now that I understand your task, I can say that you really didn't need to me. You did quite well on your own." She paused and swallowed the last of the beer. She had made it last for an hour or so. It couldn't have tasted good to her. "I can also say that I think I needed to talk with you. Thank you for listening and understanding."

She rose, and I did too. We shook hands and, in that gesture, she leaned into me and gave me the briefest of hugs. "Thank you for caring about the dots. For connecting them correctly."

Chapter Thirty-Five

Mercer and I sat at the High Life bar, the light of the Pabst sign illuminating a third of the room. I've never understood how a dark bar can get so much light out of a cheap beer sign. Some nights, it's way more light than you need.

I'd been telling Mercer about Marie Huddleston, and I'd ended up telling him I pretty much knew what had happened.

"We know what happened. The Simpson boy killed the girl."

I wanted to say, "Wrong Simpson, and both girls," but I didn't. I had given the preacher until the end of the day to sort it out. So, I shrugged.

Mercer had parked his bike out front, and he kept looking out the big plate glass window at it. "I just don't want anybody to ding it."

"Then why park it on the street?"

"Because I can't see it if it's anywhere else."

This is the conundrum that is life. You don't trust that it's safe if you can't see it, but where you can see it, it isn't safe. Why do we humans bother?

"Hey, barkeep. Put the sound up on the television," yelled a voice.

Breaking news from Channel 5. Andy Rye was out in front of a dark building. Or in the dark, in front of a building. You couldn't tell.

The sound came up. "Again, the body of Minister Paul Simpson, pastor of the Free Church on White Bridge Road, found dead, apparently of a self-inflicted gunshot wound. Mr. Simpson has been a mainstay of the Brenda Baldwin family during the investigation of her rape and murder. Police have not commented on whether a note was left, but we will be here all evening in case of breaking news. For now, Paul Simpson, dead of a gunshot wound."

"This is Andy Rye, channel 4 news."

Mercer turned to look at me. He dropped off the stool and leaned on the bar. I kept my eyes facing forward. "Jackson?"

"Yes, Don?"

"Do you know anything about this?"

"Out of my jurisdiction, Officer. Out of yours too, as a matter of fact." I did not look at him.

I wanted to say, "It'll all come out in the morning. Or all come out in the wash." Except I didn't know that it would. All I knew is that the preacher executed his own justice. And that I would distribute the information about why. To Mr. Pittsfield. To Metro. Then to Don.

Sometimes you have to park it where it'll be safe. And then trust it to be the right decision.

A few days later I had returned to my afternoon post at the corner booth next to the money pinball machine at Hannigan's. I was dragging my last french fry through a too small blob of ketchup when a shadow fell across my hand. Expecting Katie, I didn't look up. "Just put it on my tab, ok?"

"How much do you figure you owe?"

It wasn't Katie's voice and, when I looked up, I was startled to see Simpson's wife. Or housekeeper. Or whatever she was. Her hair wasn't tied back as it had always been. She had on a long brown coat that matched her eyes, and she wore just the slightest trace of makeup. I also caught a light whiff of some floral scent.

I stood. That's what they say you're supposed to do when a woman arrives. I don't know that there's a book on what you do after that. Especially if you've had a hand in her husband's death. Or whoever he was to her. I motioned to the bench across from me. "Have a seat?"

She took off her coat, revealing a smart orange sweater set and nicely tailored glen plaid pants in an equally autumnal shade. I looked and didn't see a wedding ring. Katie had walked over and looked quizzical, in a waitress-like way. "I'll have a draft," the woman said to Katie. Then she turned back to me. "We've never formally met. You're Jackson Trade. I'm Bridget Rollins."

I wiped my hand on a napkin, then shook hers. "I guess I had assumed you were Mrs. Simpson." I pointed to my bourbon glass and looked at Katie as she pulled a draft for the Rollins woman. "Unless you kept your maiden name, that is."

She took the beer from Katie, and I took the bourbon, and we sat. Finally, she leaned back, her hands circling the base of the beer glass. I had thought her a stern, slightly forbidding person. Now, outside of that house, wearing stylish clothing and her hair loosed, I could see that she was quite attractive, and not as old as I had assumed.

"I lived in the parsonage with Paul, but we were not married."

"Wasn't that problematic for his congregation?" I could imagine that "problematic" would be the low end of the hysteria register.

"That's not to say we didn't pretend we were married." Her fingers wiped the condensation from the side of the glass. I imagined I could see just the faintest hint of a tan line where a ring would go. I looked at her, and her eyes smiled at me. "Yes, I had a ring. Just a simple band."

"Then I don't understand." Really, what she told me was perfectly easy to understand. It was just hard to believe.

"I knew Paul in college. We were a couple." She smiled, but it wasn't a smile. It was an acknowledgment. "Kind of a couple."

I knew he'd been a violent guy at basketball. Was he violent elsewhere? "What kind of a couple?"

"The kind where he apologized a lot."

There was nothing about her that suggested "victim." But is there ever? Was she someone who had been caught in an abusive relationship? Everything I knew about Paul Simpson said he was completely capable of such a thing. "Paul seems like a guy who had some problems. Did you pay for them?"

"When you came to visit the first time," she said, "I thought there was something about you that I understood. You had a look about you, like you'd been through hell and come out the other side."

"Maybe I did."

"Because of that, I thought you were somebody who could be trusted." She took a sip of the beer. "I told that to Paul."

"And what did he say?"

"Paul didn't trust anyone but himself." She put the beer back down and looked at me, as if trying to find words. "He told me I was wrong."

She lifted her beer glass in salute and drank it down. All of it.

"And then what?"

"And then you went on your way. You did what you did. You came back and told him what you did." She looked from her glass to me, then back again. "I heard what you told him that night. I heard all of it."

I should have known that, once I thought of the look she gave me, the look when I said that he was contemplating the way of all flesh. "And then, after thinking about it, he killed himself."

"Well, he's dead." She didn't smile when she said it. But she didn't seem unhappy either.

"But you and him? How did that happen?"

"He was a senior. I was a freshman. He flattered me. He took me on as his project, as his protégé. And we ended up, because we were young, in bed.

"At first it was exciting. For both of us. And then it was, what would you call it? Abusive? It wasn't fun anymore. But there was no way to stop it." She seemed to shudder. "For years, there's been nothing there. He had a need to control me. Maybe I wanted to be controlled."

"I wouldn't be that hard on yourself. I don't know why I do half the things I do."

"By the time he decided to take up his 'calling,' the church, I had reconciled myself. This was the way my life was going to be. I was Paul's woman. His wife. Except we had never been married." She shook her head no, either to Katie's silent question about another beer or to her own logic. "Maybe I thought pastoring a church would change him."

"You can talk yourself into anything. You can make the worst situation into the best. You can tell yourself that it will all turn around." I was talking to her. Maybe I was talking to myself.

"I heard everything you said that night. The Pittsfield girl. The Baldwin girl. The boy. His brother, the way he set him up. And his mother. That was the final straw." She shook her head. "His mother. All that time ago."

In that moment, eavesdropping, she knew she was living with a killer, the kind who had done it more than once. The kind that doesn't mind, because in his mind it's the thing that has to be done. It isn't pretty. It's just necessary. Like fouling out of games was necessary. Probably because it felt good too. Yeah, the fouls and the murders. Both of them.

The news might have made someone else leave on the spot. I asked her why she didn't.

"Oh, I did. I left immediately and went to Belinda's mother. I told her."

That must have been quite a conversation. The preacher's wife telling the murdered girl's mother that it was the preacher all along. "That was either very brave or incredibly cruel. No, wait, that came out wrong." But it didn't. I wondered if it wasn't a cruel thing to do. "What I mean is, the news must have devastated Mrs. Baldwin."

With her fingers, she traced the shape of the missing wedding band. "And then the two of us went to tell Darrell Lee's mother."

She was looking at me now, her brown eyes taking on an entirely different gleam. Her look was neither a question nor an answer. It was a statement. It was saying, "Do you know what I am telling you?"

In a way, I was afraid to know. So, I did what I do well. I ordered another bourbon, and Katie brought it over. "I can't imagine what the two mothers went through. The death of a child. And then to find out that the murderer walked in and out of their houses as a trusted friend. An adviser. Their spiritual counselor." The bourbon felt hot against my throat. It burned, the way the truth burns lies away. "And then what? You waited for Paul to kill himself."

"That's the choice you gave him, wasn't it? End his life. Or run and be caught."

"He took the one I suspected he would."

"You found out about the basketball. That was very clever, Mr. Trade. Of course, at the time it was sort of a joke around campus. But do you know why he never changed, never quit fouling out?" She watched me with that same look in her eyes. She wasn't really asking a question. "Because he knew that he would always play the next game. They would put him in, and he would do what he did."

She took a Lucky Strike from my pack and lit it with a match. The smoke reached the sunlight and curled in graceful arcs where the afternoon sun shone through. Below the light, she and I sat. I waited.

"I understood Paul. He was taught from his earliest days that he was the favored one. He had been touched, his father said, by the hand of God. He was blessed." The nicotine wasn't relaxing her, but she took a long drag and pushed it out her nose. "That's why I knew he would never kill himself. He would try to disappear and start over."

If I was misunderstanding where this was going, I didn't want to make a mistake. "What do you think changed his mind?"

She stubbed out the cigarette, and wreathed in smoke, put her hand on mine. Her eyes were the same. They pierced through the smoke and bore into mine. "A man like Paul does not change his mind."

I understood. Or at least, I understood the end result. I didn't know how, but somehow three betrayed women had insisted on the kind of justice Paul Simpson had evaded all his life, the kind he certainly had coming. I knew that Bridget Rollins wasn't going to tell me any of the details. But she had wanted me to know. "Why tell me all this, Miss Rollins? If the story is that Paul didn't do what we all think he did, and if there's no going back on anybody thinking he did what he did, why tell me this story?"

She rose and put her coat on. The question hung in the air like her cigarette smoke.

"I told Paul that you could be trusted. And I believe that. I told Mrs. Baldwin and Mrs. Lee what I knew because, as mothers, they deserved to know. You may know someone, perhaps another mother or father, who deserves to know as well." She turned to leave, then stopped. "There are no happy endings here, Mr. Trade. But there can be endings that are just. It's not my business to sort it out."

I felt a chilly draft of air as she opened the door and left, a trace of perfume and smoke drifting gently over me. Katie knew my signal and brought another bourbon. I needed to brace myself against a long, cold night. But the night could never be as cold as justice served, nor as unexpected.

Also By TJ Arant

If you made it this far, I hope you like Jackson enough to go on another adventure. Book Two, *One Trade Too Many*, is available at the link below, as is *A Christmas for Trade*, a novella recounting Jackson's in-country Christmas during the Vietnam War. Both are exclusive to Amazon, and available via Kindle Unlimited as well.

One Trade Too Many http://getbook.at/OneTradeTooMany

A Christmas for Trade http://getbook.at/AChristmasForTrade

If you would like to keep up with publication news and other information, plus receive a free novella about Jackson's first case, just head over to https://BookHip.com/CNFHFK for a copy of TRADER. All you have to do is tell me where to send it.

Printed in the USA
CPSIA information can be obtained
at www.ICGtesting.com
LVHW042139100923
757797LV00023B/193

9 798215 064320